HAVEN

LILAH LANCE

TALON PRESS

UNDERWORLD KINGS BOOK II

To the girl who knew your fear of staying the same
must be greater than your fear of change

CONTENT WARNING

This book contains:

- A morally gray Alpha-male
- Mature themes
- Explicit content
- Graphic Language
- Mentions of human trafficking/kidnapping
- Violence
- Graphic descriptions of domestic violence and sexual assault

1

SONYA

"I JUST DON'T UNDERSTAND WHY YOU DIVORCE HIM? YOU ARE HIS WIFE, Sonya. *Who else is he supposed to hit?*"

Those were my mother's words.

She called me to tell me she was disappointed in me for leaving my abusive husband. Soon to be ex-husband. Over the phone.

The one who had held me down and violently choked me out and tried to do it at a public party before his cousin, Lucas, had intervened.

That had been a few months ago.

And it hadn't always been this violent, but there was something to be said about how little boys who got away with minor offenses became men who got away with attempted murder.

Now, I was staying in one of Lucas's apartments he'd lent for me since he was the CEO of a real estate company Mercury Group.

At my age Lucas was no stranger to helping out people around him.

He'd offered me this space as a safe haven while I filed for divorce from his 'good for nothing cousin' as he said. Distant cousins.

I didn't think Lucas was even remotely related to the monsters I had been around.

"I mean when I was your age men hit us all the time—this is

normal. This is the world for women. We do not deserve good things. Being beaten is your place as a woman."

I had barely answered the phone when she started going off on me.

And of course, because my mother was unhinged, she pivoted tactics when I didn't respond to her saccharine sweet brainwashing about how my role was to be beaten up in life.

This was common.

My mother was a Turkish woman from Nişantaşı, Istanbul.

A lifetime of being groomed to be perfection in the world had brainwashed her to being a victim of misogyny and internalized hatred against women.

So naturally, the universe had given my mother two daughters. One of them, my younger sister was her clone.

And me...Sonya Kiraz Amin, twenty-nine, slowly disintegrating into society.

The one she married off for her wealth.

"Sonya, you are *useless*, ungrateful, and a stupid girl. You cannot even take a little slap to the face—*I taught you better.* And you are getting fatter now that you don't have him to control you. I have seen your photos...they are disgusting..."

It always surprised me in the past how she was my mother, as my ears burned from when she spoke.

I didn't know how to process it when for months Lucas and I had talked and he'd told me time and time again—it was not my fault.

I could feel the familiar sensations of shutting down fighting with the new sensations in me of standing up for myself.

I was *learning* to stand up for myself.

After nine years of forced marriage to a millionaire that abused me? All thanks to my mother selling me out?

I felt my ears and throat burning to respond to her.

Burning to say something.

But my mother was too far gone. Money, time, and wealth had transformed her to this...vicious bitch.

"I mean, really Sonya, you left a man with money because you couldn't take a punch? You were asking for trouble. Asking for problems. Everyone knows women are always causing problems in the world..."

As my mother went on and on—I realized I could just hang up the phone. I could. I didn't have to say anything.

I didn't want to know how she got my number.

I just knew I wanted to change it.

I never wanted to speak to her or my sister ever again. Not when they'd laughed, belittled, and encouraged it to pay their bills. The frustration and rage built in me drowning out all other thoughts.

"Excuse me," I said to my mother in the most polite voice I could manage in my American accent.

Because I didn't know if she was recording this call on the other line illegally and if she would release it to the tabloids. And I didn't want that.

I didn't trust anyone anymore.

And maybe? That was something the twenty-one year old me should have learned faster. At thirty? I was catching on quickly.

"You have the wrong number."

I hung up. Blocked her. And requested Lucas's assistant Jenny to change my number. *Again.*

I contacted my attorney and checked on my restraining order against my family and against my ex-husband—Michael Devereaux.

Lucas, had found me and Michael in a scuffle.

Well, in a one-sided fight like it always was. Someone had been staring at me at a party as people do and Michael had thought I had been attracting attention.

As always. It was my fault.

He had dragged me into a corner of the halls and tried to demand why I was a whore. Why I did this to him. Why I embarrassed him.

Lucas had been with his friend Andrei DuPont and the two of them had ripped Michael off with Lucas laying into him while Andrei made sure I was okay.

It had been the first time in nine years that anyone had seen it and anyone had stepped in.

Up until a few months ago?

Everyone knew Michael was beating me.

Hurting me.

And not a single person stepped in.

Everyone turned the other cheek.

Everyone.

Until that night.

And maybe that was the night that I realized that's all I really needed. All I really needed was for one person to reach out to me in the grave that I had dug for myself in my head and yank me out.

Lucas had done that.

I realized out of the Devereaux clan, Lucas might've been the only gem.

He let me borrow an apartment of his temporarily and let me camp out here while Andrei introduced me discreetly to his wife— Talia. The three of them knew.

And *only* the three of them.

Lucas lent me his team of lawyers and he didn't care about picking a fight with his family.

Lucas had more money than all of them and he had nothing to lose.

In the last few months? I had gone from fearing that I would make too much noise, counting the steps it took for me to go to my bathroom to my bedroom. And praying that Michael never came home. Now? I lived alone.

I was finding that the hardest thing I had to do during the day was shop for groceries.

I was rediscovering…sipping slowly and eating even slower.

And now that I didn't have to live in fear?

I was learning how much it pissed off others to not be able to control me anymore.

Every single aspect of my life had been controlled. Until now. Lucas checked up on me when he could but Talia who was pregnant did all the texting. I visited her in her penthouse with Andrei sometimes.

And I lived alone. For now.

Eventually I would find my own place but Lucas insisted I stay here. For security. To process my divorce which would no doubt be difficult with Michael involved—and of course, the police reports, the witness statements, the constant barrage of questions, and thanks to Michael's family? Bad press.

Which had reached my parents in England.

I texted Talia.

Mum called.

I waited for her reply patiently. And I stared at the turkey and provolone sandwich on a roll with shredded lettuce, a line of mayo and a little bit of mustard. Four hundred and eighty calories on a roll.

And I wanted to tackle that next.

I didn't know where the quiet resolve came from. That was the sandwich Andrei got for me the night we went to the police station. He and Lucas were larger men and they'd been hungry.

They'd gotten me a sandwich I stared at until Andrei motioned to it.

"Try it, it's good," he had said.

Lucas had been quiet. Both of them ate like wolves.

I had been trained my entire life to eat like a former ballerina would. Nothing.

Nothing substantial at least.

Over the years I pretended if I stopped eating I would become invisible.

I could blend into the walls.

While I waited for Talia I reached for my sandwich. My turkey and cheese and provolone on a roll.

It probably had been a buttered roll.

I mentally added another one hundred calories. But I stared at it. This is my little routine for the last couple of weeks.

For the first couple of days, I didn't really eat anything, but now, I was hungry, and Lucas's apartment was actually around a bunch of restaurants.

I could smell it wafting into the apartment and it was so tempting. So I just stared at my sandwich.

This sandwich was salvation.

Very slowly I put it to my mouth smelling it. Inhaling it. Taking my first bite as my eyes watered. I kept going slowly. Slowly. I chewed it and when I swallowed everything in me protested.

It was a project for me to take in food now. But it was a lot easier.

I kept going. I didn't throw it up. I didn't ignore it. I acknowledged my fear like my therapist said.

I kept going. Slowly. I even sipped a juice box slowly.

It took me forever to finish the sandwich. It was just me and turkey and provolone cheese on a roll.

When it was finally done my phone pinged from Talia.

> I can shoot your family for you. Best if you just refer to them as that bitch instead of Mum.
>
> Mums don't try and get their daughters killed for money.
>
> Only cunts do.
>
> :)

It helped having a support system. I smiled down at her message drawing strength from the validation.

Talia Nash was a wealthier heiress who had given her father's company over to her younger sister Natasha.

Nash Group was known for being well versed in the art and securities world and right now, Talia's priority was just being a mother—and Andrei's wife.

Mine was to heal from my mother. The rigidity of my old life.

I had been here for weeks just leaning on my friends. My new ones. Some old ones.

Especially as I fought the urge to purge. To never eat again. And to become invisible. I stayed. I finished my turkey sandwich. And you know what?

Maybe I'd get another one. And another one.

And I'd *try* again.

Until my turkey and provolone and shredded lettuce with a line of mayo and mustard became the norm.

I was turning thirty soon. Trying to re-learn how to live.

Trying to re-learn what it meant to exist despite having gotten my a bachelors and wanting to pursue law—only to have it turned upside down by getting married.

I learned all the languages, all the training, all the practice I had done as a former ballerina—all of it was just preparation for me to be the perfect trophy wife.

Not to be my own person.

Years and years of being controlled and taught to obey—led to this. Oppression. Hyper-vigilance. No identity outside of my former last name that I wanted to throw out the window.

Being trapped in a prison of my own making before finally divorcing Michael after nine years.

Nine years of it being beaten into me I was a failure. I wasn't good for anything. Being erased. Abuse did not have a specific class. Abuse was everywhere.

Being told I wasn't worth it. I didn't know how to get out until Andrei and Lucas ripped me out. Lucas especially who hated his family.

Years of trying to make a legacy out of bloodshed and nothing.

Nothing left to stand on but on my own two feet.

And now?

Now I had to sip my water slowly and sit here in an empty apartment with luxury furniture and pray my divorce proceedings would go smoother than my marriage.

Some things were worse. Right?

I leaned back against the headboard trying not to shatter.

2

AIDAN

I WAS IN TROUBLE.

Being the oldest brother of two, Killian and Kieran, I was expected to never be in trouble and if I was they would never know.

Ever.

As the eldest O'Hara, it didn't matter if I was.

Killian and Kieran hadn't been there to witness our father Cormac's worst crimes. And they wouldn't know what was happening in my empire. Ever.

Like right now.

I had multiple rival gangs popping up all over crime ridden Chicago, and the longer I tried to be diplomatic the more people died on my watch.

At thirty? I was more tired than a man should be and pretty fucking fed-up.

As head of the O'Hara crime syndicate I knew better than to let cockroaches roam. I had been given my family's legacy without any choice. Without any say. By a former CIA Agent, Gabriel Monroe, who had wanted something from me.

A woman. Lara Ford.

In an intricate twist of events? Lara Ford became one of the prime reasons my business was so successful and legit.

Now? Gabriel and Lara were two of the people closest to me in a world I didn't really enjoy.

But ended up trudging through like mud in snow anyway.

Like right now I showed up to a bar where a shootout happened with two of my guys and the Belova gang. Bratva. Russian mob.

I could smell the copper scent of blood with whiskey mingling on the floor when I walked in and I wanted to gag.

"Belova's went rogue?" I asked one of my guys. They nodded.

A family tied with the Bratva.

There was four families spanning from New York to Chicago and they had a hard time understanding the word 'territory.'

Viktor Belova and I needed to sit down and talk. I fucking hated new blood.

They thought *we* were competition.

We didn't want shit to do with them.

I mean, I hated the old guard too, the new blood was always really eager and they didn't really understand their place until I stepped in.

I really didn't wanna step in, but I was a firm believer that cockroaches just needed to be eliminated as soon as they popped up.

And speaking of cockroaches—the police commissioner texted me again.

I guess it was awkward when the police commissioner realized that the strategic position I was in meant that I controlled a significant amount of legitimate businesses all across Chicago.

When I had taken over the family business, I had brought us out of the darkness and out of things like human trafficking and into a criminal intelligence empire.

We maintained ourselves now on legacy alone. But I owned enough real estate in Chicago to have weight. Leverage it across the board. I kept tabs to make sure we never ended up in a shit situation like the past.

When my father committed horrendous crimes.

Now? I made sure we were moving into a different era.

A mixture of Titans and O'Hara's that had survived the old guard now took up the reigns.

I maintained order in my territory. And I knew that I was a valuable ally to anybody who wanted it.

I had the political leverage. I had the legitimate businesses. But I also knew that people would use me against other people that I knew. So I kept that quiet.

And he wasn't getting shit from me.

I rolled my eyes adjusted my gloves in the Chicago fall. It was already sinking in temperatures.

Insanely so. It reminded me of nights when my father used to leave us outside to teach us how to have thicker skin. It definitely worked. Sometimes too well.

I worried about my brothers. Killian and Kieran were in New York.

Kieran had decided to step away from the family business.

Between drugs and sex and women?

He was running himself to the ground and I trusted my friend Gabriel who he worked under to take care of him—but Gabriel had a business to run. Kieran worked for Titan Security, along with Killian.

Killian was my second in command most of the time. And then the other half of the time, he worked for Gabriel as well.

Both of my brothers were under his watch, and I trusted him.

After Gabriel had killed my father?

I always trusted him.

The irony never did escape me. The bitter wind blew against my cheek again and I burrowed into my jacket.

The Windy City was no joke.

And neither was my problems as I navigated it.

At my side Alexei Markovik emerged like a wraith. At six feet tall Alexei was like my right hand. Platinum blonde hair, striking blue eyes like winter, and his face covered in the cold, his lean and limber figure sharply stood out from everyone.

"You wanted me?"

His Eastern European accent was still thick.

I nodded motioning to the bodies. "Get their wives something. Take care of it and meet me back at home."

He dipped his head.

At twenty-one, he was as loyal as an Enforcer got.

I met him maybe seven years ago? When he'd tried to rob me and got caught—back then he'd been a gangly teenager. Too tall for his own and too eager eyed.

I would've cut his hands off but I noted how hungry he looked. How bruised his body was. The brand on his wrist telling me he was the product of my father's trafficking. Alexei said he was from Belarus. Was. Probably an orphan picked up off the street shipped back to America. And I knew that look on his face the moment I saw him.

Another one of my father's victims. Another crime to atone for.

Another sin to catalog I had to fix.

That was my life. A monster among monsters trying to right every single wrong.

I felt it all the time.

I was him.

So I took him in, introduced him to my family and he'd taken to Kieran off the bat. Everyone did. And he'd never left.

Alexei would stand by my bedside while I slept if he could.

I sighed as I looked around the lights flashing from the cop cars, the dead bodies, and Alexei in the middle of it.

Even as my stomach growled I ignored it.

It could wait.

Being an O'Hara for me meant the struggle of an empty stomach and bearing the brunt of my father's legacy of blood and death.

Managing a syndicate with legitimacy and some form of penance.

And wondering…if I really made all the right choices.

Or if I was running from the inevitable of becoming a monster like Cormac was.

I would stick around as Alexei handled his job.

I had a meeting with another idiot in the meantime.

I didn't know why the police commissioner bothered speaking to me. We both knew he'd go to Gabriel to.

Years ago, exactly seven or so, a young former CIA operative Gabriel Monroe had busted into my father's prostitution ring in New York.

He had rescued a woman—Lara, shot my father, and offered me a proverbial bloody crown.

And I took it.

In the last seven years?

Gabriel had built up a private security company elite in its name—Titan Security and took both of my siblings out from Chicago and into his wing to be better.

They were fucked up in their own ways, but better off there than with me.

Gabriel had mentored Killian. In turn they made sure Kieran didn't accidentally off himself.

I sighed as Alexei finished and we strode over to my town car. Discreet. Ultra-modern. Annoying and uncomfortable like everything else.

Even now the only thing worse than annoying gangs—were cops who thought they were better than everyone else.

3

SONYA

"Eleanor Caroline Kennedy Devereaux left every single ounce of her legacy to you."

I forgot wealthy people kept their family names for centuries.

My attorney's voice came through like I was underwater.

Her neat bun and crisp gray suit looked molded to her as she watched me with kind eyes.

I sat back stunned with Gemma, a close friend of mine, her elegant blonde hair pulled back in a chignon in her designer dress looking every bit like the regal queen she was.

Gemma who now looked confused as me as my attorney who sat in my apartment rattled off that I was now...

"Eleanor Devereaux just left..." Gemma repeated. "Sonya owns half of the city."

"Something like that," the attorney rattled it off adjusting his glasses a bit more. "Every bit of this belongs to Mrs. Devereaux now—"

"Miss Amin," I corrected. "Just Sonya..." I hesitated as it slipped out. "I'm changing my name back."

"Sorry, on this document I'm going by what's written so...just for now, Mrs. Devereaux referred to you as Michael's wife despite your divorce proceedings she was worried if she put Amin, they would make you wait until your divorce is finalized which judging by how horrid Michael is—"

"She didn't want that." I finished.

The last thing I was expecting was Eleanor Devereaux leaving any of her wealth all to me.

I understood what my attorney was saying even as my hands trembled.

The half turkey sandwich I ate for lunch again—that had become my comfort meal—was now staging a revolution in my stomach. The plate sat on the counter half-finished and forgotten.

"But why?" I found myself asking slowly. "I just had tea with her some Sundays."

I remembered them like it was a weird dream where she would stare at my bruises and my body and never said a word. As I wilted.

Only Andrei and Lucas had said something.

Talia had done something.

Gemma hadn't really known until recently when she'd met me through Lucas.

"She left you a letter explaining herself and I have everything for you."

I took them from my attorney. I took all of it. Keys. Letters. Envelopes. Books.

As she kept on talking, I felt Gemma watching me with concern. Gemma was an heiress. I had just met her but we'd connected really well. I was…nothing.

I had been someone. A former diamond heiress.

The daughter of a wealthier family now brought down to nothing with a meager savings. I kind of wanted a smaller quieter life after the one I had led.

Sometimes I forgot what that was and why I even existed.

I had spent so long making myself invisible, that I didn't understand how to exist. And I was slowly learning how.

After signing all the necessary paperwork, Gemma ended up getting us lunch.

She was always good about making sure we were fed.

As somebody with the same societal expectations to stay rail thin, she ended up reaching out to me and always getting us enough food to feed a small army.

Over pad Thai and red velvet cookies Gemma went over everything with me and he drafted up an email with any kind of questions I had.

And turns out there was *a lot* to go through.

She said she would help me look over all of the properties and go over everything in the city. And she was more than willing to.

Between her charity gala, and everything else in between?

She juggled this by standing by my side when I got the news.

"This is good for you," Gemma said conversationally. "It's a great way to take back your power."

"Is it?" I asked weakly struggling to eat an egg-roll. It was at least one hundred calories per egg roll and I didn't know how to stomach it. But I had only the turkey sandwich today and I had to remind myself this was not normal.

This was not okay.

Shame was a societal need taught to girls to control our bodies.

"Yes," Gemma had a light French accent even now after schooling in the States. She adjusted her chignon and her skirts. "I think now you have money, you have means, and you have power. This is good for you. It gives you agency."

I nodded dumbly. "I have never been able to choose things for myself."

Gemma's smile was bittersweet. "And what a time to start."

I puffed out a breath. "I'm trying—"

"You can try by eating that egg roll you've been staring at."

I took a bite and almost moaned. "I feel like I'm re-discovering food and I don't know why I spent years avoiding delicious things. This is great."

"You should try it dipped in the sweet and sour sauce." Gemma motioned with her chopsticks. "I can add in some for you—" she didn't even wait.

And suddenly I was chowing down on egg rolls.

"Have you only eaten turkey sandwiches?" Gemma frowned at me. "You should go downstairs, there's a really nice deli down the street."

"I haven't felt brave enough to order my own sandwich, I use that food app you showed me and I just get the same thing so often the sandwich shop has started writing home-made notes."

Gemma laughed lightly. "Butterscotch's is run by a sweet woman. I'm sure she thinks you're starving."

I was.

Most of the time.

But I couldn't stomach too much.

"Maybe when I feel brave enough I can go outside every single day and try a new bakery," I wondered out loud. "Maybe I should make a list of all of the number one restaurants in the city, and every single week try to hit up one of them."

Gemma's eyes lit up. "That's proactive."

"Thank you, Dr. Khan says it's good for me." Gemma and I went to the same therapist.

I'd recommended it to her from Talia.

And instead of just sitting there, and focusing on everything that went wrong, I just wanted to focus on everything that could go right.

Because this was hard enough, I didn't need to make it any harder by starving myself the whole entire time.

"I think it's great you're trying," Gemma shifted a little in her perch on the couch. "You inspired me to do so much for myself. I cut my whole family off…"

Gemma Aurelia Valois *Marchand* was from one of the wealthier families of the world. And she had left all of it behind after her abusive stepmother, harassed her for years.

A couple of weeks after I left my ex-husband, I met Gemma. And I think the two of us talking just connected at the right times in our lives.

She was five feet eight inches of just absolutely stunning blonde with a model-like physique and inherent elegance in her features.

I felt like a sheep compared to Gemma.

But she was also the kindest woman I knew who would tell off anyone at the drop of a hat.

It was nice getting out of the circle that I had been a part of to now discover new people and new things out there in the world.

The tabloid still went crazy, but I realize I didn't care so much about them with good people on my side.

And also, the tabloids were gonna run their mouth, whether I was a part of it or not.

Best to just not care.

"And maybe I just think this is a thought, whether you want Eleanor's money or not, she did leave it for you. I think you should take it and do something with it. Not only help yourself with it, but you could always help other women. I know that Alisha did that."

Alisha was one of Gemma's good friends and I had recently met her. A social media influencer turned model who had opened a charity for women's education.

That was an idea.

"I don't even know where to start. What would I even do with it?"

Gemma shrugged lightly looking innocent with her opal eyes on me even though I sensed she was already planning.

Knowing Gemma she would know what to do with billions.

"You could always make it a safe haven for women in similar positions to yourself. It would be empowering. You could have a nurses on staff and you could have so much going for you. I don't think you have to stay like this forever and I can also help you find a new place to live. I know Lucas doesn't mind you staying here, but I'm sure it's not the same as having your own space."

It wasn't.

"Like a safe haven?" I repeated.

She nodded. "A safe haven for people to turn to and just kind of heal…" She smiled slyly at me knowing she had me. "Think about it! And eat your egg-roll!"

A safe haven.

It was later on that day when the knock at the door came. Gemma had left no less than thirty minutes ago.

If the knock had come a little bit earlier, I would've assumed it was Gemma.

With the empty Thai food containers the table and my feet propped up still eating chocolate chip cookies, I had been staring at Eleanor's letter when the knock came.

The bell.

It was so loud it startled me. But I had to remind myself that everything startled me. I flinched whenever people tried to touch me. So I was practicing on that.

If Gemma had not left so long ago, I probably would've called out if it was her or not.

And I was grateful that there was something in me that felt like the hair in the back of my neck were standing up because I checked the doorbell camera before I opened it.

Lucas had warned me to never open the door even for him, without verifying.

Every. Single. Time.

And I was grateful I did.

Because what I saw on the other side made all of the air whoosh out of my lungs. I couldn't breathe for a moment. I couldn't even speak properly.

Nine years of marriage to a monster, and I felt absolutely nauseous seeing him through a tiny screen.

My restraining order was still processing.

So it was just paperwork. It was just words.

And I knew better than to think that he would obey anything because his parents would let him get away with absolute murder.

"Sonya!" How did he know I was staying here? I rarely left the apartment and even getting mail it was sent to Lucas.

Did he have someone watching me? Or Gemma?

"Sonya! I know you're in there I just saw Gemma Marchand leave your apartment, I fucking knew you were here."

I froze. Everything in me shut down. My brain. My body. Part of me reached for the doorknob slowly trying to open it. Old instincts at war with new ones fighting the urge to obey.

To obey.

Obey what? My hand twitched as I struggled with myself.

No. I couldn't open the door. I physically was rooted to the spot.

Dr. Khan said I had trauma responses that were really common in victims of domestic violence. That's what I was.

And I couldn't open the door. I couldn't speak. I thought if I froze in place—I could become invisible and nobody would see me.

The door rattled then and only then did I take a step back.

That door wouldn't open to him. Not with the three deadbolts Lucas and Gemma made me turn and the code inside to let them in.

Lucas was a man of privacy and he didn't like anyone bothering him.

I was grateful now. My hands shook and I heard nothing he said. But everything all once.

"I know Eleanor gave you everything! I wanna know why! Who did you pay? How did she give it to you?"

What?

I'm so confused right now.

"Sonya, open this fucking door!"

I scrambled back and the first thing I did was text Lucas.

> Michael showed up to my door. He's outside right now.

There was a moment of silence as I debated what to do. I didn't know about going to the police. It looked like they weren't doing anything. Or unable to.

> Miss Sonya, this is Jenny. I'm Mr. Devereaux's secretary. He's in a meeting right now, but I'm alerting your attorney, and the security staff of the building at this moment...please standby.

It took less than five minutes for me to hear male voices and security shouting at Michael as he roared. "Do you know who I am? Let me go!"

I stayed frozen reading Jenny's texts.

> Are they there?

> Yes. They're taking him away, thank you.

> My apologies. I have no idea how he got in. I'll speak to building staff. And get another guard on your floor.

I stared at my phone frozen to the spot. Rooted until Lucas finally called letting me know he was firing the 'stupid staffers who let Michael in' and then he wanted to know if I wanted to move.

Again?

No. But I did want to go and check out Eleanor's properties.

"For some reason he's obsessed with Eleanor's will," I told Lucas.

He snorted like it was funny. "Mikey always did think everyone's else's toys were shinier…"

Because Michael had always been groomed to be a monster.

And I didn't have any emotional space for that in my life.

4

AIDAN

"It's too early for murder."

I muttered over my coffee as Alexei stood across my desk waiting his next orders. I motioned to the emerald arm-chairs in the room.

When I bought this mansion for a hundred mil I thought it would get me some semblance of peace.

So far, it was always fucking freezing and all the windows made me nervous.

Right now the sunlight was streaming in the floor to ceiling large black panes, making Alexei look like the grim reaper standing there in his all black and platinum hair.

His face a little too thin and leaner now with all the pressure we were under.

Besides Viktor Belova killing two of my guys, I had gone after him picking up a few of his interrogating them.

And then I had my guys kill 'em.

Across the city. All over it.

Sending a message.

I was a firm believer in an eye for an eye. It didn't make the world blind. Not to me.

"That should send him a message," I muttered to Alexei standing there. "Alexei sit down every time you loom over me it rubs me the wrong way."

He grumbled but did as he was told. I had ignored the commissioner because I just didn't wanna deal with him right now. Not when I was laying out bodies all across the city. It was annoying.

"I have something for you," Alexei said softly. His Eastern European accent was thick. "I think something is happening. Something beyond the Belova men."

I frowned. "What makes you say that?"

Alexei wasn't usually the type to worry. He was sensible but rational for the most part. So I knew he knew some things.

"I spent the last few weeks asking around the city. That day, when I saw the bodies, I thought they looked a little strange. Like they had gotten into a fight and it didn't make any sense for them to start fighting for no reason. We don't have any issues with them."

"We never do, but that might not be enough for him."

Alexei shook his head. "I think it's something else."

"Like?"

"I think someone else is doing this."

I stopped everything. "You think someone else is trying to cause a turf war? Or?"

He shook his head. "No, I don't think so. If it was a war, and if that's what they wanted, they could've just come after us. It's not a mystery where we live. But that's not what it felt like. When I went and saw the bodies, I was curious so I started asking around."

Alexei was my best. One of them. Besides the numerous other men around the house and the ones working for me on the street, Alexei knew what I wanted like the back of my hand.

"Dmitri and Viktor are brothers. But they have enough of the southside to leave us alone. They have no reason to come after us. There was no hint of anything before this."

"Except now there might be with me going after their guys." I said casually. I wasn't nervous. I believed in thinning the herd.

"No, I mean," Alexei struggled with his English sometimes. "No, I think is not what it is. Something is wrong. Let me look into this. Something does not make sense to me."

I was pretty sure if I kept pushing him he would hit me with a Russian proverb about something living under ice. And I didn't really wanna decipher it today.

"Fine, let me know." I didn't even get a chance to finish my sentence when the most shrill and cartoonish ringtone went off in my pocket. And the sound of cats meowing filled the entire office space.

I stiffened closing my eyes swearing his name up and down.

"Of course he fucking—" I answered the phone. "Are you fucking kidding me right now? You changed my ringtone to this shit?"

Kieran on the other end practically cackled. "Better you than Killian, he'll actually kill me if I did that shit to him."

I groaned rubbing the bridge of my nose. "What do you want? I thought Killian got you and straightened you out for Titan?"

"He did," Kieran always sounded too chipper. Too bad I knew what he did hide and what he didn't want anyone else knowing about. "But Killian's been busy."

But at the very minimum he was sober now.

Alexei smirked in his chair looking at his lap.

"He's always busy."

"Killian's busy with a girl."

I leaned back in my chair. "No shit."

"Yeah. Nisha Graham, super cute nurse. Works under Gabriel or some shit. But anyways, he got me squared away, but I heard you'd be coming into the city to help Lucas."

I bit back a groan.

"I'll be in the city in a few weeks. Handling shit right now but Killian will take care of everything. He's supposed to come see me eventually."

"Yes, sir." He mocked and I resisted the urge to hit him wishing I could teleport through the phone and smack him. "I don't know, doubtful he ever wants to see anybody."

The idea of Killian out of everybody in our family, having a girl-friend in the family was not something that I could even comprehend. Out of everyone in the family that operated the way that they did?

He was the one who ran ice-cold. Darker. Leaner and meaner. Killian was vicious with how our father raised him and now? He was with a lady?

Hm. I'd have to look into that.

23

"I know you didn't call me to tell me Killian's got a girlfriend. Even if you are jealous he's focused on her."

He made an impatient noise. "Not jealous."

"He is jealous," Alexei muttered and I smirked at him. Kieran was always hogging our attention as kids. It was what he did. We entertained him because he'd been the baby.

As Kieran rambled over the phone I smirked over at Alexei.

Killian had a girlfriend and Kieran wanted to have a heart to heart.

I GOT CALLED TO NEW YORK WHEN LUCAS DEVEREAUX HAD BEEN SHOT. A minor problem—attempted murder.

And while I was juggling Lucas and potential threats, Killian thought it would be an opportunity to introduce me to his girlfriend. Nisha Graham.

In person.

I was standing in the hospital corridor, the sterile scent making me a little nauseous, when Killian's leaner form appeared. Next to him was a softer looking woman in green scrubs and she was holding his hand.

Nisha.

The fluorescent lights caught her raven hair, making something in my chest tighten at the way she bat her eyes up at Killian.

That same sheen our mother had when she'd sit at her vanity, brushing her hair while Killian and I watched, playing at her feet.

Little memories. Sharp ones that cut through the shadows of everything that came after.

Gabriel's best friend and the on-paper CEO of Titan Security, Reed Whittaker, had a brother working here—Adam.

Same green scrubs as Nisha wore, though she was tiny compared to the rest of us.

Maybe five-five, with an hourglass frame that made Killian look even more imposing beside her.

She looked completely soft compared to him.

The exhaustion lifted from her face as she smiled, and I caught Killian watching me with those mismatched eyes—one aqua, one amber.

Eyes our father had tried to beat the uniqueness out of him for. His heterochromia had been just another thing to hate, another reason to make him feel wrong.

And over the years he'd caught enough flack from our late father to turn into someone I didn't really recognize.

Killian being with Nisha was nothing short of a smaller miracle.

"Aidan, this is—"

"Nisha." I knew who she was the moment she smiled up at Killian like he would get her the moon. Judging by how my brother looked at her? He would.

Cracks in his icy exterior that surprised me filled me with a shock I couldn't hide, but I wore my mask tight.

"I've heard a lot about you. Never a good time, is it?" I kept my voice neutral not wanting to freak her out. Alexei was in the car still. He usually freaked everyone out so I told him to stay put.

"All good things I hope," she murmured, her small hand disappeared in mine. "I don't mind." Her smile was warm.

As she said it Killian smiled a little looking at her with pride. I tried not to show my shock.

Most people shrank away from men like us. But she met my gaze steadily with warmth and appreciation.

"How'd my brother land you?"

I was genuinely curious. He never talked about her but she seemed warmer than anyone I'd ever seen around our family.

Nisha surprised me with her light laughter. "I can assure you I landed him, he's been wonderful."

Had he been?

The words wonderful and Killian were never included in the same sentence unless he killed someone.

"Is that so?" I didn't even bother looking at Killian. He was too busy looking at her. "I don't think Killian fought back once."

To my surprise Killian turned a little redder and almost looked embarrassed as Nisha tugged him closer to her.

She was comfortable touching him, which also surprised me because he didn't like anybody doing that. "No, he didn't. Killian's great. He's told me so much about you…"

As she spoke? I kept my mask on, but on the inside, I was kind of marbling at her. It was obvious to me that they've been together for a long time. Killian really liked her.

Not only did he tell her about me, but about Kieran. About us as his family.

Nisha smiled up at me with warmth in those eyes of hers. Her features were softer and familiar to me in a way I didn't know how to place.

She wasn't putting on an act. And Killian?

I had never seen my brother like this.

I passed Nisha my number in case she ever needed it. I had to go—Reed wanted to talk to me about Lucas. Which wouldn't go well.

"If Killian ever decides not to be great, you can call me. I'll straighten him out." I meant it. Because she was…I saw the way he watched her—she was important to him.

And I wondered how much she knew about my family.

I saw Killian shift in real time. "I'm not sure that's necessary."

Nisha squirmed. "No truly—"

"I need to borrow him for a few days," I watched her. "You can help my brother back then. Text me if you ever need anything."

It was all I could give her.

She was Killian's.

He loved her.

Done deal. Plus, I rarely gave my number out and once Alexei found out about her he'd just run an entire background check on her.

As Nisha smiled up at me, I saw something flare in Killian's face. Hope.

I swallowed hard as she spoke to me. He was searching for my approval with those eyes of his.

I knew a good woman when I saw one after doing the work I did. I tipped my head at him.

He had it.

I bit back a smile at the relief in his features.

He was introducing Nisha to me…because he wanted to be with her. He wanted my approval.

I tried not to let the unfamiliar sensations clenching my chest fill me in at the memories of a younger Killian trailing behind me.

That little boy had grown up to be this six-two monster who sank his teeth into things—and right now? He was holding Nisha tighter as she spoke to me.

5

SONYA

Dearest Sonya,

By the time you receive this letter, I'm afraid I will no longer be around to tell you of my guilt.

A cowards way out if you will.

I regret to tell you I was too aware of how my grandchildren raised my great-grand-son. I was. But I felt as though over the years I had hope that he might change.

Maybe your love or softness would heal him. Teach him new things. Then maybe he might learn from your culture to help make himself a better man, but I was a fool for thinking that.

As I write this letter, I have just been informed by the numerous individuals that you have filed for divorce. And of course, every idiots righteous anger.

When I had been younger, divorce was not something that most women considered.

But I was proud that you had.

It has been brought to my attention that without you no longer in the imaginary competition that all of the people around, we seem to have for my money, I realize over the

last couple of weeks I hadn't known what to do with any
of it.

I kept searching for answers. And it seems today I have the
right ones.

As of today, I am leaving everything I have to you. I watched
the way you were treated for years hoping something
might change—but I was too foolish to understand it.

Now? I'm atoning for those sins.

My mother had died in childbirth from what I thought was
complications after birth.

Not from an abusive man.

Not from the father who loved me.

And I realized a lot of what I knew was wrong.

I'm sorry, Sonya. I couldn't do anything for you when I was
alive and I had this dream of my mother, a woman with
fewer rights than me, and what she might have wanted in
the situation's she had been in this world.

And I realized I couldn't save her as much as I couldn't
save you.

I want to be able to right those wrongs. All of them.

And so everything I have is now yours—use it well. Use it wisely.

And if my family kicks up a fuss?

You now have the means to take them down by any means
necessary since you are wealthier than all them.

My dear, I cannot apologize enough.

I hope when you come to the Hyacinth Manor you find my
room in tact and my favorite painting there your favorite
in the house

Love, Elle.

Atonement was an interesting word.

That was Eleanor's last message to me when I did go to Hyacinth Manor.

Eleanor's original family, the Kennedy's were insanely wealthy New York elite.

Among the Hyacinth Manor? I was now the owner of the Primrose Hotel, Laurel Apartments, and the Evergreen Mansion in Greenwich, Connecticut.

Each of the four properties represented factions of Eleanor's wealth. Catering to different clientele and now?

I had a host of new things to do.

But Hyacinth Manor was the oldest standing mansion in New York, spanning four stories and looking like white elegance in a French styled castle.

It took up an *entire* city block.

The windows glittered, and the wrought iron gates held the Devereaux lion on it in gold the hyacinth flowers around it at the center. I didn't have to knock. I had the key-code.

And it was *mine*.

To enter the city again on my terms. On my power.

And to take it back.

"Michael is holding up the paperwork on his end, he claims to have meetings and is unable to sign his end of the paperwork…"

"No surprise there," I told my attorney.

"Don't worry, we'll get everything squared away and I'm reaching out about the restraining order…"

It came as no surprise for me to find out during my early morning, conference call with my attorney that my soon to be ex-husband was holding up all of the paperwork on his end and dragging out divorce proceedings.

Even though it had been mentioned that I did not want any aspect of his money or his time, he still continued to make up as many excuses as possible.

Which I saw coming.

My therapist and I had talked about Michael's need for control. Lucas was not wrong.

Michael only held onto things when he couldn't have them. Once he had them, he would destroy them.

It was a trait that I learned ran on his side of the family, he was the only child of two extremely wealthy parents, who never said no.

And so he never believed in no. In any situation.

Memories of Michael holding me down to get what he wanted

and needed no matter what I wanted were another reminder of why I chose to be alone.

Memories of his fist into my body and never touching my face so I would still be pretty haunted me.

Memories of holidays spent away that Michael had pushed me down a flight of stairs and I had spent it at the emergency room—Michael had told his relatives I wasn't feeling good and they in turn spread gossip about me saying I thought I was too good for them.

While I was in the emergency room.

That had been the Devereaux family.

By contrast—Lucas was nothing like his family and he preferred to distance himself from all of them. Which I was grateful for.

My attorneys made sure that every aspect of Eleanor's properties and everything that I have been given had been insured.

They explained to me that Eleanor's fortune was something that the entire family had been vying for. Her family had come over on the earliest ships to America and had wealth back in England.

The later generations had changed their names and remarried and Eleanor had wealth beyond her wildest dreams and nowhere to put it.

She had invested it in into one of the oldest standing mansions and all of New York City. But also all throughout the globe.

All of which now I had access to that people were trying to contest within the family.

But they wouldn't win because Eleanor had signed all of these documents in front of other people.

And so they were witnesses to testify that she had done it under no duress, but of her own choice.

I explored the entire house alone, and Gemma's concept became more of a possibility for me. It became more of a reality. And I was just reaching out to her for ideas for it. The manor was huge.

There was a smaller elevator in the back as well that worked and to my surprise, everything had been modernized. But it had one lacking. Security.

I would need to contact someone for that.

I began making a list on my phone of all the things that I needed to do. And I did find Eleanor's room.

I sat on her bedroom surrounded by blush pinks and cremes. Some hints of sage green.

An elegant chandelier seemed to occupy every single room and I knew—I knew that I couldn't stay here because it was just not what I wanted. It was too solitary.

Even for me, I liked living in an apartment just to be around people. This manner was just a little bit too spooky for me.

I had hired people to pack away some of her things after I looked through them.

I did find the painting that she mentioned, but it was hard not to.

On my way here I had done research on that painting since it was featured on the house when someone had done a piece on it. *Spring.*

It was the largest painting in the house and it was in Eleanor's bedroom.

It was one of a pair. The second one had been lost. But this was the first one. An oil painting of two lovers on a swing on a rainy day.

The woman wore a dress billowing out and the man holding onto the swing while her arms wrapped around him.

The artist had captured two lovers seeking refuge in each other.

And part of me watched it wondering if my time for love was over.

It had to be.

I was thirty. Not a woman in her prime anymore.

I had a failed marriage. An abusive husband.

I placed my hand over my stomach aware I still ashamed of the things I couldn't control. Things I never told anyone.

Finding out I couldn't have children even with the help of modern medicine, did nothing to make me feel better. I had dreams of having a baby girl.

Dreams of a life outside of being just a wife.

None of those dreams would ever come true.

But that didn't mean that they couldn't come true for other people.

Gemma wanted me to funnel all of my energy, in the building something better for everybody else.

Just because I couldn't have the things I wanted didn't mean that it had to be the same for everybody else.

And so, I sat on my course of not only meeting in interviewing people, but just trying to find the right fits for the team.

Trying to find all of the right people, and I began filling it over the next couple of weeks.

One of the people I potentially wanted was Adam Whittaker.

He was the brother of Reed Whittaker, a man who owned a private security company and who also happened to be dating Gemma's best friend Alisha.

I had met Alisha a few times and I'd rather liked her, and so I spoke to her about potentially getting Reed to do the security upgrade to Hyacinth Manor.

Now renamed Haven as a charity focused group.

Reed agreed and came by one morning, all six-feet four of him taking up all the space in the manor with Alisha.

I had shown Alisha around while Reed quickly went around taking inventory.

Within a few days I had security cameras and other features including internet installed, and Reed had done the same to my new place—a townhouse on the Upper East Side that had once belonged to Eleanor as well.

Alisha had come over with the girls for me to live my best life with them. It had been nice letting go with women in my world.

I needed it.

"If you need anything at all, Lish has my direct line," Reed had said as he'd scanned every bit of the manor leaving no stone unturned.

I also interviewed Reed's brother, Adam who was a medical resident and he said he would consider the offer as well.

I thought both of them were a really good fit for the team, but I also needed a few others.

Adam recommended Nisha Graham a coworker of his who happened to be a nurse.

Today I was meeting her at a Turkish coffee shop, deliberately choosing a spot that I found really cozy, but somewhere where nobody would see me.

The tables were speculating and losing their loving minds after I had inherited Eleanor's Fortune.

I didn't need to give them any more gossip.

I was now building a network.

I didn't need Michael to be in my business about it.

The raven-haired woman with warmer eyes who walked in a blush pink sweater I knew was Nisha. I stood feeling self conscious. She was pretty.

Fuller figured in a way I envied as she smiled. Her curves in her softer outfit made me feel her warmth.

I didn't even breathe as I said something to her.

Her eyes widened on me. "Your accent is beautiful."

Was it? The compliment really caught me off guard. Michael's entire family wanted me to take English as a second language classes for a very long time to erase my accent.

They wanted me to imitate what they sounded like, but I never could.

Another failure.

"Thank you…I'm Turkish," I was.

I didn't know where I fit in culturally. Not anymore.

"My parents live there, but I moved to the States with—" I stopped abruptly.

I had received a formal education in Switzerland but marrying me off to Michael Devereaux had been an attempt to secure wealth.

For them.

Not for me.

"I live here now." I finished stopping myself.

And her eyes widened again and I saw a faint hint of embarrassment written all over her face.

I wonder if she *knew.*

If she read gossip magazines. If she was aware of what people thought about me.

Nisha gave me a gentle smile as a waiter walked by us to a nearby table.

The food smelled so good here, I thought this might be a good stop for me to get something for myself.

Something to go back to my roots and find what I love.

Michael hated anything other than American food and convinced me I was sub-human if I ate my cultures food. Or anything that involved eating with your hands. He turned his nose up at it.

I would relish it today.

But I saw Nisha absolutely pale the moment the waiter walked by. Her face drained of color.

"Are you all right?"

"I'm sorry," she gasped, pressing her hand to her mouth as she darted up. "I need to—"

She didn't finish as she rushed to the restroom.

It wasn't even a second thought for me to just follow her.

In the bathroom, I could hear Nisha throwing up and I felt a little uneasy wondering if I picked the right place or not. Did I...was she sick because of the smell?

Michael always said it smelled horrible.

My stomach was twisting as I watched her, my arm instinctively moving around her in the stall, holding her hair back. She shook her head weakly.

"It's okay," I murmured under my breath.

"I haven't told anyone..." she managed. What?

"It's okay—" Whatever it was. It was fine.

"I'm so sorry," she whispered. She sounded embarrassed. Why? I mean, I was apologetic she didn't like Turkish food. "This was not how I wanted to meet you—"

"No, don't apologize," I interrupted. "You're fine. There are worse ways to meet people, believe me."

I quickly grabbed some paper towels out of the dispenser handing it to Nisha. "Are you...ill? Or do you need anything?" Maybe that's all it was.

Nisha shook her head. "I'm not sick..."

Then?

Was it me?

I felt nothing but anxiety in that moment like she was not trying to offend me, but she really did not like anything. And I was a little afraid.

"I'm pregnant."

Oh. That had not been the answer I was expecting. And I almost felt a hysterical little smile tug at my lips as my hand moved over my womb.

"Ah. Morning sickness?"

Nisha smiled a little. "Although it seems to have missed the memo about sticking to mornings."

I didn't know how to tell her I was grateful she wasn't going to insult me in any way. Or that it wasn't my fault.

"I have heard," I said. When I was trying to get pregnant at the insistence of Michael's family...I did every kind of research I could. Every single thing. "How far along are you?"

"About sixteen weeks going on seventeen. I haven't told anyone else yet."

"Is he—"

"He's in my life," she answered ducking her head a little flush on her cheeks. "He's wonderful."

"Your husband?" I didn't know if she was married or not I didn't want to ask but it seemed right to now.

"No." I felt bad when I realized what I had asked, but I was just curious. And I quickly reassured her.

I didn't want her to think that I was. I just hoped that there was somebody else taking care of her when she felt like this.

Because I knew if it were me, I wouldn't have anyone.

"I'm not one to judge you. Lord knows I have enough complications in my own life. Are you going to be all right?" And not only that —but my problems were blasted into society papers.

"Just disgusted now. Sorry, I tried to be perfect—"

"You don't ever have to be perfect—" I was quick on that one.

"But I met you for a job interview," Nisha said weakly. "And here I am, throwing up in the bathroom—"

"You're all right," I heard myself say. "I'm not too concerned with the perception of perfection these days. I'm learning to get that go. Perhaps it's something we could both work on, hmm?" I tipped my head in what I hoped was understanding.

Nisha didn't understand how I was struggling to and she didn't need to, but she never needed to feel like she had to be perfect with me. For anything.

She ducked her head again with a small smile. And I felt myself straighten instinctively, adjusting my rounded shoulders.

"Were you a dancer?"

Nisha's eyes were on my shoulders.

"Are you—" I didn't think she was. But she would have to know if she took it. Or was around ballerina's. Even former one's.

"No, I'm a musician—or I was—I just noticed the way you stood just now, your shoulders, your back...I went to school with ballerinas."

Ah.

My mother had sent me to ballet classes growing up. On top of the already heavy curriculum's and intensive language prep. I spoke seven languages and did ballet and had a degree.

All to have been here. I never talked about it.

Besides, I wasn't proud of any of it. It was never my dreams.

"I was...I did ballroom dancing after I couldn't do ballet. Too hippy..."

Nisha looked offended for me. "If you're too hippy, I'm a hippo."

I laughed finding her delightful. Out of all the places I could've found someone to be friends with it would inside a woman's bathroom. *"Nonsense."*

"Why did you stop?"

I shrugged lightly not wanting to give too much away. "Life. I got married. I got divorced."

Nisha nodded and then I realized how intelligent her eyes were when she said. "Your ex-husband didn't like your dancing?"

I suppose since I already asked her about her boyfriend it was fair game. "No, he did not. My ex-husband didn't like anything about me."

That was the truth.

I didn't want to tell Nisha about what it had been like being married to somebody who inherently knew that he was doing my family a financial favor. Something that had just been arranged for the sake of advancing other people and not me.

I didn't know how to tell her what he was like. And I didn't know how to tell her what he had done. I also just didn't want to talk about it.

Instead, I told her about Haven and the Hyacinth mansion, and what I wanted to turn it into. I told her about my vision and what I wanted to do with the women who I wanted to host there.

I knew that it was going to be difficult and I knew that it was a challenge, but I was determined.

Combined with Gemma's expertise I could do it.

"You'd still hire me even if I was pregnant?" Nisha asked.

"Yes, I'm not in the business of shaming women for wanting a family."

Or for not being able to have a family.

"Nor would I not cover your maternity leave. It's hard finding the right people and I'm not an employer who would hurt you at a vulnerable moment. You can think about it…" she motioned to my stomach. "And for now, maybe some lemonade might help?"

"That sounds amazing."

And for a moment I saw a light in Nisha's eyes. One I wanted to make sure every woman around me had.

Just because I had been treated the way I had didn't mean, that everyone else had to go through it as well.

No. It was about using Eleanor's money to make changes.

No matter how small or large.

I smiled at Nisha. "Come on, I think they have something tart here which should help."

6

AIDAN

TO SAY LIFE GOT BUSY WAS AN UNDERSTATEMENT.

We made it back to Chicago. Someone had tried to kill Lucas because of his business with the Titans—Gabriel had stepped in to leverage that.

I had to deal with my guys letting me know Dmitri Belova wanted to meet me now formally.

I was juggling new threats in the city and old ones, and Alexei—Alexei was adjusting to all the things too.

Like Chicago pizza vs New York.

"After trying New York style, it's good too," he commented on the car back to my home.

I snorted. "Don't let anyone here catch you saying that."

"Why?" He looked at me confused. Sometimes I forgot how old he was. I had picked him up at maybe fourteen years old. I wasn't sure how old he was but he swore he was twenty-one now.

He'd tried to rob me and normally?

I would've just put him out of his misery and shot him. But there was something about him that reminded me of Killian so I took him in. Now, he was at my side all the time.

"The stuffed crust is nice too," Alexei said conversationally driving us now.

I shook my head. "Reed introduced you to it."

"No. Mr. Monroe."

Gabriel. Fucking figures. "Tell me he got us some information."

"Yes, it's very interesting." Alexei snapped into work mode. "I was right. The pattern of how everybody is taken out does not make any sense. I think that something is going on inside of the Belova family. There are rumors Dmitri is sick."

"Sick how?"

"I do not know. Gabriel says doctor's cannot find what is wrong with him."

"But he's definitely dying."

Alexei nodded as he explained. "Viktor is next in line, but Dmitri has a daughter. Eden Ekaterina Belova. And she is closer to her father than Viktor."

I paused for a moment turning my head.

"What are the odds a Bratva princess would stir up shit just to get Viktor taken out?"

Alexei's smile was grim. "That would explain why Dmitri has no idea what is going on."

"You think she wants Viktor taken out so she can rule?"

Alexei shrugged. "It does not make sense. Dmitri would give either to her or to Viktor—"

"So then why?"

"I do not know, but I am going to the streets as you say."

I blew out a breath. "Yeah."

"In Russia we have a saying—"

I groaned a little. "You're from Belarus."

"Yes, and Russian." Alexei stared pointedly as he parked the car in the underground garage I had.

"I can't take another proverb about ice bears right now, Alexei I have five hundred fires to put out."

He grumbled about something in Russian that I didn't under-stand and unfolded his long, lean limbs from the car before following me up the stairs. "I am right, you will see too. Watch, I think Eden Belova is behind this. I have seen her eyes. She is intelligent..."

As I walked up to my office, he was talking to me about our potential suspect.

MEETING THE BRATVA WAS NO JOKE.

But I refused to do it at Dmitri's place. I wasn't a fucking idiot.

Not without Alexei there who covered his face with a black mask when he went to meet him with me.

"Do not mention his daughter," Alexei whispered. "I had information she likes to party—"

"But you said it was her—"

"I do think it is her, but I do not think he knows. I do not want you to be play a fool, how you say? A fool. Do not do it. Let him think he does not know. And we will do our digging."

Fine. I puffed out a breath feeling the wind cutting over my cheeks.

All of my guys were parked outside and two of them lingered as I walked into the pizzeria.

It was completely closed safe for us.

Red and white checkered tablecloths, fake grapevines wrapping around plastic lattices.

It was so fucking cliché.

It would've been laughable, but of course the Russians would've picked an Italian restaurant because God forbid they actually spent real money.

I was starving, but there was no way I was eating anything out of here.

Dimitri Belova sat in a seat all by himself, but I didn't miss the two guys covering behind him a couple of feet away.

I definitely clocked them, but I didn't bring an entourage.

Not when I had Alexei.

He moved like a wraith around me and that was all I needed. I had trained him to be a fighter. He was good at what he did.

And right now I trusted what he said about there being someone among the Belova's who was a threat to Dmitri and Chicago's political infrastructure.

He stood as I walked in. "Mr. O'Hara."

"Dmitri."

I didn't give a shit what he thought. After being raised by my father, I felt the shift happening in me as soon as I saw him. They need to protect. Most people joined what I did, to prove something. I had been very lucky.

My name was built already on legacy.

I didn't have anything to prove.

And so I operated off of the values of protecting my brothers. And immediately the moment I saw him, the shift happened in me, and I switched from being who I was turning into a monster.

"Someone's trying to start a war on my land. And I think it's coming from you."

I cut to the chase. I was starving and I wasn't here to talk to him. I was here to handle business. And then I would leave and eat a fucking pizza.

I sat down even when he didn't dropping myself down aware the two guys behind Dmitri straightened and turned to see who had the audacity to talk to their boss.

Dmitri raised a brow slowly sitting down as he looked at his guys then me. Like he was impressed or he was like 'get a load of this guy' but I didn't give a shit.

I had been around longer than him.

The O'Hara's carried weight.

The Russian's were new blood.

And new blood wasn't welcome here.

"I heard you were direct."

"Then you also heard I'm not in the business for war. If you don't find out who's provoking this among your people, I don't have time for politics. I'll shut it down."

"And you think my people are responsible? That's a bold statement of you to make." I didn't miss the way Dmitri eyed Alexei. "And who is this?"

Unlike his men, Alexei was close to me. Right at my side. He didn't speak. The dark shadows inside of me purred as I adjusted my wool coat.

I could eat seventy pizzas after this.

"Your fucking Grim Reaper." I tipped my head pissed the fuck off now. I was so annoyed at everyone. "Find out who your rat is. I heard about your medical conditions. Your bills. Your brother Viktor. I know everything. So I suggest you get your shit together." I motioned to his face. "You took out two of my guys—"

"You killed many of my men on the streets—"

"And I'll kill all of them. Starting with the two right there."

Sometimes I forgot how easy it was. Sometimes I forgot whose son I was. But my moments like this, I never forgot. It always came easy to me.

Alexei didn't even hesitate to pull out his gun faster than the other two.

"Nu-uh," I said softly. "I wouldn't even try with Alexei."

Belova looked appalled I would even try.

I met his clear blue eyes head on.

"This is my city. It has been my families for hundreds of years. Just because I'm not scummy like you? Doesn't mean I wouldn't even try. I know someone on your team is playing the field. I suggest you find out which one. You have a week. When I hear back from you—it better be with a name."

7

SONYA

"HE WON'T SIGN THE PAPERS."

"What do you mean, Michael refuses to sign the papers?"

I was standing in my new apartment, complete with security features now that made me feel safer.

And Michael didn't know I lived here.

"He wants to try and contest Eleanor's will—"

"That's garbage—" I swore. The familiar tension of who Michael was crept into my spine. He was always trying to control me in someway or a

"I know, and I'm going to shut it down. But it's gonna take some time. He's trying to claim that the six month separation period that is required. Didn't start because you were technically still living in his property until the incident."

"Even though I had been gone longer?"

"Informally, but yes, his lawyer is a dirtbag as well and he's using the system. The delays, the contest, every piece of paperwork just understand this is his way of being—"

"An evil man?"

"Well…yes."

He didn't have control over me physically, so he wanted to maintain control through his lawyers.

Even though I had documented to the police everything that happened that day that he tried to strangle me in public.

And then there was the detailed accounts of the one hundred and fifty two pages of violence of the last nine years. I had a diary on my phone and I went back and logged all of it tirelessly with my lawyers.

With all that information being leaked out into the press—it was suicide for Michael to continue and yet he was.

Because his image meant everything to him.

"I need to go after him for slander and defamation," my attorney was saying. "I'm trying to get those articles of you taken down."

The ones that constantly insinuated that I had somehow slept my way to getting Eleanor's inheritance. It was so disgustingly vulgar, that it was everything that I saw coming from Michael.

"He wants to demand an asset division of Eleanor's things even though he knows he won't get it."

Not with the pages and pages of documented abuse.

"I'm trying," she said. "I will. But somehow he found out about you going to your therapist and so he's trying to utilize everything that he can…"

I puffed out a breath.

I needed admin which I had worked out. Lucas had offered up a list of potentials. Including coordinators, assistants, and managers for staff.

Along with a full time medical team. Access to a clinic or care network I needed to go visit and work with.

I needed to talk to Reed about potentially hiring a full time security guard or several probably women around the premies so they could blend in.

He said he would go over a few of my options with me.

But there was so much to do that Gemma ended up gathering names and interviews and she had taken it as well upon herself.

"I'm wealthy and bored, sometimes." Gemma said over the phone. "I need to do things."

"Are you all right with doing everything?" I paused.

"Yes, now pass me all of it so I have something to do with my life that isn't mooning over my relationship."

Gemma had gotten together with her long time bodyguard Nathan Wyatt and the two of them lived together in her Upper East Side Townhouse.

And so Gemma had done about seventy percent of the work within a week which was insanity, but it was her job. It was something she was more familiar with than I was.

I had never felt more alive moving with purpose.

I had graduated to my turkey sandwich with some chips.

Gemma wasn't wrong.

Money meant having choices.

And I had that now.

"QUITE LITERALLY THEY SAID I CHANGED AFTER MY MARRIAGE—" I WAS venting to Dr. Khan. "I was just called an immigrant stealing some American families fortune even though I am a US citizen."

"The Devereaux's side of the PR machine is working overtime," Dr. Khan frowned. "I did get a few calls asking me for interviews about your mental health."

I gaped.

"The ethics of which are so disgusting," she shook her head clearly infuriated with my ex-husband's family.

"On social media they are spreading news about conspiracy's on how I was manipulating Michael and he can do no wrong. How am I supposed to deal with being hated despite what I have been through?"

I had been the one who woke up night and day to Michael's violence.

"Your attorneys are working overtime you said?"

I nodded.

"It might be worth speaking with Reed Whittaker, he sounds like a gentleman who can handle it."

"I completely forgot," I admitted. "I've been so busy with Haven but he was helping Gemma..."

Dr. Khan agreed. "It sounds like he might be able to assist you with your technical problems and he has the connections to help your lawyers fight this."

And so taking her advice I went back to Reed who agreed to help passing me over to someone named Liam Sullivan.

Liam called me one afternoon to talk to me about everything. I broke it down for him.

Over the phone Liam blew out a whistle. "Yeah, gimme a day or two to have everything pulled up. I can get enough dirt and everything else you need."

"Just like that?"

He sounded like I said something funny. "Just like that."

We began to connect over text or phone.

Liam being my point of contact and he was a polite man. I realized then this was the same Liam Sullivan dating my friend—Lara Ford.

I had met Lara through Gemma. Lara was the owner of a burlesque club—*Teaser's*.

Over the years, I had been there a few times. All of them I had been sneaking out. Under the guise of being with Gemma.

Now? Lara's boyfriend Liam became my life raft for all things combatting cybersecurity issues.

Liam became the person I texted whenever I saw or heard anything and in turn? Not having to worry about that let me focus on building Haven.

I called him one day to just thank him over the sheer relief I felt.

"Thank you, I cannot say that enough."

He chuckled on the phone one day and I heard a woman's voice in the background. "Gimme a second, Sonya."

And I realized I was probably interrupting his life which was why he texted. Before I could apologize I heard him shout. "*Muneca*, I got it. I got it...yes...yes."

I didn't realize Liam had a woman in his life.

He was on the phone. "Sorry about that. You don't have to thank me, taking your shit-bag ex is good enough."

"Even still, I am grateful."

He laughed again. "Nothing makes me happier than seeing guys like your ex eat shit, you're all good."

It was only after my conversation with Liam my phone rang again.

47

To my surprise it was Nisha and she sounded like she was breaking down.

"S-Sonya...can I come...stay with you? I need to leave my place right now."

8

AIDAN

BELOVA COULDN'T GET BACK TO ME IN TIME.

Not at his fault, I left one of my guys Devlin in charge of Chicago temporarily while I left for New York.

Reed had called me.

Killian and Nisha had broken up.

In short—Nisha ran away from Killian to one of her friends a woman named Sonya Amin.

"He didn't tell Nisha he was still mob," I explained to Alexei on the plane ride to New York. "He didn't tell a fucking civilian who we were and she's terrified. She's run off and now we have another civilian who happens to be stirring up all types of trouble in New York with her divorce, asking questions—about me."

Alexei was quiet as I said it.

"Yes, but your brother is a good man," he said after a moment.

"I'm not saying he isn't good. I'm saying he's a fucking idiot for keeping this from her. And now I need to go and meet with whoever this Sonya fucking Amin is to do damage control."

Killian conveniently forgot to mention to his sweeter and cake, girlfriend, that he occasionally murders people for a living.

Kieran, who had been sent to the hospital for a potential drug overdose, had accidentally told his nurse who was Killian's girlfriend, that *we were mob.*

49

Casually.

Nisha had ran.

Killian had freaked out on Kieran.

And now I had to put out multiple family fires.

We arrived in New York and the first thing I did was go see Reed in Titan Midtown where he basically explained with a regretful expression and Kieran—that Nisha had ran off.

"She ran off." I repeated dryly. "And now Sonya is asking why the Chicago mob is in New York?"

I covered my eyes feeling them twitch as I fought back whether or not I should laugh or cry.

Only things would get this complicated for me.

"Did he learn nothing from Lucas?"

Reed blew out a breath looking exhausted as he laughed without any humor.

"I need to talk to Sonya, don't I? That easiest way to fix this. I can go meet with Nisha and figure this out and explain everything to her."

"She won't see Killian so that's the best bet," but even as Reed said it? I read between the lines.

So my brother was actively losing his mind.

I blew out a breath. "Where is he?"

Reed blinked. "He didn't text you?" He ran a hand down his hand. "Listen, Liam was the one helping Sonya with me, if you need to find Killian, he'll help you."

"Liam Sullivan?"

Reed dipped his head. "He's dating Lara. According to Alisha."

Reed's girlfriend Alisha Malhotra was friends with Lara Ford. The one woman that had changed my entire life.

Nobody knew who Lara was but my family and Gabriel. And nobody would ever say a word about it.

I didn't think Reed knew.

Lara had been a trafficking victim of my father's Gabriel had rescued. When he had? He'd also saved me and my brothers.

Now? I owed her everything since she'd rebuilt the same club she'd been at a victim at into a multi-million dollar burlesque club. With a vision and Killian.

"I'll start with Sonya." I'll take my chances with the unknown.

Better Sonya Amin than Killian who was probably a loose cannon now.

ON THE DAY I WAS SUPPOSED TO MEET SONYA SHE PICKED A NEUTRAL spot.

Some cafe she said she liked called Butterscotch's. I texted her back and Alexei ran another check on her.

I already knew everything I needed to know about my brother's girlfriend.

I knew that Nisha Graham had been kidnapped at a really young age, and she been brought to the states. Her adoptive parents had abused her.

She'd put herself through nursing school and she ran some online blog about baking.

That was Killian's sweet *adorable* girlfriend. All smiles and sunshine.

Everything he was not. I hadn't even gone to see him.

There was no point.

I knew my brother and the moment I did see him? He would erupt. My focus was Sonya Amin.

The gatekeeper between me and Nisha—I was the kind of man who solved problems at root cause.

Root cause was Nisha.

Fix Nisha? It fixes Killian. Alls well.

Sonya Amin was a different story. A waif like thin ballerina who'd been married off to the highest bidder of some sort. Michael Devereaux who was her estranged soon-to-be ex-husband was now hounding her for everything under the son.

She didn't talk to her family. She effectively had nobody except for the support of the people around her like Reed who actually genuinely liked her.

But Reed's girlfriend Alisha was friends with Sonya. So he was biased.

She'd been married for nine years. No kids. And by the looks of it? Michael was a piece of shit.

Lucas texted me filling me in on the rest of what I needed to know about Sonya Amin. Or soon-to-be Amin. And now?

I had all the cards in my hand to meet her.

In the photos I saw of her she was model like beauty with sharp angles and a polite smile.

Her brunette locks always styled to perfection, darker green eyes that met the camera with a sultry look.

She was hot.

But not my type.

Too thin, too much trouble I couldn't afford, and I was here for Nisha. Just Nisha.

This was a job. Nothing else.

I stood in line waiting to get some food because I was starving again when I heard a male voice behind me.

"Aye, sorry about that, you come around here often?"

A husky female voice that sent a shiver chasing down my spine said. "Sorry, I don't speak English." Her accent was musical.

"Where are you from?" Guy was persistent. I'd give him that. I eyed Alexei on his phone no doubt texting Kieran. The two got on well.

"Not here. Sorry."

Her accent was thicker and she moved closer to me. I knew because nobody dared to stand more than one foot close to me and she was right there.

"I can use translate apps to talk to you—"

"No—"

Jesus fucking—

I turned around staring down at a woman about Nisha's height, but she was the prettiest thing I'd ever seen.

When I'd been younger I'd had this crush on this actress who'd been an elf or fairy or some shit in this fantasy series franchise.

She looked like that woman.

Sonya.

The photos fucking lied.

Her eyes were darker and deeper than emerald and now batting up at me as she murmured an apology ducking her head down.

I forced myself to step to the side a tiny bit and motion for her to get in front of me.

"Hey, we were talking—" the other guy started.

But Sonya was already shooting me a grateful look on her too sharp too pretty face and cutting ahead.

"The conversations over." I tried to get between them and he touched me. Or he tried to.

Alexei cut in between us so fast I knew the guy took two steps back as my Enforcer eyed him down hungrily.

He said something in Russian that didn't sound too nice and it definitely wasn't a fucking proverb as I turned to Sonya.

Sonya Amin.

In the flesh.

She was shorter than I thought she'd look in the pictures. But I was learning, the pictures were lies.

Now she didn't look too thin she just looked haunted. And she was watching me, batting those dark eyes up to see what the commotion was.

"Thank you."

She did in fact speak English.

I felt a smirk curving my lips. "No problem." I motioned for her to go in front of me as it was her turn at the register.

"Welcome to the Butterscotch Bakery, my name's Mint how can I help you?"

Sonya ordered her food. "A turkey sandwich please, with the cheese. Provolone. Little lettuce. And some mayo. One bag of the chips. The spicy…yes…"

That was my order. She missed the tomatoes though.

"And tomato…" she added.

Nevermind.

The lady at the register was hitting buttons on her screen.

"Would you like a cookie with that? We're running a special today and all sandwiches come with a cookie and water bottle."

Sonya thought about it. Like she was upset. But she nodded.

"And what flavor cookie would you like?"

Now Sonya looked perturbed. She looked at the case and back and then again. "Ummm…"

She looked at the register girl who was blinking owl eyes back. "Whatever is your favorite."

Red-velvet. With the icing. Of course.

I blinked at my own thoughts.

"Red-velvet." The cashier said. I smirked.

The register wrung her up but then Sonya turned to me. "I can buy you lunch, since you—" she motioned to the guy behind me Alexei was still eyeing down with a bored expression.

I bit back a laugh. "No, I'm straight—I don't need anything."

"But you—I insist." She turned back to the register. "Can you make it two sandwiches? And with the cookie."

I blinked as Sonya paid for it with her smartwatch or some shit before I could blink and then she asked me. "Do you want something else? For your friend?"

I shook my head unable to formulate words at this woman's kindness. And then she ordered three.

"Sorry, make that four orders of the same thing because…they are bigger."

Oh, she was adorable. She paid for it easily and then she smiled at me over her shoulder and…just walked off to the waiting area.

She walks off?

Who is this woman?

I walked after her as Alexei followed and the two of us were around her. Sonya blinked up at me and then Alexei a little flustered.

"Yes?"

"You speak English." I lowered my voice. "I won't say a thing, but you didn't have to do that."

"It's okay," she stumbled over her words. Her perfect English gone and I wondered if I made her nervous. "You helped me, so I just want to do something nice."

Without expecting anything in her return. Now in her wool coat, in that deep green that brought her eyes out, her fingers trembled a little.

I make her nervous.

I didn't want to scare her but if she knew who I was it would. And I knew for a second then Sonya Amin didn't know me.

Initially, that had been the entire point. The entire point was to make sure that she didn't know who I was. I had the upper hand. Now? Face to face with her? I did not have the upper hand.

She was pretty. A nice lady. And fucking stunning up close.

Looks aside, focus. She's got questions. You need Nisha.

I felt my throat working as she watched me carefully and Alexei broke the silence.

"You are Sonya Amin?"

She blinked at him and I would've slapped him upside the head if we weren't in public. I shot him a look and he blinked.

"What? She looks like the picture. You are Sonya? We are here for Nisha. And you."

Her bow shaped lips, pink and pouty parted just a little as she took me in again and I saw the shift in real time.

In real time.

The relaxed posture gone, her smile dipping, her eyes widening now with a panic. And her entire face completely shuttered.

That is what I did to people.

This.

I watched in real time her reaction when she realized just who she had helped.

"You're Aidan O'Hara?" She whispered.

I tipped my head.

That was me.

And then I watched in real time as she looked away and I told myself it shouldn't have hurt as much as it did.

I was here for a job.

Not for a pretty lady who didn't like the sight of me.

9

SONYA

SPEAK?

I couldn't even think straight.

"You're Aidan O'Hara?"

Was it just me or did he wince?

He was handsome. More than a man should be allowed to be. Over six feet tall, with dark locks of hair, inky black and eyes that were too beautiful. Bright citrine. Amber. Lush.

That was the word.

He looked unreal as he licked his lips and watched me.

This was Killian's older brother?

Nisha never mentioned he was…beautiful.

"In the flesh." He muttered shooting an annoyed glance over at the pretty younger man next to him. His platinum blonde hair despite being a windswept mess, his eyes were clear as day and he smiled a little at me.

That only made Aidan more annoyed.

"I am Alexei." He held his hand out. "Thank you for buying us food. Do you want to sit down?"

He motioned to a table and I nodded dumbly aware I just accidentally purchased lunch for the man I was supposed to meet. And his… assistant?

When Aidan had motioned for me to skip him to avoid the man

asking me out, I had thought he was enormous. He smelled of something masculine and spice and I found myself unconsciously leaning into him.

And then he'd come closer and I got to take in a chiseled face, jawline cut from marble like one of the Greek gods in the paintings Eleanor had around her home.

"Like I said," Aidan said in a cooler tone still being Alexei. "You didn't have to buy us anything."

I swallowed unable to even speak. And then our order was called out and I felt nothing but grateful as I went to go grab it. Alexei, the blonde, reached for it to help me as Aidan let him do his thing.

Definitely assistant. I didn't dare look at him.

For years I kept my head down never making eye contact with a man and right now? Aidan O'Hara was stirring up something in me that felt as unfamiliar as eating to me.

I felt my hands trembling and my body waking up...to him?

My English had deserted me. Words in any language seemed inadequate around him.

We sat down and I felt almost nervous now. Why was I shaking so hard? I couldn't open my sandwich or eat or anything. I was just frozen. Both of them moved in sync with each other with Alexei sitting in a way that looked like he was blocking Aidan from the public.

Maybe a bodyguard?

"I want to see Nisha." His sandwich sat in front of him untouched as those amber eyes aimed at me.

On his face? Those eyes looked ethereal even as his words cut through me.

"My brother made a mistake. I understand you have questions, but this isn't the time for me to answer them. At least not out loud."

He motioned around. Alexei looked between us as he slowly opened his food and began working in on one of his sandwiches.

I was hungry just watching him, even if he took a bite like a wolf.

Neither Aidan nor I moved. We didn't even take off our coats. We just sat there facing each other off.

"Y—You cannot—see her." I was struggling. My hands were

shaking so hard I shoved them under my thighs feeling all of seven around him. "No."

I said it. I practiced it so many times.

Nisha had come running to me and she'd told me brokenly she was terrified. She was pregnant and terrified. Two things this man did not know.

I knew Nisha had been happy with Killian, and she loved him—until she found out he was *mafia*.

That was not a small thing.

I could not imagine finding out the man I loved for months and was having a baby with was…a criminal.

It was frightening for her and she'd come to me for refuge. And I gave it to her at the townhouse. She was staying with me for the time being. And I was here trying to formulate a singular sentence with Aidan O'Hara.

He blinked. "No."

"No."

Alexei was halfway through his sandwich munching quietly. He had the manners of a wolf.

"What do you want in return for me seeing her?"

"I want nothing. I just want to keep her safe."

That was a fact.

"She is safe. Killian would never hurt her."

There was a certainty in his voice, and I don't know why I just didn't believe him.

I didn't think that Killian would be the type to willingly hurt his girlfriend, but I also didn't know him.

I was learning to operate off of trusting actions versus words. And right now, the actions did not match the words.

"He lied to her." I sat up straighter feeling a flicker of fire in me. "He lied to her and he did not tell her who he is—"

"Let's not do that here." He glanced over with a flicker of his eyes before turning back to me. "I'm here to tell you what you know isn't the entire truth. He's clean. As much as he could be. He's a Titan and most of his money comes from there. He's solid."

Is he?

"He wasn't *solid* when she came running to me crying." I found my voice. I was practicing my spine straightened. "She trusted him. And he lied to her. What do you want me to say? Everything is fine? Yes, you can see her?"

"I want you to let me see her. I want to talk to her—"

"And what will you do when you do?"

In my mind, I just imagine the worst case scenario of what happened to me. It was when I would go to my mother, it was the first time I still remember it I went to her, and I told her what Michael was doing to me.

And she laughed.

My mother laughed and told me I was being a big baby and she said "boys will be boys" and that I should just take it.

A sour sensation filled my throat into my stomach at the memory of that.

I went to her three more times for different things and each time she would get more and more angry.

Why are you bothering me with this nonsense, Sonya? Did I not raise you better? He has money?

Who cares if he hits you?

He can do whatever he wants to you, you're his wife.

Maybe if you were able to have a child with him, he would not beat you so bad. You failed him as a woman and now you deserve to be punished.

None of it was true.

And I imagined what it would be like if someone like Aidan looked like a man who was used to getting his way got into a room with a woman who didn't know any better.

I couldn't fight. I was barely a hundred and fifteen pounds which was underweight. I could only yell and maybe then not too loud.

But I knew in my heart?

I would never what happened to me happen to another woman. I had cruelty in my life.

I didn't want that for Nisha.

Aidan's jaw clenched, the sunlight making his eyes look eerily bright and his hair almost blue. "I want to fix this as much as you wanna protect her. And she won't see my brother."

So she got him. This man.

59

I had not met Killian O'Hara, but meeting Aidan told me what kind of a man his sibling was.

Alexei who had been downing his second sandwich looked between us like he was watching a tennis match.

He was the least threatening bodyguard I had ever met.

My throat worked as I said in a low voice.

"I don't trust you to not hurt her. I have met men like you. I know you. She is already in a not good place and I came here to meet you to shed some light on what is going on. So if you want me to consider anything—I would like answers from you on why I should ever let anyone like you close to her. When we both know, you are still keeping secrets."

He paused. And I could tell I upset him. He wasn't used to being denied. Just like my ex-husband.

He is used to getting what he wants.

Just like Michael.

And at that thought my spine stiffened.

He wasn't Michael. No. But I didn't know him. Handsome man aside? I didn't know this man.

I just met him.

And even if he made me feel things? I thought about Nisha, pregnant, crying and numbed out in my townhouse. I couldn't let her go.

Years of being taunted by my mother reminded me that even the best of people? Did not want the best for you.

Who else is he supposed to beat?

You are his wife. You need to understand your place in the world, Sonya. You are a woman, he is a man.

Who else is he supposed to walk all over?

My rage felt like flickers of a flame as I sat on my shaking hands. I bit my cheeks to stop my lower lip from wobbling. Until I tasted copper.

I was sitting in the room with Aidan and Alexei and the crowd milling around us. But I was mentally somewhere darker.

The shadows in my head took over.

I watched Aidan O'Hara expectantly. When he spoke his voice was gruff. "Sometimes we keep things from people to protect them."

"And sometimes it's because we don't trust them to be able to handle the truth," I said. "But she can. She can handle it. Just like I can."

"You can't handle the truth," now he looked at me differently almost mockingly. He looked angrier, annoyed with me, annoyed with the situation as Alexei ate quietly.

"You're a former ballerina. You've been to private school your entire life. You're from a wealthy family. You've never gone hungry a single day. Not without choice. You sit here on your high horse and you make judgment calls about me. Even before I walked in here and you knew who I was, you had already made a call about me. You already thought some type of way. I never even had a chance. So let's not pretend like you're not judgmental. *You are* judgmental. *Especially* in your six hundred dollar shoes."

Amber eyes leveled at me.

Michael once stomped into my rib cage with his Italian loafers. He'd thrown me onto the floor and kicked me so hard it broke my left rib.

This hurt differently as he said it.

The kind man who told me that I could move in front of him was completely gone, and instead in his place was a dangerous predator. And I suddenly realize that if I thought Michael was, Aidan O'Hara was infinitely worse. Because Aidan O'Hara had already committed crimes and had gotten away with it.

I didn't need to know he had.

He wore the look of someone who could watch me die and not care.

"The moment you saw me and you knew what I was, you had already made up your mind. But that was fine because I didn't have to come and see you. I didn't have to come and meet you today. I did it because I needed to be polite because that's my brother's girl."

He said brother with some hint of warmth in his eyes that was gone as quickly as it appeared.

"See, Mrs. Devereaux—"

"It's Amin." My temper flared.

He continued like I hadn't spoken. "I can do whatever I want. This meeting is a courtesy. This meeting is not a necessity for me. I can take what I want and when I want."

61

"You must feel fantastic about yourself," I shot back. "Bragging to a woman about whatever *you* want to do."

He leaned back with a smirk on his too pretty lips.

"It's easy to judge something when it isn't packaged all pretty, princess?"

I don't know it burned as he called me that.

"I am not a princess." I steeled my spine against this man not knowing where it came from in me but I dug deep as I said it. "I don't judge you because of your title and because you are *who and what* you are—"

I was aware I couldn't exactly say it out loud.

In hindsight, this may not have been the best place for us to have this conversation, but my spine straightened.

Alexei stopped chewing his food and I wondered for a while second if he was just going to kill me.

"I judge you based off your inability to speak the truth, to just say what you need to. To trust in loving someone enough to know they can handle what you have to throw at them. Your brother didn't. He kept things from her. And when she was blind-sided she ran from him. That is what I know."

I was shaking even harder as Alexei paused in his third sandwich having stolen Aidan's, his clear blue eyes batting at me with respect.

"And now she is my home, she is afraid and somehow even if she does not want to meet him? You are no better. I am not judging you. It's hard for me to speak English. Not because of you. You come here and demand to see her. You don't try to explain yourself. The entire point was for you to fix not to come here and say I am a ballerina and *you are not.*"

I don't know where it came from but there it was.

"You bring up my past like you can use it as a weapon. Like you can make me feel ashamed. Why? Did you think that you were coming into a negotiation? We were here to talk about a mutual friend. Not your enemy. You do not know how to speak to normal people, do you?"

I caught the flicker of surprise in his eyes as I said it all.

And I wasn't finished.

"You are not seeing Nisha." I didn't even feel an ounce of satisfaction as I said it and his eyes darkened.

"After seeing how cruel you are as a man, I would never let you anywhere near my home," I continued. "I will tell Reed I did not see you and this did not work out. Nisha will always be safe with me. I suggest if you do not want problems in your *illegal activities* you will stay away from me. I still have some weight to my name—both of them—and I am not afraid of you to use it."

The spirit of Gemma Marchand has possessed me.

Only Gemma had that type of sharp tongue.

I stood up then adjusting my coat and walking out before my hands shaking so hard gave me away.

I had no idea where any of that came from, but I felt like after spending months and months with sassy women all around me, it was inside of me now and I could not let it stop.

I did not feel bad as I walked away.

I only felt for Nisha.

How could I even tell her this?

10

AIDAN

"She has...what you say?"

Alexei pointed to his canines. "Vampire."

I would've snorted had I not been shut down by the elven lady.

Alexei watched Sonya walk away and now I didn't hold back. I did smack him upside the head.

"Fangs." I corrected him. "She has fangs."

"*Da*. Big ones." He started in on the cookies while I sat there peeved.

I didn't even remember anything that she said I just remembered how it made me feel. I did walk into this like a negotiation. Was that not what this was?

"You speak to her like Belova," Alexei said taking an enormous bite of the red velvet cookie. "But she is not Belova."

No.

She was a five foot five Asian woman with a bite.

It had been a few days since I saw Sonya now. Alexei had discovered red velvet cookies and ordered dozens of them and I was pretty sure he was single-handedly operating off sugar.

It was nice up until she knew that I was a monster.

I never factored in the fact that English was not her first language so maybe she just had a hard time talking to me. Maybe I just made her nervous.

Should I have provoked her? Probably not.

And now I was nowhere near fixing Killian's problem.

"You should not go to women like that," Alexei dropped his wisdom. "In Russia—"

"No." I cut him off. "No proverbs."

He shrugged looking amused at me. "We go to Killian now?"

"No," I shook my head feeling annoyed more than ever.

"So in Russia—"

"Alexei—" I rubbed my hands over my eyes.

"No, she is like mother bear."

I opened my eyes as he looked as philosophical as he could look at the age of twenty-one shoveling red velvet cookies into his mouth with a gigantic jar of milk in front of him.

Reed had lent us this apartment inside of K2 to stay at and right now Alexei was the only one having the time of his life.

"I'm beginning to think you only come with me to New York because you like the food here."

He turned a little red. "Is good. But she is."

Back to Sonya. "I haven't seen Killian because there's no point. If you go to him now he's probably drinking and pissed off. I know how much she means to him, and we have to fix this before we can go to him." I paused. "Nisha isn't her cub."

"She is." Alexei argued with his mouth full. "She turned the mansion into a home for women. You know, like a safe place. Reed said so. I ask him. He says she is protective. If Killian's wife runs to her scared? She is there because she is afraid. Maybe you do not speak to her like you speak to Belova's."

"*How* do I speak to her, *Aristotle*?"

"Who?" He blinked.

Right.

He had no formal education. I don't even know if he knew how to read or write properly but I was betting it was the level of a fifteen year old. So there was that. One problem down another to go.

"You need to go to her like a man." Alexei nodded. "You know Devlin?"

Yeah. I left him in charge of Chicago.

"He has woman."

I frowned. "He does?"

Alexei nodded all sage like eating his fucking cookies. "He says he did not go to her like he was mafia. But like…a man. And she likes this. He says he brings her flowers—"

"I am not bringing Sonya flowers."

Alexei shrugged. "Then maybe you can bring her food. Devlin says he does this as well."

"Devlin is dating his woman. There's a difference."

"Yes, but you want to date Sonya."

I blinked as all of me careened to a halt. He sat there like a swami holding court with milk. "What?"

Alexei shrugged again like it was a no brainer for him. "She is pretty lady. She fights you. You respect that."

"How the fuck do you—"

"I fight you." He blinked at me soaking his next cookie. "You respect me. And Devlin. And Killian." He took an enormous bite.

This was true. I did like people who disagreed with me.

Mostly because I knew they weren't kissing my ass.

But this was different.

She got under my skin in a different way. She wasn't somebody that I could intimidate. Even though I saw her hand shaking, she didn't back down. Her accent got super thick and beautiful when she got angry. And her eyes flashed whenever I called her a princess.

The truth was that's what she was. She was everything that I wasn't. She had everything that I didn't.

She didn't know me.

It rankled me she thought she did.

"She doesn't know me—"

"Mhm."

"She doesn't understand our world—"

"Mhmm."

"She doesn't get where I'm coming from—"

"Mhm."

A pause.

He swallowed his cookie. "But you will go will go see her."

I had to. For Killian.

Even I understood deep down this was the first thing that he'd really ever wanted.

I remembered how he introduced her to me. Like he was a shy seven-year-old introducing me to his favorite toy. Like he liked her.

And I did not mean to go see him to know that he was not in a good place.

I would do it for him.

I blew out a breath tipping my head back on the couch.

"Jesus fucking Christ, Alexei."

"I have already picked out the flowers…I think her favorite color is green…" he held out his phone and showed me two options. "I get both since they are pretty and you have money."

"I'm going to kill you."

He just kept talking like I hadn't even said anything. "I also purchase all the cookies and sandwiches she likes so we can deliver them to her townhouse. The one on the East Side not Haven. I believe Nisha is staying there."

As he kept talking I closed my eyes preparing myself for another fucking verbal duel with Sonya.

The elven princess.

"Man, fuck this shit."

11

SONYA

I WASN'T EXPECTING THE FLOWERS AT MY TOWNHOUSE.

Marta came inside and said we had a guest.

Nisha was asleep upstairs and I frowned at the endless sea of all shades of green. There were some hints of soft pink roses in between that, but they were all wrapped in cream ribbons.

"Is it your birthday, Marta?" I asked her confused.

"No, Miss. You have a gentleman at the door. Mighty handsome I'd say."

I frowned. "I'm not expecting anyone."

I went over knowing Marta knew better than to let in Michael but I didn't know who else it could be.

But who I found in the foyer was the last person I expected. The moment I saw him standing there in his wool coat, looking entirely too uncomfortable, I was on him. Ushering him with a group on his arm into the library.

"Did anyone see you?" I hissed looking out the window aware Michael might not know I was residing here and I did have cameras, but alas—I did not want anyone knowing I was cavorting with...a criminal.

"You mean did anyone see me creeping around your manor?"

"Now is not the time to joke, my ex-husband will use you against me." Just imagine the titles right now of the gossip rags.

Ex-Devereaux flame gets fortune with criminal

Sonya Devereaux shacking up or slumming it out?

Heiress leaves high roller husband for mafia boss

I felt hysterical laughter, bubble up inside of me at the idea of them. And then I turned back around to face him.

"You are back."

"Yeah. Look, I didn't know Alexei ordered the entire shop. And nobody saw me." He held up a ball cap. "I looked like a delivery guy. I'm not completely stupid. Figured your ex was a nightmare so I came prepared."

I didn't know how to place him with a baseball cap in his hand. He was over six feet something of pure male grace and he took up all the space in the room with his darker presence. Amber eyes catching the morning light now through the cracks in the curtain.

I loved this library, I had hand picked all of the trinkets in here, including all of the lambs and everything else. But right now, his presence felt just a little bit unsettling. Like I was letting him into my private world.

Now I felt a little uncomfortable, because now I was standing there with him in my library like a couple of days ago, we hadn't gone to toe to toe.

Nisha was in the house right now.

I didn't know if he knew or not, but I didn't find out and tell him.

"Why are you here?"

This was awkward and he looked just about as uncomfortable as I felt.

We were completely polar opposites, and I forced myself to focus because I had never had anything romantic with a man and I never intended to.

Especially not one who looked like he could eat me alive.

Not that one.

"Look, I came here because I know it's not a negotiation."

I stopped. Aware it was just the two of us inside the library and now the door was closed. I hadn't been alone in a room with a man in so long I almost forgot how it felt.

Except I waited for the interfere and it never came. Which was surprising considering the last time I met him we had a verbal match.

"I came here to talk." He looked almost resigned as he said it. I was uncomfortable. He wasn't used to this.

This wasn't what he normally did.

I was sure that as a man who was in charge of his own empire, he was not only used to getting his way, but he was never used to hearing pushback.

But Michael had never shown up with flowers after he made a mistake. In his mind he didn't make any mistakes—I did.

This was new for me.

I motioned to one of the couches in the library.

And I sat opposite him folding my hands under my thighs so he wouldn't see them shaking.

Between us was the wooden coffee table filled with flowers and my magazines.

He looked out of place in my home.

"To talk," I repeated.

He dipped his head and my heart thundered at how he looked now that he said down with his lazier grace.

"I just came to talk. About my family. About Killian. About our business."

I swallowed. His business.

"Your family is—"

"Mob." He tipped his head. His bluntness made my breath catch. I told myself that's what it was and not his jawline, the lines of his throat I wanted to run my fingers on like art. Or the way his Adam's apple bobbed as it worked.

He exhaled.

"It sounds really shitty when you say it out loud. I just considered it business. But instead of hiding what I do I'm just very open about it. If I ran a corporate business and I was killing people like politicians do, I would keep it under the rug. I don't do that. I'm just like everybody else, I'm just a bit more forward about it."

That he was. Extremely forward.

70

No social mask for him.

Part of me respected that. Envied it.

"My empire is no different. If you wanna know, since I came into power, I took out everything my father did. So it's not so much crimes as it is just getting shit done. I handle real estate, and I handle legitimate ventures—"

"Yes, but you—" I broke off. How did I ask him this? "But you hurt people."

He shrugged deceptively casual. "I do. But I don't hurt people for no reason. If someone comes up to me and tells me that their daughter was assaulted by the cops, what do you want me to do? You may go to the police and ask them for a restraining order? We both know that shit doesn't work. It only works if you have somebody with you full-time protecting you. I prefer an expedited method on solving my problems."

Aidan O'Hara explained that people had all types of names but at the end of the day Killian didn't tell Nisha—

"Nisha's the equivalent of a softie. At best. I know he was stupid for telling her, but I wanna talk to her and explain everything out to her. I feel like she sensible she's just scared—"

"She's frightened."

He paused. "I know. Which is why I'm here to ask you to let me see her. I think if I talk to her, it'll make her feel better because she has answers and she won't see Killian. And I'd like to respect her wishes at the bare minimum."

"Why?"

I knew full well Aidan O'Hara had the ability to break into my home and demand answers.

He chose not to.

He shrugged lightly. "Because I'm not a total tool and I think she deserves a choice. She also deserves the truth, but she won't see Killian because he scares her. And I know that guts him alive because he loves her. So I'm second best choice."

Amber eyes flickered over me then curiously.

"I think it should be her choice and I know she's here—" I stiffened. "So I'll let you go and talk to her and I can come back at a better time for her. Once I do, I'm gonna go mediate with

Killian and before I leave this damn city again—I'll fix it and go."

What?

"You're not from here?"

"Reed didn't tell you I live in Chicago?"

I forgot honestly. "You look comfortable in the city. I thought you were from here."

"My family was based out here once."

"What happened?"

Something happened. I saw it on his face.

"Someone killed my father and I took over Chicago and Killian took over New York. It's split between us but it's less for him. I moved everything out there and we're slowly moving into legitimate ventures. More property taxes, instead of human trafficking."

I blinked. He was so forward and casual about his...life.

Now he was telling me the truth and it wasn't that I couldn't handle it, but I had never been around somebody who spoke so casually, and so honestly about his life before.

Everybody in my life always played games.

Everybody always hid things. In a way he reminded me of Lucas because Lucas spoke like this too.

"Do you commit crimes?"

"Sometimes."

I processed that. "Do you hurt people?"

"Sometimes."

"And women..."

He seemed to consider himself very carefully before he answered my question. His eyes held mine, and he tipped his head as he said it.

"Contrary to popular belief I'm not a complete monster."

I could hear a pin drop in the library as I gripped my thighs feeling myself shaking, tumbling into my own shadows.

"No, I don't hurt women." A lazy smile graced his lips. "Not unless they ask nicely." At my expression he smirked wider. "Can I see Nisha?"

I ducked my head feeling heat on my cheeks at the mental images he conjured up.

"Yes."

12

AIDAN

Nisha was pregnant.

I knew looking at her.

She was trying to hide it.

Thats why she ran.

I forced myself to stay calm because deep down in my head, I knew why she ran from Killian. It was never about the mafia. It was about her *kid*.

Alexei's words rang in my head that these were women, who were protecting people.

That was their mental state.

Killian and Nisha were keeping secrets from me.

And Sonya?

She definitely knew. This is why she was so protective. And it all made sense then. I rose when I saw her and I knew, I took her by surprise.

Alexei was sitting in the kitchen meeting Sonya again with Marta feeding him.

"I'm sorry," I said it to Nisha. Her dark hair looked a little duller and the light around her eyes dimmed.

She looked like she'd been crying. "I'm sorry, Nisha. I shouldn't have let that happen—"

"You didn't do anything—"

"I did—" I broke off, the weight of responsibility heavy. "I did. I know this isn't easy for you. But I appreciate you giving me a chance to explain."

"I'm not sure what there is to explain," she said, her voice steadier than I expected. "Killian lied to me. For months. Kieran told me by accident—"

"I think you deserve to know why."

"Why?"

My smile felt grim. "Because my brother loves you, and he's losing his mind without you. I don't think my brother intended to deceive you..." I began, feeling the weight of family secrets on my tongue. How do you explain generations of damage without scaring someone away?

"Killian, he's...not good at talking." The laugh that escaped me was harsh, bitter. "But you probably knew that already. He's always been closed off, especially compared to Kieran."

I paused a bit gathering myself.

I don't understand why I had to be so honest now. But it was working.

"He didn't tell me anything about you for months. I only recently realized just how serious he was about you. He wasn't always meant to be who he is now. For a long time, he was an outcast. Our father..." The hatred rose in my throat. "He didn't like Killian."

"He mentioned that to me..." Her soft voice surprised me. "He told me months ago that your father was...he wasn't a good man."

Cormac O'Hara was a monster.

He beat scars into Killian's skin. When Gabriel had found me my father had almost killed me several times. I had the scars to prove it.

We all did. Except all of us had gotten tattoos over them to hide it all.

No need to brag.

My father had trafficked girls, believed in human slavery, and held up his end up murdering innocent folks at the hands of businessmen who needed it.

Lucas's father and mine had worked together years ago to ensure everyone who spoke out against him had died.

Lucas and I swore to be better. Nisha had no clue.

74

"That's a polite way of putting it."

I talked to Nisha a bit more about Killian.

"Killian's always been the one helping everyone else. Always there for others as a way to not be there for himself. He doesn't know how to treat himself...until you."

Until you made him human again.

"My brother isn't eloquent. He doesn't know how to tell you that when Kieran left the family business, he stepped up. Took over. I didn't know if he knew what he wanted. I just knew...it was what he did. We've changed, Nisha. Stopped most of what our father did. Now, our family is mostly just that—a network within Titan. We don't always participate in..."

"Killian, he deals with real estate, legitimate ventures. He helps Titan, runs his own industry. Now, the only real criminal in the family is me. I can't say my brother doesn't do things for Titan that on paper are...morally bankrupt. But the only member of the mafia in the family is me. What Killian does for everyone else? That's sanctioned."

"I know he messed up. I messed up too. I should've sat down with you guys, but I was too busy. I should've talked to you."

"I don't know what to do. I ran away from home...after my life...I never wanted to run again. And...I'm angry with him."

"That's fine, you can be. But I think the longer it went on, the harder it was for him to tell you. But I'm not here to convince you to go back to him. I only wanted you to understand his point of view. Not that I do..." Frustration crept into my voice. My brother, always silent when words mattered most. "Killian hasn't said a word to me."

"How can I trust anything he says now?"

"I can't make this decision for you," I said, gentling my voice. "But I know he's doing everything in his power to make sure nothing happens to you."

I kept my voice carefully measured, watching Nisha's unconscious protective gesture over her stomach. "I know it would help if you at least spoke to him. If you choose to."

She nodded slowly, and I noted how she cradled her secret. "I...I don't know if I'm ready. I just found out you're in the mafia..."

"I can't explain the entire thing to you, all I can tell you is, Killian

75

isn't fully in or out. He's been in the middle of everything for a long time. But it's up to you what you want to do—"

The muffled thud hit my ears like a gunshot. I stilled.

I was rising before I could even stop it, unable to stop myself from walking out of the room and into the kitchen where I heard it coming from.

I heard Alexei's voice in Russian, and I heard someone shouting. I was moving before I could even stop myself with Nisha right on my heels.

Sonya.

The sight that greeted me in the kitchen was one I haven't seen coming. My eyes took in Sonya first, her distress, those emerald eyes wide and hands shaking.

I clocked everything rapidly. Alexei's gun drawn. Marta the housekeeper glancing between the Sonya, and the man in the room causing the chaos.

I focused in on him.

Shorter than me.

Blonde. Blue eyes. I didn't need anyone to introduce him. I knew Michael Devereaux when I saw him. The way his nose turned up. The way he looked at me like I was scum, his cheeks turning red with mottled rage.

"What the fuck is this, Sonya? *You have men in this house holding a weapon to me? Are you fucking kidding me right now?*"

Oh. Hell. No.

"*It is none of your business who I have in my house,*" Sonya raised her voice her voice quivering and her body shaking. "You are violating your restraining order. And you need to leave."

He's definitely going to leave.

After I break his kneecaps.

Michael was the living embodiment of the same type of abuser my father was. I looked into him already. He represented everything I had spent years fighting against.

With Nisha pregnant in the room? I needed to get her out. And then kill this motherfucker.

"What the fuck is this Sonya?" Michael's voice grated against my ears. The kind of entitled rage I knew too well. The kind my father had wielded like a weapon.

I needed to get Nisha out. That was my first focus. Everything else was secondary.

Alexei's teeth were bared. "Boss—"

"You have men in this house holding a weapon to me? Are you fucking kidding me right now?"

"It is none of your business who I have in my house! You are violating your restraining order. And you need to leave. I'm calling the police."

I felt the growl building in my throat. "I suggest you watch your fucking mouth, Devereaux—"

"Don't tell me what the fuck to do—"

"*You're* not allowed here," Sonya's voice shook, but she stood tall. "And I am allowed to have *whoever* I want in my home."

And I swear I saw my father's face on Michael Devereaux. I knew how my father treated my mother. I knew that he just used her for what he needed. I still remember walking in on my mother the day she killed herself.

Hanging from the ceiling of her bedroom.

Killian behind me lost and quiet. He remembered nothing.

But that was why my father didn't like Killian.

Only I knew deep down what I would never say, Killian's eyes weren't ours. He didn't resemble us too much until he laughed. And I knew, what I overheard. Years ago.

Even if he was my half-brother? I considered him blood. And he would never know what I knew. I would never tell a soul.

Now? As I watched Michael I was aware of myself snapping. Nisha was right behind me.

"*Allowed?*" His gaze snapped to me, puffing up like all weak men do before they fall. "Who the fuck are you?"

"I suggest you listen to your *ex*-wife. Because if you don't, I'm the man who's gonna be escorting you off the fucking property." I turned to Alexei, keeping Michael in my peripheral vision. "How the fuck did he get in?"

Marta's voice trembled. "I'm sorry sir, I thought he was the mailman."

"Don't let it happen again."

Marta was fired. She just didn't know it. I'd get this shit in order real fucking quick. Something was building, moving through me, the urge to protect Sonya and make sure she was taken care of was a new one—but it was one and the same knowing my brother's girl and his fucking baby were in the room too.

I couldn't shoot anyone like this.

Alexei moved toward Nisha after my quick order in Russian. *"Take her."*

He needed to get Nisha out.

I'd handle the fucking cockroach in the room after.

13

SONYA

It happened so fast I didn't see it coming.

The moment Alexei lift with Nisha—the moment the door closed to the kitchen, Aidan was moving. A tank in his shirt and tattoos fully exposed to Michael's shock.

I had seen Lucas lay into Michael months ago.

Andrei blocking me from witnessing it.

There was nothing blocking me anymore.

"I fucking dare you to say half of the shit you did to her? To me." Aidan's voice was dark, his amber eyes pitch black now. "I fucking dare you."

One moment, Michael was standing there in his privileged indignation in his Italian suit and the next he was pinned to the kitchen wall with Aiden's arm against his throat.

In an instant it was dark against whatever Michael was. Because he certainly wasn't light. Not when he'd rammed his boot into my side. Not when he held me down to take what he deemed was his.

Not when he slapped me around enough times and left me in the house alone only to tell people I was spoiled and entitled.

Not when his family insulted me for being a brown woman married into a white family and degrading them.

Not once had I ever seen Michael as light.

But now?

79

I didn't see Aidan like that either.

"Shut the fuck up."

My heart was pounding at the sound of Aidan's voice as he leveled a wicked grin at Michael his cheeks red as he shoved his arm into his throat.

"You are such a fucking cunt, Mikkey. *Everyone* in your family knows it. Look at you talking to me and your fancy fucking suit. Like I'm dirt. *When I fucking own you."*

Aidan shoved his arm as he searched Michael pockets with one hand throwing his wallet and keys to the floor.

"I fucking own this city and the next one, and everyone under it. But see, you don't know me like I know you, do you?" Michael face was turning bottle red as Aidan pinned him and I saw Marta frowning.

I felt no sympathy for Michael.

None.

I was angry with Marta. I was. Maybe in another life, I would've been upset or I would've been shocked, but right now I was more furious than anything else.

What was interesting about healing was that, the more you healed? The less you tolerated what you had in the past.

The more your past disgusted you.

We had cameras set up.

We had so much security, I didn't understand how he got in. Either she got careless and didn't check or she knew who it was and felt entitled to let him in.

One moment I had been conversing with Alexei who was a hungry boy, and the next Michael had been swearing and demanding answers enough for Alexei to draw his gun so fast.

But watching Aidan look at Michael like an unleashed predator?

"Who the fuck do you—" Michael's growl cut off him thoughts as Aidan took him in both hands and slammed him back into the wall, making the cabinets rattle and I put my hand over my mouth.

"One more fucking word out of your mouth—"

"You piece of—"

"You guessed it." If I thought Aidan would hit him in the face I was wrong. He went straight for his sides. Two hits. And I winced covering my eyes at the sound of fist meeting flesh.

"Fuck off, Mikkey. I don't have time for you today. You're going to willingly walk out of here, or I will call the fucking commissioner down here to take your fucking ass out. And the press. With the way you've been hounding my girl, I suggest you get the fuck out of here."

Michael's throat worked as he wheezed and glanced back at me only for Aidan to block his view.

"*Now.*"

He let out a breath as to my relief my ex-husband stumbled out of the room. To my shock, Aidan turned around looking more annoyed than anything else.

"You." His eyes now black laser-focused on Marta. "Why did you let him in?"

She stumbled over her words.

"No, talk."

"I—I thought he was welcome—"

"Why?" Aidan rolled his eyes in annoyance. "Are you a fucking idiot? Do you not watch the news? *This is your boss.*" He pointed at me. "Are you not aware of every single fucking thing that happens with her?"

He didn't even wait for her to respond.

Instead he looked at her pointedly and said. "Get your shit and get the fuck out. And if you so much as go to anybody, and tell them anything that happened today, you will never work again in the city. I will make you go so fucking far out into Siberia to find ANY KIND of work."

Marta paled and I felt the words leave my throat. "What—"

Aidan didn't let me finish when his eyes met mine. "You might have mercy and empathy—I have none." He flickered back to Marta. "*Get the fuck out. Don't look at her, look at me. Get. Out. Or I won't say it nicely anymore.*"

And I stood there as Marta scrambled to gather her things and leave on the heels of Michael.

Leaving me stunned, rooted to the spot, and Aidan standing there looking peeved more than angry.

He just—he just uprooted my entire world with his casual darkness and shadows. With violence and unflinching protection, and I don't even know what to do about it. I didn't disagree with anything that he had done.

Because I had been on the receiving end of it, and I knew what it felt like to be helpless.

My kitchen felt smaller somehow. Charged with an energy that I couldn't put a name onto.

I wasn't upset with Aidan.

Most of me was just shaken up that Michael not only knew where I lived, but Marta had dared to even let him in.

But I didn't feel any of that towards Aidan.

I didn't know how I felt. If the two people who just left felt like poison, he felt like a breath of fresh air.

I felt like we were standing across from each other, with the island between us, and I didn't even know what to do. I just watched him and he looked at me. I felt frozen in place.

"Are you all right?" He bit it out like it was costing him. "Are you upset?"

I shook my head. Now, I was shaking, not with fear, but with something else.

I had just met this man. He had come over with flowers and I had only met him three times. Now I was questioning everything I knew about him. Everything I thought about what I knew in society.

Despite our initial meeting, he had shown me more respect than my ex-husband had in nine years of marriage.

He apologized when he was wrong. He listened when I said no. He went out of his way to protect me.

And I was cataloging every single bit of him.

Every single thing about him, dark hair, tanned skin, amber eyes bright on me taking me in like he was hesitant and waiting to hear what I had to say.

Was he moving closer? Slow enough that I could step back if I wanted to, like I was a war animal, he was afraid to scare. But I wasn't afraid of him.

I was learning in my time with him relatively quickly. That good and bad were not delineated in black-and-white.

A moral compass was a shade of gray.

I told myself I didn't know this man as I wrapped my arms around myself. I told myself I didn't understand him and we were two worlds apart.

But I did understand him.

My tongue darted out to lick my lips as they dropped to his.

Nine years of not knowing what a man was like other than Michael and for once I felt my entire body screaming for something.

Michael had been my first—my only. And that had been painful, rough, degrading. Humiliating.

It had left me scarred more than I thought possible inside and out.

I hadn't ever felt like this since I had been a teenager.

"Why do you keep looking at me like that?" He said in a gruff voice. He was closer. "Like you don't know me but you do."

I just inhaled his cologne, watched where his pulse jumped in his throat as he drew closer. My head craning to look at him.

"Why did you step in?"

He almost frowned at that question. "I might be a monster in your eyes, but I don't fuck with cowards either."

But that was the thing, I didn't think he was a monster.

I have been married to one. I had lived with one. I knew exactly what monsters were.

It was Michael beating me every single day of my life. And when he didn't get a chance to do that, he made sure he controlled every single aspect of it.

It was my mother and my family encouraging it because they were still getting payouts from Michael's family. It was Michael's family covering it up and letting me deal with it because if I was the punching bag, nobody else was.

I think Aidan was pretending.

I didn't think he was a violent man.

I think he was a protector being violent to take care of Nisha. Me. And somehow I feel into his orbit.

My throat worked. I had never felt like this. Never had a man leave me speechless. Never made eye contact or held my ground.

It was entirely unfamiliar to me, but as I looked up at him, I wanted something. And I didn't understand it.

Heat. Uncertainty. Desire. Was that was this was?

A crush? I always teased Gemma about having a crush on her bodyguard Nathan. But now?

Did I have one? On him?

"I'm not afraid of you," I whispered.

"You should be." His voice was low like mine as he watched me eyes narrowed. "I'm not your type. And I'm not your kind."

My throat worked. "I don't want my kind."

I didn't fit in with them either. He was so close now I could feel his heat, and everything in me screamed for something.

For a moment neither one of us moved.

"I want a choice."

"And what do you want?"

Him.

I wanted him.

And it was freeing. It was liberating. It was like a firework exploded in my chest as I thought about it, lighting up all of the dark corners that everyone else had created inside of me.

I liked him because he didn't tear me down to build himself up.

After our misunderstanding he fixed it.

He fixed things. With me. With Nisha. With his brother.

I didn't know who moved, I just knew I felt us touching skin to skin, too much, too fast—not entirely enough as his mouth crashed onto mine and a low moan left me.

This. I needed this.

I felt like a starving woman as hot heat and tongue infiltrated my senses and I couldn't think of anything else.

His hands were rough, hot and heavy handed gripping my hips and the other holding my face as he ate at my mouth and I was gasping.

Michael never liked kissing me.

He complained I smelled bad and so I brushed my teeth three times a day and used mouthwash in between meals.

But that was just an excuse.

I knew that now.

Michael said I didn't know how to kiss. Aidan? Kissed me like his life depended on it. It was all heat and tongue, and I couldn't think of anything else.

He kissed me like if he didn't? I would disappear and I returned it. I made out with right there in my kitchen unable to stop.

His tongue sweeping over mine until I took it into my mouth and sucked. I was lifting into his arms in another instant and his mouth working down my jawline as he set me onto the island. His lips moved down to my neck.

His hands roaming all over me with a hunger I echoed.

So I didn't know where the panic came from then. But this was uncharted territory for me.

Michael never had sex with me.

Marital rape was not sex.

The first time he slept with me, it felt like I was being burned from the inside out. I'd screamed and he'd shoved his hand over my mouth. I had been bleeding for two days afterwards. That was sex for me.

Right now as Aidan kissed his way down my neck, I stiffened and felt the shaking start. The fear gripping my throat, ice rushing down my veins as he did. It was a familiar noose I knew of thanks to Michael.

I went from wanting him to falling down a rabbit hole.

One where I was pushing him away and blanking out at his wide amber eyes. Not blue. Dark hair. Not blonde. Something in me fractured like shattered glass as I stopped breathing.

"*No.*"

The words left me as I shook wrapping my arms around myself. Just like that the fear filled me and I felt the familiar sensations of it gripping me.

I couldn't stop shaking as I looked away embarrassed of my own reaction.

"No."

He stood back and didn't move both of us like wary animals again.

"Nisha...she—she's..."

I couldn't speak.

Words failed me. It wasn't my fault. I knew that. But I closed my eyes trying to breathe and not have a full on panic attack after a man kissed me.

I closed my eyes feeling tears stinging them.

"We should…we should go—"

Aidan just stood there quietly before dipping his head. "When were you going to tell me she was pregnant?"

And my heart sank to my stomach.

I didn't know what to say to him.

"Did you not trust me enough to know I would do the right thing?"

He leveled those eyes at me as I ate my own words from the previous meeting we had.

"Sometimes we keep things from people to protect them," I gave his own words back.

He smirked a little, nodding his head at me not sparring me from the shadows in his eyes.

"And sometimes it's because we don't trust them to be able to handle the truth," he finished. "But I can. I can handle it. Remember?"

I swallowed and nodded giving in. How could I not?

"Let's go find Nisha."

And if possible?

I liked him even more.

Even if Michael Devereaux had set the bar so low it was in Hell?

The last person I expected to have a crush on was Aidan O'Hara.

14

SONYA

"AIDAN IS HELPING YOU WITH MICHAEL?"

I was sitting eating pizza and gummy worms with Nisha in her bed in the guest room.

"Yes."

I swallowed as I told Nisha about Marta and Aidan's actions. Her eyes widened as she ate another gummy worm.

"He wasn't supposed to be here," I whispered, her gaze fixed on some distant point. "I have a restraining order against him. This is the second time he's violated it."

"Why does he…" I trailed off.

"Michael is from the Devereaux family? Do you know who they are?"

"Lucas Devereaux—"

"That's his cousin," My fingers nervously plucked at the silky fabric of my blouse. "Distant cousin. Lucas does not like his family. They're all some variation and shade of deranged. Michael is a product of his parents, spoiled rotten from birth. He's never had his mother say no to him. She's so proud of her son and who he is, he routinely breaks the rules and his mother bails him out of everything."

"Yikes," she whispered sounding younger than her twenty-four. "That sounds like a nightmare."

She has no idea.

"When I was married to him, the first time he..." I motioned to her lip. "It split my lip...and she told me to put more gloss on so nobody could tell."

That had been my first message that something was wrong. That these people would've allowed it. It was years of makeup and long sleeves, and pretending like nothing was going on.

That was my normal.

Who else is he supposed to hit?

Who else is supposed to do it too?

It's not rape if he's your husband.

It's not rape because you're a failure.

You can't even give him a child.

You can't be a mother. Why should he be a good husband?

You deserve this.

This is your life.

And the burning sensation in my chest was back.

"She knew what he was doing and she asked me who else did I think he was going to do it too?"

My mother had said the same.

"She said it was my duty as his wife for him to take his anger out on me."

I felt my lips curl at the memories. For years and years of knowing something was wrong and not being able to do anything about it— and now?

Now I never had to deal with them again save for Michael terrorizing me.

I didn't know Aidan was connected.

I didn't think he would be.

Until today? I didn't understand who Aidan was. Not really.

"I tolerated it for years because I didn't know who else to go to. And then we were at a party, and Lucas and Andrei happened to see. I thought Andrei was going to kill him. If not Lucas."

Lucas had laid into Michael and his parents had thrown a fit and Lucas had merely shrugged it off.

Out of his entire family, Lucas held onto the most power. The rest of the Devereaux's paled in comparison and from what I knew? Lucas despised his entire lineage.

Fucking wastes of space.

His words. Not mine.

"He's why you started Haven."

I nodded.

"I didn't realize how much of myself I'd lost until I left. It is why I started Haven. I couldn't bear the thought of other women going through what I did, feeling as alone as I felt."

That's why I vouched for Nisha.

Why I let Aidan into my home.

"How is Aidan going to help?"

I wasn't expecting that quiet question.

It threw me off guard.

I didn't know. I didn't know what he intended to do.

I shook my head not knowing how to respond, turning to Nisha who looked so small sitting there wrapped up in her blankets.

"I've stopped believing in simple notions of good and evil after watching what Michael got away with in broad daylight. I don't think people operate in right and wrong," I whispered. "And I think today was the first day someone stood up for me in my eyes to Michael... my own family didn't even do that."

Not really. Lucas had. But...Aidan...Aidan felt different.

"And he isn't even on the right side of the law and he defended me."

"Michael..." Nisha whispered. "The rumors are true."

I nodded.

"I was twenty-one...my parents wanted connections. They didn't mind sending off their only daughter to secure them." Her eyes were dark as she spoke.

"We're a smaller jewelry family, up and coming. My parents thought marrying a Devereaux would be great. They didn't care which one. Michael's cousin Lucas was in the military and so Michael was...my only choice. Sometimes we do not get a say in our lives. I didn't want that forever. So I got divorced. And you should have seen Michael. He was furious. Like it was embarrassing. My friend Andrei and his wife Talia helped. Lucas stepped in as well. But…my family did not take kindly."

Not at all.

My mother had cursed the day I was born up and down and the moment she realized she was going to be financially cut off? She switched her tone so fast.

I couldn't describe to Nisha what it was like.

After years of abuse?

My mother had one singular phone call with me that would haunt me for the rest of my life.

Sonya, you know I did not mean any of the things I said to you. I was only joking. Don't be angry with me. Come now, we can make things work. Right? You can tell Michael's family you are still in love with him…

My mother made me want to vomit and slice my skin open until I could feel the spoiled ink in my veins from them leak out.

My mother and sister who had exposed me to this. My father just some enabling figure who let it all happen.

They were all the same.

"And now Michael doesn't leave me alone and he's been dragging the divorce out. Something Aidan does not take lightly," I kept my voice low. I couldn't talk about it without getting upset. "I think perhaps if his younger brother is anything like the older, he would not take lightly to losing you as well."

And Killian if he was anything like his brother? Aidan coming by made me realize why Nisha was upset.

She loved Killian.

"Killian sounds lovely. And might I remind you, since you have been here…you've not said a bad word about him."

"I have nothing bad to say about him." Nisha shook her head and I was right. She was…upset he had lied. But she loved him so much. I saw why after meeting his older brother but I didn't know how to tell Nisha—I liked Aidan too.

"But you're afraid."

"I'm terrified of bringing a daughter into his world."

As soon as she said it? She couldn't know how hard it hit me.

In some secretive part of me? Some darker aspects I was grateful I had never had my daughter with Michael.

The idea of her ever seeing him do what he had done and think that is normal.

"Maybe he might be too." My eyes looked down at my lap struggling with my thoughts now. "Aidan knows about the baby…so I'm guessing at some point Killian will too."

"I'm not upset if he knows—" she started.

"I'm saying he might be."

I broke off. I was aware of that.

"Are you going to talk to him when he comes to see you?" I had to say it. Aidan…he would talk to Killian after this. He would go to his brother.

"When?" She whispered.

I nodded.

Nisha was quiet. I could tell she was struggling with her emotions as much as I was struggling with mine. She didn't realize that we were kind of the same person. But we were in two different parts of our lives.

I was thirty. She was twenty-four.

We were both coping with our lives in our own ways.

I didn't tell her about kissing Aidan. It didn't seem as important as her finding her way back to Killian. I had never met him but after meeting his brother? I knew what kind of man he raised. Because Aidan had raised his brothers.

He never mentioned a mother. His father had been murdered.

They were like his kids. His brothers. And he would take care of them.

I mentally added yet another reason to the list of all the reasons why I shouldn't have had a crush on Aidan O'Hara. But I did.

Nisha whispered from her end of the bed chewing on another gummy worm.

"I am."

"Do you think you'll see Aidan again?"

I swallowed feeling my throat work.

"I don't know."

But I did want to.

15

AIDAN

I found Killian drinking himself away in his penthouse.

That wasn't surprising.

On the way to his penthouse, I ended up calling the police commissioner in New York, called in my favors to make sure Sonya's house had some sort of piece of shit cop detail in front since it mattered.

Got her restraining order expedited. She'd have it in the next week because it would matter in court.

I let Gabriel know what was happening with her divorce and he said he would make some calls.

Kieran told me he was sorry for telling Nisha, but he had no idea. As annoyed as I was with him, I didn't blame him for what he didn't know.

I just thought that he was happy to have somebody in our lives that wasn't the three of us.

He was the only one out of us that talked about having a family. One day.

Me and Killian never considered it. So it made sense why he connected with Nisha. Until now—Killian might've not known what he could have.

Like me...with her. And her emerald eyes.

The entire ride to Killian's place I ignored thoughts about emerald eyes in my vision.

I couldn't focus on her right now because my brother was drinking himself into a stupor.

I let myself in to find him there.

"I'm not in the fucking mood." That was the first thing he said. He knew I'd been in the city, he didn't get in touch with me which shouldn't have surprised me.

"Well you're about to be. I talked to Nisha." I stalked up to him.

Introducing me to her was one thing, getting her pregnant and not telling her who we were was totally different.

His eyes mismatched and eerie turned to me then at her name coming from my lips.

"What the fuck were you thinking?" I was furious with my brother. I taught him better. "You didn't tell her! She's out of her mind scared. She quit her fucking job!"

Nisha had been through it.

"I know." Killian's temper flared as he threw his glass. "You don't think I know I fucked up! *You came in here to tell me how much I did after you got to see my girl? You know what the fuck it costs me to hold back?"*

And just like that I was on him.

"...you should've told her the moment you knew about your fucking kid."

His brows rose in front of my eyes as I said it.

"You think I'm a moron! The way she hides it from me! She's pregnant and she's fucking terrified! I don't know why you didn't say a word to me or at least Gabriel–"

"My kid..."

He blinked at me like he was sleepy. Like he was confused.

What the fuck was he confused about?

Did he not think I would find out?

"Bringing a fucking kid into our world without even considering telling the mom what the fuck she was getting into—"

"What kid?" He choked it out like it cost him.

What...kid?

What?

"What fucking kid?"

93

He didn't know.

He doesn't know.

Killian's not the only one keeping secrets.

Nisha's been keeping hers too.

His eyes met mine, a haunting look dawning in them.

"Oh, fuck me. Both of you…fucking *kids."*

Killian snapped on me then. *"What. Kid? What the fuck did you just say?"* Killian broke out of my hold and he looked at me with horror dawning in his eyes. *"She's pregnant."*

"You didn't know—"

"She's pregnant." Killian whispered, horror coursing through his face. "Nisha's *pregnant."*

Oh, fuck me. "Killian—"

"And I fucked it up?" His hands went to his chest as he looked gutted. Absolutely gutted.

"Killian, breathe—she's four months pregnant."

"That's why Sonya got involved. She knew—"

"She knew and she was worried about Nisha and the baby—"

"Four months."

"Nisha found out and didn't say anything—"

"She was going to tell me."

In real time, I saw my brother lose it. Lose it.

"Killian, listen to me—"

"No, you listen to me."

He was all up in my face then and I knew I was fucked. He wasn't going to listen to a word I said.

Not anymore.

"You had me sitting tight thinking she didn't want to see me. She needs to see me. I'm the fucking—She needs me. I am hers. *Do you understand me? You won't keep me away from her. Not anymore."*

And what I saw in his eyes then I had never seen before.

"Nothing is going to keep me away from her. Not anymore."

16

AIDAN

Nisha says she went back to her apartment with
Killian for the time being.

They're going to move into his apartment later.

I DIDN'T KNOW WHY I WAS STILL HANGING OUT IN THE CITY.

Especially not when I was texting Sonya back and forth so I could
just go back to Chicago now that Killian had gotten his girl back.
Right?

I told myself this was about family legacy and patterns that I
recognized from the past.

Not about a pretty lady with green eyes and doll features that
really got under my skin.

I told myself that I was taking around to see the fallout of what
happened with Killian, and how Sonya's restraining order worked
out. I told myself everyone needed me in the city to handle their
problems.

Not because I was hoping to see her again.

Devlin was handling Chicago, and I felt confident I could go back
and it wouldn't be up in flames.

"Are you going to see Sonya?"

Alexei was hanging out on the couch in the apartment. His blue eyes blinked at me, his sharp features dulled by him eating pizza. Again.

I was beginning to think the little shit had a thing for New York style.

"You want to see her?" He asked.

I shot him a look. "Do *you* want to see Sonya?"

"Yes." He said it plainly. "I like her. She is funny and strong."

That she was. She had that long sable hair, not quite dark brown, not quite chocolate but something in between that shimmered under the lights. Dark, emerald eyes that bat at me whenever she was shy.

And even then I realized why she'd freaked out after I kissed her. I knew it off the bat.

Michael Devereaux was a piece of work judging by the police reports. And the pages upon pages I'd been pouring over.

"He abused her."

Alexei went quiet as I said that.

"Devereaux."

"Lucas is good man, but his family not so good."

I looked over at him. "How come you never talk about your family?"

He shrugged. "They are dead."

I was silent. I forgot sometimes we were just as blunt as the other.

"She buy this." He pointed to the five pies in front of him. "I text her too."

I blinked. "The fuck you mean you text Sonya?"

He showed me his phone. Sure enough, I ran through text messages he was sending her. Some emojis. Some gifs. Some memes.

"You send her memes?"

"I like this." He pointed to one of a polar bear cub dancing . "She likes this one too. She send me food."

And then the doorbell rang.

"Who the fuck is that?"

He smirked. "She sends me many things."

No fucking way I was jealous of my kid.

No fucking way.

He went to get the door as I stared at his phone where I saw Sonya typing the three little bubbles appearing. She had liked all his texts.

That little shit was texting my—No. She wasn't my girl.
But she was…texting him easily.

> Did you like the salty pickle chips?

> I think they're good. I'm trying new foods out. You
> might like that.

I looked up at Alexei walked in with bags of takeout and snacks.
He had a goofy smile on his face.
    "What did she say?"
I scowled. "Read it yourself."
Texting Sonya like he knew her. Pfft.

∽

> Stop sending Alexei food.

> You're spoiling him.

> And why is that a problem?

THIS FUCKING WOMAN.

> He can't be eating five pizzas a day.

> You're right.

I breathed a sigh of relief I didn't feel.

> I'll be sending him twelve from now on.

> Are you trying to piss me off?

> That depends. Is it working?

I stared down at my phone confused.

> I feel like I'm existing in an alternate reality right now.

> Is this real?

Did you try the pizza?

No, Alexei ate two pies by himself and he's going for his third. If I touch it, he might bite my hand off.

I don't starve him you know

No.

Of course not.

Is sarcasm a Turkish thing?

I thought the Americans invented sarcasm.

"You are talking to her," Alexei sounded gleeful as he wolfed down his food.

"I don't fucking know where all of that food in you goes," I shot back catching myself smiling down at my phone like a fucking teenager. When was the last time I just sat there texting a girl?

Never.

I never texted women.

I called when I needed them and there was no shortage of women that wanted me in their bedroom.

Just nothing permanent.

And that extinguished any kind of anything I felt for her when I realized that she wasn't a one time thing.

She wasn't the kind of person that I could just sleep with and then just leave and go back to Chicago. Not with her issues. Not with mine.

She was friends with Nisha which meant if Nisha and Killian had worked things out she would be back in my life.

Fucking Sonya was a no go.

Not like she'd fuck me anyway.

No. Sonya was the kind of woman you made love to. Like for hours. The kind that you found out if she had beauty marks, and what her body looked like under those layers of long sleeves and propriety.

Not...fucking her.

My phone pinged again.

It was a gif with a round bear cartoon shoveling pizza into his mouth. Where the fuck did she find these?

> That is you.

> > I bet you're laughing it up in your ivory tower, princess.

> > You can't face in person.

> I am not a princess.

> Yes, I can.

> And I can take you out.

> > Don't tempt me with a good time.

> When and where?

I blinked staring down at my phone.

Did I just inadvertently ask out Sonya?

I looked at Alexei watching me from his perch with a smirk.

"She sent you thai food?"

"Lo mein," he corrected. "I needed a break from the pizza."

"Stop treating Sonya like a fucking delivery service."

My phone pinged.

> You're not being mean to Alexei, are you?

I snapped my head up to find Alexei texting.

Jesus fucking—

> > Tony's, the one Uptown on the West Side. In two hours. Be there.

> > Or else I know you're a coward, princess

> Fine. Do not bring your frown with you.

I smirked down at my phone.

And then I realized what I'd done.

"I think I just asked her out on a date."

"Mhm."

"Shut up."

17

SONYA

A DATE.

With a man.

Foreign words to me as I got dressed.

I had spent so long wearing what other people had approved of and what other people wanted. I didn't even know how to address myself right now for a *date*.

For pizza *sure*. But I had never dated anyone before. What did I wear? What did I do? Did I put on perfume? Did I do my hair?

Half up? Or half-down? A pony-tail?

I didn't know what to do.

I was fidgeting until the last hour when I did go outside in the cold of New York's lights and sounds. I made it to Tony's which was one of the better Italian spots in the West Side.

He was already there. With no Alexei in sight.

And the rest of the place was empty.

Hm. I wondered if he'd forgone his guard tonight or if Alexei was hanging out somewhere I couldn't see him.

His eyes lifted up, bright amber on me as he motioned to the case. He was still darker and powerful, stunningly beautiful—but he seemed more approachable on a pizza date.

"I haven't ordered yet." His sculpted beautiful lips tipped in a smirk. "Don't even think about paying."

I shot him a look as we both went and placed our order to a smiling woman behind the register.

"Hey Maria," Aidan said low.

"Mr. O'Hara," her eyes warm and brown and weather face twinkled on me. "Who's this?"

"Uhh," I was struggling already. There were so many options. I didn't know what I wanted right now or how to answer his questions.

"This is Sonya," Aidan answered his jaw a little tight. "I'll take a..." he placed his order and then motioned for me. I was still struggling.

"Can I have the chicken...with the mushrooms...and the jalapeños...and the..." I picked out a few veggies. "And those spicy chips you have."

She blinked at my order. "You want a whole pie?"

Aidan had gotten one. Should I? Or should I get a slice? Should I get more? Should I get less? What did I do?

"She'll take the pie."

Aidan didn't look at me as he said it instead picking out water bottles and the spicy chips I liked.

I nodded eagerly as Maria smiled at me again with a knowing look. Aidan paid for it while I quietly tried to take the items from his hand but he didn't let me.

As we sat back down we both took off our coats and I blinked at his green sweater and mine. Both of us were in similar colors and I supposed we looked like a couple. Matching. Together.

Was that was this was?

I ducked my head realizing I was staring at him. Again. After I'd kissed him back. And freaked out.

My throat worked.

"How do you know this place?" I asked.

"I own it." He smirked with amusement twinkling in his eyes at my expression. "Sort of. Killian technically owns it. All the properties in New York belong to him. Which in turn all funnel back to me."

I frowned. "You own it under an...illusion of it being legitimate?"

"No. It's all legit. But it doesn't always fuel legitimate ventures."

I was surprised by his honesty.

"And you own the business in Chicago?"

He nodded sipping his water with a smile on your face. "You interrogate me more than cops do."

I squirmed a little. "I am curious. It's not every day you meet a—" I broke off. I didn't want to call him a criminal as his smile dipped a little. But I didn't know what else to call him. "What are you called?"

"Aidan."

"Funny," I shot back. "But no, seriously."

He shrugged looking nonchalantly like a normal man. And I supposed that's what he was. "I'm still just a person."

"True, but I was expecting a smoke machine."

"And a cape."

I nodded. And then to my surprise? A grin spread his lips wide and I blinked at his dimples.

He had dimples.

I didn't even know I found that attractive until I saw his on his clean shaven face and I realized how bad I had it when my stomach turned. Twisted.

Butterflies erupting in a space that I thought was hollow.

When I first met him, I thought he was dangerous because of his job.

Now I knew he was dangerous for a completely different reason.

Now I knew it was because I really thought I could like someone like Aidan O'Hara.

And that was scarier than anything I'd felt in a long time.

DAYS AFTER MY DINNER WITH AIDAN WHERE WE TALKED UNTIL THE FULL moon came up, I was in my townhouse searching for an assistant.

I had an interview with a younger woman named Valentina Leighton. She was in college but her classes were all online and she came over for an interview.

"You're really young," I commented when I met her in person.

At maybe five feet tall with raven hair and bright blue eyes she blinked up at me looking like a nervous mouse.

"Are you sure you want to do be my assistant? Or an intern maybe at Haven?"

She ducked her head almost embarrassed. "Yes, Miss Amin. Either or is fine with me."

Her interview went swimmingly and she gave me a soft smile when I told her I'd think about it.

When she left I had gone into the kitchen to grab something to drink when the doorbell rang again.

Valentina had just left so I thought it was her having forgotten something. I didn't check the camera because it didn't occur to me to.

I thought it was Valentina.

It wasn't.

The moment I opened the door I realized my mistake.

Instantly.

A older man stood on the other end with a woman next to him and before I even took them both in, he said. "Michelle, go."

And then I was swarmed.

A scream left my throat as they both attacked me—both of them moving so fast I couldn't even stop it.

The man's disgusting scent hit me first and I felt his fist—the woman grabbing my hair. I hit the floor screaming and crawling into a ball. Stars exploded behind my eyes and I screamed until it seemed endless.

I went limp stealing myself for blow after blow as the man yanked my hair up.

"You're gonna call Nisha and you're gonna tell her you fell down the fucking stairs and you can't feel your arm—"

What? Nisha?

He eyed the woman who approached me with a glint in her eyes. I tried to fight her off as he held me down and she twisted my arm—the shriek that came out of me tore from my throat as I felt the sickening pop of my socket being wrenched back.

Immediate blinding pain tore through me.

White hot agony like what I felt so many times with Michael. Another scream ripped from me as he held a phone to my ear.

"Do it."

18

AIDAN

I was going to forcibly leave New York.

That was the original plan.

Originally.

Now?

Killian's phone call from hell haunted my nightmares.

Nisha said Sonya fell down a flight of stairs, but why would she call Nisha? Are you close?

I'm not, but I can be.

I never tore off running so fucking fast Alexei at my heels as we rushed to Sonya's.

My heart was hammering against my rib cage so loud, every scenario possible playing through my head.

All of the violence I had seen over the years, every single thing that I had ever endured, it was all replaying like a nightmare loop in my brain.

Her door was wide open and my heart bottomed out.

Nonononononono.

I didn't even notice myself hitting the proverbial wall, but Alexei didn't. He tore off without me rushing in with his gun out. He cleared the room and my eyes focused on the passed out body on the floor.

Small. Broken.

Arm bent in the wrong direction. Oh. Holy. Shit.

"Alexei, call Dr. Perla. I need—I need..."

I couldn't even formulate any words. All of them left my brain as I look down at her. Every single connection I had in the world was useless not looking at her.

In my efforts to get my family together and juggling everything that I did, it didn't occur to me that when Nisha had been staying with Sonya—she'd had a tiny problem.

One where her adoptive father Samuel had been released from prison. Killian had suspected he'd been gunning for her. But Sonya had been the last person I suspected he would target.

Alexei went to her limp body before I could his fingers out checking her pulse and I didn't realize I was holding my breath.

"She's alive. I will call Perla."

I sank to my knees feeling the unfamiliar sensation of being completely powerless wash over me.

Samuel did this. Nisha's former fucked up family. I knew because Nisha? Was nowhere to be found.

There was no way she was just missing. I didn't even know how to touch Sonya. She was frail and light right now, I knew she was alive, but her arm...

Rage flickered like ember inside of me at the thought of what I would do when I got my hands on the people who did this to her.

Alexei it seemed had called Kieran whose eyes so much like mine blinked down in horror.

"Shit, is that Sonya?"

Alexei explained what was happening to Kieran just as Killian burst in. His eyes landed on me and the Kieran who looked at him.

"Nisha's been kidnapped." Killian paled as Kieran said. "I'm gonna help you get her back."

Sonya was moved to the hospital where she was treated and she didn't wake up until after they'd treated her.

High on pain meds she made an animal noise.

I was on her in an instant.

"Shhh," I brushed her back feeling the panic in my chest at the image of her lying there broken. I thought she was just some woman. Just some girl I met. I had pizza with her the other night. It was just a silly little date.

Nothing serious.

No sex after.

Nothing.

Not this.

She was restless and they just let her sleep it off because there was no point of her waking up in pain. Whenever she did stir I caught the bruises all over her face.

The rage in me was flickering and burning higher and higher and higher until I got the text from Killian.

Killian and Kieran along with their team had gone out and found Samuel and Michelle Graham.

You want him alive?

Yes.

I would finish it.

When I got to the old Graham house where Nisha had been raised, I found the two of them strung up in the basement.

Killian's handiwork was to string them up to the ceiling like animals. Both of them screaming when they saw me.

To my right, one of Killian's guys, Sean grimaced.

"Boss."

I was still the head of the demon.

And they touched my girl.

I rolled up my sleeves feeling the restless monsters in me twist and turn coming alive at the sight of knowing they touched what was mine. My family.

Nisha was pregnant. Sonya was mine.

In that moment—that's when I knew. I knew I wasn't letting her go. I grabbed one of the knives from the side with my hand. These were old friends to me.

I knew exactly what to do with it.

And I'd start with Samuel.

"You went after my girls." I kept my voice low as Sean shut the door. "You went after all of my girls." Nisha's kid was a girl. Kieran told me. And it left Killian gutted.

"You tried to break her arm," I watched Samuel who was sweating under my gaze. Killian's work was nasty. He liked to drag it out. "I should take yours for hers."

And I didn't even flinch sinking it into his collar bone and dragging it down.

I gotta admit—I was fucking demented.

I loved watching Samuel scream.

Especially imagining if Sonya had died? And I'd lost her even before I got to kiss her again?

Absolutely not. A feral grin lit my lips as it sliced him open.

Blood dripped onto the concrete as I worked. Through both of them. And I wasn't going to stop. Not until they bled out.

They could beg and plead and beg again.

And I would never let it go.

"When I'm done with them, I want their bodies laid out."

I turned to Sean wiping my hands. "I want this bitch cut open." I pointed at Michelle. "Nisha's file said you were aware of every single time your husband molested her. You are just as guilty. And women like you don't deserve to be women."

I grabbed a bigger knife and went to work on butchering Michelle. With all the screaming she did, I relished it slicing into her starting at her stomach.

I didn't think people understood I was my father's son. I watched my father do this from a young age.

And then I went at Samuel until they were hacked to pieces and I was covered in blood.

The best part? They were still breathing. Barely.

I sighed. "This used to be way more fun when I was younger."

Sean looked like he was going to be sick. I smirked despite feeling their blood all over my hands.

Out of all the team, Sean had a softer heart than the other guys. He didn't like this—so he was the one we kept close when we did get like this.

This wasn't about revenge.

This was about keeping up my image.

You didn't threaten our future, you didn't threaten our women, you didn't come into our territory, thinking that you meant anything.

I still had a reputation to maintain.

I wiped my hands down.

"Make sure the city knows about this." I motioned to the two of them. "You can leave them lying around wherever."

Sean nodded. Whatever was left of those two anyway.

I had to clean up.

My girl would be wondering why I wasn't there when she finally came to.

19

SONYA

I was in bed with a man.

Moonlight was streaming into the room.

And this was my nightmare. One of them.

My throat felt like sandpaper, and I could taste a lingering bitterness from the hospital inside of the back of my mouth. The soft pajamas felt scratchy. And I felt like I couldn't breathe properly.

Nine years of conditioning screamed at me to run, to hide, to make myself smaller.

The pain that accompanied those thoughts was met with panic. Fear like no other clogged my throat and a helpless noise left me.

I felt the bed dip and a weight appearing at my side that felt too familiar and another noise—barely a scream left me.

My body remembered other nights, other rooms, other hands.

My eyes flew open bracing for clear blue ones.

Michael's eyes. Pressing himself into me. Fear choking me alive.

But the eyes in front of me weren't blue.

They were amber. Solid amber. Bright. Beautiful. Like whiskey caught in sunlight. Rumpled white dress-shirt. His tanned features sculpted from marble.

"Sonya. Don't make that sound."

His hand moved around my throat hauling me to him, but there was no violence in the touch. Just...anchoring. I close my eyes of the contact of heat against my skin.

"It's okay. You're fine." His eyes stayed locked on mine, letting me see the truth in them. "I promise."

I was shaking so hard I couldn't even—

"Breathe, Sonya. Inhale—"

I obeyed. Not from fear, but because his voice cut through the panic.

"Exhale."

I did.

"A—Aidan."

Aidan *O'Hara* was in bed with me. The last thing I remembered was interviewing that girl to be my housekeeper. Valentina. And now? I had no...wait—

My townhouse. The break-in. The assault.

"A-idan."

"I'm here. I gotcha. You're safe, you're fine...it's okay."

Now I knew I was either dead or dreaming.

Because I didn't exist in a reality where that was even possible. Not him. Never him.

Not the crime lord of the O'Hara syndicate.

But he was here, the scent of his cologne invading my nostrils, my lungs, spice of some kind on him.

Nobody smelled that good.

It should've been illegal for him to walk around that handsome.

But he was real.

He was laying me back down, against silk sheets, and I looked around the room for a moment to realize that my surroundings were a deep emerald color.

And this was not my house.

This wasn't even my room. Everything felt a little off.

There were no plants.

There was none of that lush pink in my house.

The mattress was too soft, and the air was too still.

"Where...where am I..." And then I tried to rub my eyes and found my arm in a sling.

A sling.

And suddenly it all came rushing back to me.

I was with Nisha. Aidan's younger brother Killian had a girlfriend. Nisha Graham. She had been in my apartment.

"What happened?"

Nisha had left and then the doorbell had rung one afternoon and—

I gasped trying to move, to do anything but feel the way I did then.

"Easy, easy."

Aidan swore and next thing I knew I was in his arms. Again.

"Easy, you got hurt. Samuel—Nisha's fucked up adoptive parents— attacked you. You're fine. You're safe—"

"This isn't my home." Panic. Dread. All the things that could've crawled up my spine did.

"No, it's mine—"

"I don't—"

"It's okay."

But it wasn't. It wasn't because for the first time since leaving Michael, I was in a man's bed. In a man's space.

And the strangest part? I didn't feel trapped.

Dumbly I was aware of Aidan slowly telling me what happened as I made an incoherent noise at the sling my arm was in. Samuel attacked me. Used me as bait.

"Nisha—"

"She's fine." Aidan paused. "She and the baby are fine. Killian's with her."

I breathed out feeling some of the panic ebb. "I had a nightmare…"

I was groggy, in pain, half sleep deprived and half out of it. With Aidan O'Hara.

"We are…we are in Chicago?" I blinked slowly realizing one critical thing was wrong here. *"You kidnapped me?"*

20

AIDAN

I KNEW SHE'D LOSE HER MIND.

I just didn't know *how* much until now.

"I handled everything in New York," I quickly explained despite it being midnight, I had been half-asleep and I didn't wake up alert. And Sonya was now panicking beside me.

She was in my bed.

I should've put her in the guest room but I needed to get some sleep and I didn't want to lose sight of her.

Technically, I had taken from the hospital and I brought her to Chicago. Not only did I coordinate with Titan to work on Haven, but also, for her to ride out her divorce out here.

Was it still kidnapping when the hospital, the Titans, and everyone knew except for her?

Maybe.

As I explained to her my thought process she blinked slowly processing it all through her delicate bruised features.

It ached to see her like that and I did the only thing I rationally knew I could.

"I removed you from your situation," I said needing to clarify. "Now, you can ride out your injuries and life here until Michael chills the fuck out. You're vulnerable right now. It isn't a good time for you to be in New York."

She blinked slowly like I was a three-headed alien.

"You *removed* me from the situation?" She repeated. Like I had said something of grave offense. "What do you—"

"Samuel Graham and his wife attacked you, don't worry I took care them. Nisha's safe. And Killian isn't letting her out of his sight. I brought you to Chicago and coordinated with Gemma for her to handle—"

"You removed me?" Those eyes turned on me. "Like furniture?"

Oh, she was pissed. I wasn't expecting her to be this pissed.

Did I miscalculate?

I was used to making choices like this. Operating outside legal channels meant that I could make calls like this. Besides every time I looked at her I kept seeing her broken on the floor, her arm bent at an unnatural angle.

I kept seeing her in the hospital. And I couldn't focus on anything else.

Now? In my territory, I could protect her. I could take care of her. I can make sure nothing bad happened to her. And Haven would function with Gemma.

"I don't understand why you're upset," I tried to sound calm, but she was in my bed. She was here. She was safe. The moonlight caught her bruises making them look darker and her like a ghost.

Around me the space felt enormous and small at the same exact time and I didn't know what to do anymore.

It didn't make sense to me.

"I'm upset because you didn't give me a choice." Her accent thicker, and I caught she was upset.

"Your shoulder is dislocated, your husband wants to kill you, someone just attacked you—what choice do you want?"

I could hear the frustration in my voice, but I was also really exhausted. Nobody wanted to wake up at midnight and fight with their—house guest? Roommate?

Angry pizza lady?

I didn't know.

She looked absolutely livid trying to sit up and I was trying—I was. I reached for her easily, gently, but she squirmed away. As best as someone could on one arm. The movement made an uncomfortable sensation in my chest tighten.

"You coordinated with everyone, but me!"

"You were passed out!"

"Then wait until I wake up!"

"Oh, and what should I ask? Do you want to go to Chicago with me so I can actually fucking protect you and still do my job?" My voice rose. "You think you would've said yes!"

"Yes!"

Silence.

"What?"

I could feel the weight of the word hanging between us in the darkness. And I knew that she was right, but I kept seeing her injured.

"You would've said yes?"

"If you ask me—"

"You have a broken rib, a dislocate shoulder, and bruises all over your body," I bit out as I got off the bed. "You can barely sit up alone."

"You think you have the right—"

"I do have the right!" I shouted back now fully standing and grabbing my stuff to leave. "I have the right to protect the people in my life! I will do that time and time again."

I was so fucking pissed off as I ran a hand through my hair unsure of why I felt less like myself the more I was around her. "I keep seeing you broken, on the floor—your arm—" I broke off.

I just helped her. Didn't she see that?

"Look, I brought you here to heal, to get better, to ride out your divorce from your life—here." With me.

"Haven is my life—"

"I know that but you need to mean a lot to yourself as well!" I was frustrated with her. "I don't wanna fight you. I am trying to help you! That is all I have ever done! You can choose what you wanna eat for breakfast and you can choose what fucking shoes you wanna wear, but when it comes to the shit I'm good at—*let me do my fucking job!*"

The moment she looked at me like she didn't recognize me—I knew I fucked up.

I didn't even look at her as I walked out unable to be in the same room as her.

In that moment, the words felt off in my mouth, and I sounded too much like my father and I needed to leave the room.

I didn't talk to women like this.

The only language I spoke was getting my message across in violence. Power.

Ruthless efficiency disguised as a method of advancement. That was it.

I didn't talk about my *feelings*.

The door slammed behind me and I almost ran headfirst into Alexei who stood there in sweats and a hoodie blinking surprised.

He ducked his head the moment I walked out.

"What?"

He didn't say anything.

I stormed to the guest room. Not my room, because she was in my room. Maybe that wasn't the best thing to do, but I was pissed off too.

It was midnight. I was exhausted. I had come back with her and ninety other things happening in my life.

Maybe she was upset I had taken her from her home, but I was more pissed off at the sight of her…thinking she had died.

That she was gone.

I didn't know why it mattered.

Me, the son of a monster who taught me one language worth speaking—violence. I prided myself in not raising my brother's like that.

Sonya didn't fucking understand my life, but I understood hers. To her core.

I knew her.

And she had no fucking clue what I was. The things I'd seen.

I long since suspected deep down my mother never went missing, but Cormac took care of her. Like he did all his problems.

She was a problem the moment she had an affair with someone for Killian. I knew the moment his eyes were hers—when he sat still?

Sometimes he didn't look like he was an O'Hara.

I knew why my father took out his anger on Killian the most. And he would never know.

Sonya was a foreign language in more ways than one to me.

My style of leadership was necessary. Unilateral decisions kept people alive. Sending Killian to Gabriel.

Sending Kieran to New York so he wouldn't drive me insane in Chicago.

I had never asked them, I had given them and it had saved their lives. It's like I knew it would save Sonya's. She just didn't know it.

Was her choice important?

Not so much.

Not to me. Not for this.

I didn't ask. I only act.

Discussion would only lead to death and vulnerability. And who the fuck wanted that?

Before I left New York Killian and Kieran knew I was taking Sonya.

Everyone knew I removed Sonya from the New York scene.

Gabriel had frowned but nobody not even Nisha protested. Mostly because Nisha had been traumatized and *pregnant* and she knew the value of being kept safe. For her daughter.

Killian was having a fucking baby.

My brother was a completely different person with his *fiancé*. I didn't even recognize him.

But he didn't matter to me because I couldn't follow his footsteps.

Anybody that I brought into this world would have to stay in this world and not have a world in New York.

This was their new world. And I couldn't do that to anybody.

I didn't know how to.

I long since expected that the only way I would be with somebody is through convenience and arrangement.

Not someone I wanted. Not like her.

And in the guest room I found myself pacing the floors, unable to rest, and I realized that I wasn't gonna get any sleep tonight.

Not while imagining her haunted emerald eyes on me staring at me like I was the villain in her story.

What the fuck was I supposed to do?

I didn't know anymore.

I didn't know how to be.

Every single time I looked at her…I just saw another person I couldn't save.

And I couldn't watch her become another grave I dug, another body my father gutted, and these were the same methods that helped me build my empire.

My kingdom.

Lack of control meant death.

It didn't allow for me—a man raised by monsters—to suddenly try to speak her language.

I didn't want to.

21

SONYA

I'M TRYING TO HELP YOU.

Nine years of no help from anyone with Michael and all of a sudden I felt uprooted from everything I worked hard for.

My arm ached and a knock came at my door after Aidan left.

It wasn't him, but I didn't know who else was here.

A shock of platinum blonde poked his head in.

"Sonya?"

Alexei.

I looked down and saw somehow I was in my pajamas.

From home. The ones I had not been in at the hospital. Unless one of the nurse's had changed me at the hospital? I didn't remember anything.

That was a little terrifying right now and I felt shaken up.

Alexei stepped into the room holding something. A blanket.

"I turn on the lights…slowly. He has a dimmer." And sure enough, slowly, the lights dimmed lower as he walked in with an innocent smile on his face. His eyes looking tired but so blue I could see them glowing.

He brought in the blanket and handed it to me. "Is for you. It's good."

I took it from him looking down at my sling. My arm was…dislocated. But they'd put it back…so it was healing?

I barely was aware of any of it feeling like I was in a weird dream. In Aidan O'Hara's house in his bedroom.

Alexei looked a little shy standing there watching me in his sweats and hoodie. "You fight with him."

I had.

And he hadn't hit me. He'd just walked away looking annoyed and exhausted to be fair.

He was still in a rumpled dress shirt looking out of it when he left. Alexei stood by my bed staring down at me.

"Do you need something?"

I shook my head slowly sitting myself up. A faint twinge of pain went up my shoulder and I felt groggy. Out of it.

"Water would be good."

"I come back with water...and some snacks..." And then he was gone. I watched his retreating form a little surreal at the way I turned to the dresser next to me and found my phone. I reached for it feeling a little more than overwhelmed.

I had texts from everyone. Lucas. Nisha. Gemma. Everyone.

With one hand I sat up against the headboard realizing this bed felt massive now. Aidan's bed. My throat worked as Alexei returned quietly while I looked down at the texts and he handed me an open water bottle now.

I took it without even thinking as he sat down with a little basket in his hand.

"We have this in kitchen, it's box of my favorite snacks..." and I sat there a little dazed as Alexei brought out his snacks and I stopped on the hazelnut cookies. He passed me the bag opening it for me. "Do you want to watch TV?" He motioned to the wall where there was nothing but a wall.

"There's nothing there," I whispered.

His smirk was sly. "Not now. But boss has secrets." He grabbed a remote on the wall and then the entire wall panel opposite the bed opened. And a TV emerged.

"Oh...my..."

Alexei turned it on muting it really low and to my surprise the first channel was a poker game. I blinked as he switched until he found a popular show from when I was younger.

"I like this," he motioned to it sitting back with me on the head-board. "He does not like me in here but I think now he is in guest room and he is angry, so he is not coming back." He looked devious sitting there with the basket of snacks open.

"What am I doing here?"

He was quiet as he looked over. "He is taking care of you."

"Yes, I know…" I held my phone with my hand as I watched him. "But why…why am I…" I motioned to the room. "You know him. You know why he does things."

Alexei was quiet. "I hear you fighting with him." He looked almost forlorn with his messy hair and deep eyes. "I don't know why he does everything. He has plans and he just does them. He does not ask. That is who he is."

"But if he asked I would have said yes."

Alexei was looking down at the hazelnut cookies. "But he did not so you are upset by this?"

I couldn't believe I was having this conversation half groggy and barely awake to comprehend it but I nodded. "I'm upset he didn't care to ask me if it was okay."

"But it is okay, because you like it here."

I blinked.

"And you can leave whenever you want. And you can do whatever you want. He just thinks it's safer for you here than New York."

He paused a little looking much younger than what I originally thought his age was. I don't know why I looked at the box of snacks and remembered being a teenager and having this.

"I understand you are upset, after…your life you want to control things. So does he…he likes control over everything. Now that control is for you."

"My ex-husband was controlling."

His eyes met mine. "Boss is not your ex-husband."

No. He wasn't.

"But he does not understand you and you don't understand him…" Alexei shrugged. "Maybe instead of fight you talk to him later?" He held out his phone to me and I saw a picture of—

"That's a stack of pancakes. Why are you showing me this?"

"He likes them."

121

Alexei smirked.

Something told me Aidan wasn't the only one who liked pancakes. This conversation had taken a surreal turn.

I couldn't stop myself from asking. "How old are you?"

"Twenty-one."

"Ae you lying to me?" Call it confidence from the amount of pain medication I had in me, but it just kind of came out of me.

A flush covered his cheeks even I caught from here. "I am twenty-one."

But I don't know why I got the feeling that he was much younger.

I felt a strange sensation come over me. Aidan...did Aidan know how old he was?

I just felt like he was much younger. He didn't act like a twenty-one year old. He acted like a teenager.

"And you're Aidan's..."

"Like an assistant," he said. "But I do everything."

"Everything?"

He dipped his head. "I can do anything assistants do. I look it up."

Aidan is raising a child...

"I just don't know why you look like a teenager..." I whispered. I knew because I had spent enough time in youth shelters whenever I volunteered to know.

This entire time I was so confused as to why a grown man would be eating so much.

Even at twenty-one even if he lifted weights...he ate like a teenager.

"You like this?" He passed me another snack as I stared at the giant screen playing another movie. "This is nice."

It was...oddly enough.

"My things are all here?"

"Mhm."

"And I can leave whenever I want?"

"Mhm."

He leaned back against the headboard again and motioned to my snacks. "You can eat something...and maybe we get pizza?"

I blinked looking down at the time.

1:37am.

I looked back at him. "You're nineteen."

He blinked back at me. "I am twenty-one."

22

AIDAN

Turns out, my sleep could be absolutely destroyed from a five foot five inches tall, Turkish woman with a penchant for lighting me up.

I tried to go back and after tossing and turning by like four o'clock in the morning, I was up working out at the gym, and taking a shower before heading off for my day.

Even a brutal workout didn't fix how it felt. Frustrated. Anxious. Torn up from the inside out over her.

Something about her eyes and imaging anything happening to her, fucked me up from the inside out. All the fucking time.

I told myself it wasn't a big deal.

Sonya Amin wasn't my fucking problem. She wouldn't be and she couldn't be. She wasn't Nisha. God no. My brother's soon to be wife was a fucking butterfly compared to Sonya who was hands down a fiercer thing.

Perfect for me.

Even if she had stayed in her abusive marriage? Violence and fear did things to people. It ate them out alive.

If she left in the morning, I told myself that it wasn't my responsibility.

What *was* my responsibility, was the text that I got after my third cup of coffee in my study.

Nisha sent me a photo of tiny socks with a thank you.

On the flight to Chicago, I couldn't sleep, and I had spent it just ordering all sorts of things for Nisha.

Turns out, if you go on the Internet and search baby products, you get nine thousand options.

I just purchased everything that I could think of for her.

She was family.

She was Killian's whole world. That's where my focus was. If Sonya Amin decided to leave? So be it. I'd book the fucking plane ride back for her myself.

Even as something in me rankled at the thought of her heading back to New York and being vulnerable hit me. I had an interacted with her much and I didn't even know what it was about her that got under my skin. But for some reason, she did out of all women.

I blamed it on the fact that rather than hitting on me, she stood up to me. And I blamed it on the fact that unlike most women, I thought that she had more of a spine.

Nisha was about as sweet as cookie butter. Which was good for Killian. He needed that.

Alexei had discovered Nisha's food blog a long time ago and he acted like the sun rose and set on Nisha.

It wasn't even eight o'clock in the morning, and I was already fucking exhausted.

And then I got a call I didn't need.

"We got another body Downtown," Devlin said gruffly. He sounded annoyed. "But we got surveillance footage. You might want to come down here."

When he hung up, I got up and got my coat, as Alexei strode in looking tired but chipper.

"We're going Downtown."

He snapped into business mode and the two of us left Sonya in the mansion.

The thing was millions of dollars of fortified brick, nobody was getting fucking in here with all the security I had. And if she wanted to leave, I had an alarm on my phone that I knew, so I wasn't even worried. If she left when I got back, then she would. No big fucking deal.

I was telling myself that over and over again when I made it Downtown.

Thankfully for me, the area was relatively quiet this early, avoiding the rush.

"Tell me everything," I asked Devlin who stood over a body looking grim. The entrance of the alleyway was blocked off by my guys as the copper of blood hit my nostrils. I didn't like this shit. Not one bit.

I think it had rained early in the morning or something because I saw blood washing into the gutters, but I knew somebody had taken him out.

"We got the surveillance footage of last night. After everything we know, we just have to assume it's the Belova's." Devlin looked annoyed as he said it.

Alex was already crouched by the body, his lean form in all black, looking lethal. "I found something."

He held up a strand of deep red hair.

Both me and Devlin frowned at it. "Let me go see the surveillance footage."

In the back of the bar that my guy had been attacked in, I caught the footage of him, sitting at the bar and having a few drinks. He got enough to go to the bathroom and then he exited the bar through the front.

But right before he exited, somebody called him and so he turned back. I saw it. But I couldn't see who it was.

"He's talking to someone at the bar," I murmured frowning down in the small room. "Look, when he turns back around, he's doing it because somebody calls him back. So he goes to leave through the front door, and whoever is sitting at the bar, says for him to come back."

"A woman," Alexei said frowning. Devlin and I looked at him. He shrugged. "He was sitting at the bar but look at the drink to his right."

When I turned back to the camera, I saw that he was right, but the person sitting next to him was out of the vantage point of the camera. A chill ran down my spine.

"Dev, is that the only camera in there?"

He nodded. I was afraid of that.

126

"What if a woman was talking to him at the bar? Scoping him out. When he was leaving, he was about to get away—" Devlin started.

"So she calls him and finishes him off?" That didn't make any sense.

Alexei held up the red hair strand now in a plastic bag. "You have Rachel run this?"

Rachel Leighton was the cybersecurity specialist of Titan Chicago.

Titan had an entire team out in Chicago too. Mimicking their New York team, and this one was just as big if not bigger thanks to me being out here.

Gabriel and Reed weren't kidding when they expanded out with their company.

Every major city that I could think of had a branch, if not smaller units imbedded into the city with all orders coming out for them from their head. Titan, New York.

Reed's orders were final.

"Dev, take that down to them."

But I saw the look on Alexei's face. "You think it's his daughter."

Alexei tipped his head. He motioned to the woman sitting there. "You can get Rachel to see if she can find anything. Maybe someone was on their phone or her phone. I think we can trace her back to the others."

"And then we get her." Devlin watched us, his green eyes bright with anticipation. "When and where, just say the word."

"I'm not going to kill Eden Belova."

Not yet. Not without sending her and her father a message.

"Take it down to Rachel, explain the situation to her. Her boss will want in on this."

"Yes, sir." Devlin was off and Alexei watched him with careful eyes before he turned to me.

I didn't like the look on his face. Every so often he fucked with me and he joked around, but there were times where he got serious and I knew shit was gonna hit the fan.

Alexei's familiarity with Russian culture kept me on top of the game because I understood things and he was able to translate things for me that I couldn't.

"Eden is doing this because she wants control. Viktor is the enemy to her. I spoke to a few of the Belova's and I think they wanted to recruit me. I want to send someone into their spots to spy on them."

I listened as he explained it to me. He understood what was happening. Better than I did. In a way I just kinda let him handle this.

I just wanted to take out them all together.

"You think Eden is trying to start a fight to take Viktor out."

Alexei nodded. "It's common. Whoever this is is trying to start problems."

"When Viktor comes into power—we wipe him out."

"And she sits on her kingdom. With her father and his brother dead. We solve her problem. She magically gets peace."

"How old is Eden?"

"Twenty-one?"

And hungry apparently.

It made sense.

"I still feel like we're missing something. Where is Eden now?"

Alexei shrugged lightly. "She has an apartment inside the city."

"Send someone to tail her. A female Titan—" I thought about it. "Send Nadine. She'll blend in."

Nadine Forrester was another Titan imbedded within my guys.

She was damn good at collecting intelligence as a former spy turned Titan.

"Have her tag Eden. Maybe she goes to a yoga studio or something, something inconspicuous where she can blend in. Maybe they'll become friends. Nadine knows how to make it not obvious."

Nadine was also discreet.

Alexei dipped his head.

"What made you think Eden was your prime suspect from the job?"

"I know how they think, and Viktor is not smart. He is very..." Alexei held up his fingers like a gun.

"Trigger-happy."

"Yes."

"Eden is not."

Alexei smirked looking younger than age. "What I understand she is her favorites favorite."

"Then why give his kingdom to Viktor?"

"He does not trust a woman's place."

"Ah, casual sexism."

So we had a Russian princess who was pissed off at her father didn't want to give her a piece of his kingdom. Simply because she was better off being married to someone else then actually taking control.

Which meant she would do anything to prove him wrong.

It made the most sense because neither one of the older Belova's had a reason to pick a fight with us.

Alexei nodded. "And she is aware of this too. I asked around. I have information about Dmitri. He is…old school? He does not think it is Eden's place."

"But she wants it—"

"However she can."

"We need to tail her. Watch her. And get Nadine and her team working on it."

"One more thing," Alexei said carefully. "The hair? Means she's getting messy. I think she is sending a message."

"Tell Nadine to work fast."

ALEXEI AND I MADE IT BACK TO THE MANSION AND I THOROUGHLY expected her to be gone.

The chill outside blew in and I don't know why every time I went outside. I was always shocked by how cold it was. But it was downright frigid right now.

The heat of the mansion felt better against my skin than anything else. But I wasn't expecting anything else.

I didn't expect was the sense of cinnamon and sugar and all sorts of nice things coming out from inside the house.

"I didn't know the housekeeper was in today," I muttered as Alexei went after the scent like a bloodhound. "He's like a seven-year old."

I made it to the kitchen island walking through the dark mahogany hallways of my house, to find the least likely candidate, brunette hair, swept up into a messy bun, and flower dusting a sweater she borrowed. From me.

As in she had been in my closet.

Emerald eyes darted up and a radiant smile lit her lips. "You guys are back? I'm almost done with the frosting…"

Frosting?

And then Alexei made a happy noise looking down at the other side of the island filled with—

"Cinnamon buns." Alexei was fucking thrilled.

"I thought you might be hungry," she said to him with a smile. And her eyes were carefully avoiding me as she whipped together creamy white frosting before covering another batch of them in it. "My secret is lime juice…it makes it nice…"

I don't have to fucking guess that my kid who was all of seven years old was currently grabbing extra plates and making himself a cup of coffee and grabbing a pan for himself.

"This is good…"

"Alexei, don't be an animal," I said to him unsure of what to even do. She was cooking. In my house. In my kitchen.

She's still here.

In my house.

Her eyes met mine quickly as I sat her taking out breakfast sandwiches from the oven. "This is yours. It's real food, not coffee."

I swallowed hard at the gesture as Alexei slinked out of there holding a pan and a jug of coffee.

I raised an animal.

"You're still here." I waited until he left to speak. He shut the door thankfully. Standing there among the wood and granite, she looked… like she belonged there more than I did. The lights overhead made her hair shimmer a little and I saw her spine straighten as I said it.

Her shoulders arching in a way that spoke of years of ballet training.

"I am." Her eyes met mine then, her chin rising in a challenge and didn't that get my cock to notice her now.

And that's what I caught the shift, every time I met her before this, all the other times, I just felt a general attraction to her. Something about her had changed in the short time that I had known her. Now, she was in my kitchen, wearing my clothes, and I saw her differently.

I didn't see her as an heiress, I just saw her as a woman.

130

Now, my body was actually waking up to the possibility of even ever being with Sonya in a way that went beyond logic.

I couldn't have a fling with her.

But now…I didn't know about that.

She didn't deserve it.

Maybe she doesn't want anything serious with her divorce going on.

"I decided to stay."

"Why?"

I had to ask even as my stomach and I absolutely was fucking salivating for some real fucking food. All I had was coffee.

And my brain was too busy working through all of the reasons why one Russian princess would be after my fucking blood.

"I still think you are wrong," she started looking down at the island. "I think you are wrong in how you handled it. But you are correct when it comes to your…decisions."

"If I say no to you bringing me here, would you still bring me?"

"Yes."

Without hesitation. I saw her eyes widen a little.

"I don't always care what you want. If I think it's good for you, I'll do it. Eventually you'll be grateful because you're alive."

Her eyes narrowed. "I am not an object."

"Oh, trust me, princess. I know." I leaned back. "I never said you were. I said exactly what I meant."

She bristled in front of my eyes as I said it.

"I didn't ask because you were passed out and my only thought was getting you back to this city. Since you left your ex-husband has been by your house, a couple of times. He doesn't understand the word no and I made sure the police know about it. Your contact Liam Sullivan, he made sure the tabloids are busy with his scandals. Which makes you his prime target."

I could tell that I surprised her because she didn't know all these things. But it was true.

The woman she involve Titan in anything, she should've known better than to stay there.

Even if she had a guard all the time, it wasn't the same for her. She wasn't Gemma. She didn't need or want that. She rarely left her house and even when she did?

I don't know why she didn't just ask, but at this point I realized Sonya might be just as stubborn as I was.

That being said.

"I wouldn't care what you wanted if it meant keeping you safe. Thats the kind of man I am. I know you want your choice, but if you were in danger, and I knew keeping you here was what would keep you safe—I would do it. You won't change that part of me."

I saw how much it upset her.

But the truth was, she wasn't the kind of woman that I could be with. I couldn't be with her. Because eventually, she would have to leave here. She would have to go back to her life. And this was mine.

In my world, I was her protector. And this is how things worked. My brothers understood that, that's exactly why Killian came and asked me for my approval with his wife.

I knew I was a fucking King.

"I know you have a need to make choices. I'm not saying I don't respect you choosing all the ninety things you want to do. But when it comes to my territory and the information I have—that is my choice. This. Bringing you here. All of your projects in New York will go without saying. They will keep going. You will still get to make all of your choices. But you'll do them from here. And you'll stay here until everything is finalized and I have Michael's head on the fucking pike."

I paused letting out a breath understanding I didn't know how to meet Sonya in the middle.

I didn't.

"You are welcome to go whenever you like. Nobody will stop you. That's a choice. But I will not apologize for bringing you here and keeping you safe the only way I know how."

Her eyes met mine head on.

"That is all? You will not care if I said no?"

I closed my eyes and opened them slowly. "You have always said no to me and I have headed it. I won't rape you or hurt you—my job is to keep anything under my family's umbrella safe. If anything happened to you—Nisha would be devastated."

I was devastated.

"You have a life in the city, you have a legion of women you need to help."

I was careful about my answer. I have memories of what my father had done in the past. The crimes he had committed. The bodies he had brought in.

It was ironic Sonya was doing the anti-thesis of that.

Of me.

Another reason why I couldn't have her. I looked down at the food she made and I was aware I was starving. For more than just food. Because now my body recognized Sonya. It did. And I couldn't do shit about it.

Kissing her once had been a mistake.

A mistake I couldn't make twice.

I stood slowly grabbing an apple off the counter and avoiding her eyes. I'd have to grab real food earlier than her starting tomorrow.

If I ate anything it would force more conversation.

And then I would only admit what I couldn't hold back.

I liked her.

She was everything I wasn't.

She was everything good in the world with helping women and healing trauma. Her whole entire life was based off of building a safe space so that nobody would go through what she did ever again. It was admirable.

Because that's exactly the values I lived by. Except I did it differently.

I was my father's son.

I was violent. She was peace.

I was darkness. She was light.

I had too much life experience, she didn't have enough. And when it came to what I needed and wanted?

Sonya was none of the things I could have.

Not when the entire world was held at arms length.

"You can do great things as long as you live. And once you ride out your divorce here, and Michael's gotten what he deserves—you're welcome to do whatever you want."

And I walked out.

23

SONYA

"He doesn't speak to you?"

Nisha's voice was soft and husky as she spoke to me one morning. She called to check in on me and I felt a deeper connection to her than others.

"He does, but it's like he's speaking like the ambassador of himself. He is nice, and he is polite, but—"

"He won't talk to you for longer than three seconds? That doesn't sound like Aidan. Killian says like Kieran, Aidan likes speaking."

Not to me.

"Exactly." I flopped back on the bed feeling unsure of myself. "What did I do?"

Nisha made a sympathetic noise. "I don't think you did anything wrong, it's *you*. Maybe it's just about him. He's being weird now."

She said it as though I could do no wrong. But I knew I could.

Although, I didn't think this situation was black and white anymore.

Since I had left New York, Nisha and I kept in touch every single day. Sometimes via text, sometimes she called me.

"I mean, Killian said he knew when Aidan took you to Chicago something was going on between you guys...he says his brother isn't the type to just take someone to his home." Nisha finished in a quiet voice. "Killian says he thinks his brother really cares about you. He thinks it has to do with all three of them having different issues with their mom. Killian doesn't talk about his mom often, but he says he just remembers she was abused and upset all the time. Do you know what happened to her?"

"No." I sat up.

"Well, don't tell anyone I told you this, Killian doesn't like talking about it. But I think Aidan's mother's hung herself and he found her."

"What?" My heart bottomed out. "How old was he? Why?"

Nisha's voice went quiet as though she was remembering something. "Killian says he was maybe seven or eight. So Aidan was ten…"

Nisha explained Killian walked into the room and saw her in the ceiling. As a seven-year old who didn't understand what was happening? She probably was.

Aidan had found her. He blocked Killian out of the room.

"Killian says Aidan took over the family empire reluctantly. He says he remembers his brother going to high school. He was good in school. Maybe Aidan's trying to make sure you don't end up like their mom. I don't know what happened to her. I know it upsets Killian so you can never say a word."

"Is he there? I promise I won't. Thank you for telling me." Deep down I was more than grateful Nisha told me what she did.

"No, he went to the gym for a bit after we stretched a little. Killian did some research about me bouncing around on some bosu balls so everything he's been teaching me for an easier labor."

"It's true, it works." I laughed low realizing I had done that research. "How is she doing? Still kicking?"

"Yes, and he's overjoyed. I think she loves him more than me and she doesn't know us yet."

"He's ready to be a father?"

"I feel like that's all he's ever wanted deep down. I think all of the boys want a home. I think in a way…that's why Aidan's letting you stay there. Killian says he's never even thought a woman could. And with you adopting Alexei? I'm sure they're both thrilled."

"Alexei is basically his son."

Nisha laughed. "Killian says the same, but he says he never considered Alexei being his son."

"That's because Killian loves his daughter."

She sighed. "Ah, he does. He's so in love with her, he's baby proofing the house and I've vetoed so many things. You should him, he's adorable. He's listening to a podcast about labor and how not to cause any tearing."

I laughed wincing a little, but my chest clenched tightly at the sound of that. A happy home. A family. Nisha's daughter would be born into love. Into happiness.

Not forced into marriage. Never abused or mistreated. She'd be *loved*.

We talked for a bit longer with Nisha telling me all she craved was spicy food.

I walked to the edge of the room where I was looking out through the large windows spanning out onto the street.

It would be almost a month since I had spent the last few weeks in Chicago. Adjusting to the enormous O'Hara mansion.

Aidan lived in a nicer part of town. All around us there were enormous manors, spread out and it gave the illusion I was in some European town.

Aidan's manor was one of the bigger ones. Naturally. The man couldn't do anything in half measures.

Brick walls and black and gold windows, the trim around the house a luxurious emerald.

On the outside, it look like a multi million dollar home that line the streets, but inside every single room was mahogany and emerald.

There was a modern kitchen with sleek appliances, but old world craftsmanship.

Alexei's snack baskets were organized by snacks, and I swore I bumped into the housekeeper here a few times doing it.

I thought it would be intimidating, but the living spaces were absolutely enormous with vaulted ceilings and cozy, plush couches.

Everything was soft and warm, while also being absolutely the most imposing and threatening space I had lived in.

Power and comfort.

Strength and sanctuary.

All at the same time.

I did feel safer here. I felt like this was a different type of castle than my townhouse or anywhere else I had lived.

"…Killian thinks his brother likes you a lot. I think so too. But I think so because he took you to Chicago and he didn't say anything…"

"What do you mean?" My heart was racing.

"Meaning, according to his brother, Aidan doesn't get involved if he isn't invested. And he cares about you. I think it's hard for him to talk to you, it's the same with Killian. He had a hard time talking to me when we first met. Did I ever tell you about that?"

"No." I didn't know how they met. Just that via some connection within the Titan hospital.

"He came in with a dislocated shoulder oddly enough, and he kissed me…" Nisha laughed a little at my silence.

"It took him a few times to come and ask me out but he just wanted to kiss me. I invited him over for dinner and since that night he'd been a constant."

"What I'm trying to say is, Killian never told me that he wanted to spend time with me, he just did it. He never told me he missed me often, but he showed up every day with lunch and flowers and he drove me home. He never told me he thought I was beautiful, he just kissed me and never looked away. I figured out really easily he had a hard time speaking. Don't get me wrong, he's gotten a lot better at talking about himself, and to me. But when I first met him, he rarely said *anything*. He just kissed me and hugged me."

I didn't know that. I had met him once or twice and he did seem like a man of a few words. Or if any words.

"But I realized that what he couldn't say, he was trying to do through his actions. I think his brother is trying to do the same. I know the two of them have a lot more in common. Even Kieran, the youngest? He has a hard time too. I think all three of them don't know how to communicate properly. So sometimes I have to kind of ask him."

"You think I should go talk to Aidan?"

"I think, sometimes they need a push. Sometimes. In tiny ways. For the longest time, Killian never told me he wanted me to be his girlfriend, I just asked him and he said yes. I know it's a little strange because he's not forward, but I already had all the other things, I think it wouldn't hurt to push him a little. You're in his home. You're in his bed, sort of..." I blushed at the thought of being in Aidan's bed while he was in fact relegated to the guest room.

Michael would've forced himself into this space, but Aidan would never.

"But while, I think it's really admirable that you're considering all of this, I also can't help but realize that he might've brought you there for you to heal. And that means doing what you need to do to do that. So if you wanted to cook or you wanted to knit or you wanted to color or read, romance novels, everything you do should just be for you."

I knew that.

"Maybe I should start a blog too," I teased.

Nisha did have a successful food blog where she posted photos of her recipes and other things that she liked.

She's been doing it for a long time and had amassed quite a few thousands of followers. She had wanted to do that full time instead of going back to nursing. Instead of doing anything else.

Nisha laughed. "Hey, my lemon bars never hurt a soul."

It was easy interacting with her.

"I know Killian isn't worried about you, he says you'll be fine."

"He has confidence in his brother—"

"No, he has confidence in you. Even if you think he doesn't know you, he says he's never seen Aidan like this, which is good. It means he does like you, but I think just like Killian, he doesn't know what to do with you—Killian's back, hang on." I felt like an eavesdropper as I heard Nisha's laughter and kisses.

He said something to her, and the sounds of their intimate life made my chest clench.

Nisha had fallen in love with Killian after he'd been one of her regular patients. And he'd just asked her out and one thing led to another—and now they were having a baby.

Sure, their love life wasn't without struggle.

She had been kidnapped and tortured...and me...my shoulder had healed, but my heart was still healing from everything else.

Nisha laughed at something he said. "No, I'm having girl time with Sonya...yes...yes, it's about Aidan, your brother is frustrating..."

I turned beet red never imaging Nisha talked to Killian so candidly. This was actually my first time listening to them talk.

I didn't hear what he said, but I heard her replies. "Yes, she's in his room, but I think he sleeps in the guest room. Sonya, you can't see Killian's face but he looks shocked."

I bit back my laughter.

Nisha laughed then. "He says, you should check under his bed to see if there's a shoebox or something filled with...elves? *Who is Gwendolyn Fairchild?*"

And then she laughed harder.

"Aidan is a closeted nerd? Killian says he realized during his workout, why his brother might like you so much. And he says you look like a fantasy character that Aiden had a crush on when he was a teenager."

"What?"

"I'll send her to you, one second...oh my Gosh she's beautiful... she's an elf...a warrior priestess elf. A magical elf. Sonya, you are this for Aidan."

And then a photo popped up of a stunning woman in green robes, elven ears, and long dark hair.

"She even has your eyes," Nisha laughed. "Oh, this is so cute. I didn't know Aidan was a nerd." I heard Killian laughter in the back with her. "Yes...she's fine. We both are...Sonya's venting..."

I stared at the movie star woman from eons ago. Maybe she did look a little similar. But...why did I feel an unexpected flare of jealousy to her?

"She's very pretty," I murmured honestly.

I guess I could see the resemblance.

In the website, it said that she was a high priestess in this fantasy series.

I did not know Aidan liked this.

I couldn't imagine the two sides of him.

The one side he was for the world and for his family, but maybe what Nisha was saying is that there was another side of him that he had in private.

The same side that Killian only showed to his fiancé.

Nisha laughed harder. "Killian says you have the same eyes but yeah, anyways, Killian's going to shower now...yes, right now. While I enjoy my pickles and Sonya...but yeah, I think it just takes time. I think you need to push Aidan into some type of interaction. Otherwise, he's just going to lurk all around you trying to control what groceries you get into the house, until you tell him that everything's fine..." she broke off. "I didn't say *you* did that, baby. I'm just saying you guys have a language without words—yes, I told her your brother's weird...yes... I think Kieran gave it away...yes, baby. Yes...Sonya, Killian says just keep doing you, you're getting under his skin...yes the baby's fine."

I couldn't stop grinning listening to them. Killian sounded concerned.

"No, I—" she sucked her teeth. "Killian. Shower. Now...I swear this man listens to one podcast about labor and now he's reconsidering everything."

I laughed harder.

I didn't even know this side of the O'Hara's existed.

I did look around his bedroom and found nothing under the bed.

"Thank you," I whispered. "You two should get your time, thank you for this."

"Don't mention it, I'm always here. Text me. This last trimester is going to drive me crazier than ever. I can't see my toes."

I laughed harder as I hung up and turned to find Aidan's watch on the dresser.

He did come in and out of here sometimes.

Every so often I found his things lying around his bedroom, and I would just put it all back into one side. I discovered that I had his credit card at my disposal and I got what I needed when I needed it.

Alexei dropped by with snacks and movies.

My attorney let me know Michael had signed the first half of the documents he needed to once Aidan had gotten people breathing down his neck.

And things were progressing with Haven with Gemma keeping me updated.

"Hey baby before you go shower," I heard Nisha ask. "Does Aidan have a favorite food or snack he likes...er why? Oh, just curious. I wanted to send him a care package..."

I heard a masculine chuckle. "Don't ever become a spy, luv." And I heard Killian raise his voice louder. "Sonya."

"Hi." I squeaked. There was something about the middle O'Hara brother that was more...I wouldn't say he was scary, but just intense. Very intense.

"No, we're just having girl time...yes, I know. Killian says he doesn't think Aidan discriminates against any food type. He likes everything."

"That should be easy."

"Yes, but it should be said you should do it for you, not just for him. I genuinely like cooking, and so I do it for Killian, but he also likes everything I make."

Killian rumbled in agreement.

I flopped back on the bed. "Great, I have to figure out how to communicate with him, even though he doesn't know how to communicate."

"It's not hard...Killian has a thing for lemon...maybe lemons are an O'Hara weakness." Nisha laughed at something Killian was saying. *"Your weakness is lemons. It's your kryptonite."*

"You're my kryptonite."

"Your daughter is your kryptonite, you're going to scare the mid-wife—"

"Good—she better not touch my daughter—"

"She has to—"

I heard him say to me. "Good luck with my brother, Sonya. I need to shower. With my wife."

"But I can't see my toes—"

"I'll clean your toes too, woman."

I laughed harder at the two of them laying back as Nisha hung up after saying goodbye.

Good luck with my brother.

And I still had no clue what to do.

24

AIDAN

"YOU'RE NEVER GOING TO BELIEVE THIS."

Nadine Forrester had called me, and Alexei straightened at the sound of her voice on speaker.

"It's been a month," I muttered.

"Good things take time, and even greater things—"

"Take forever," I got it. "Tell me you found her."

"Worse, I've got a fuck ton of information on this girl. Check this out, she's a former straight a student, a ballerina, and honest to God, the kids clean." My heart sank. "Or she was."

Alexei frowned. He was invested because he was the one who called it. From the beginning, he was the one who knew that it might not be who we thought it was.

It wasn't a man.

"This is where it gets wild. She's twenty-one years old. I found out that she virtually disappeared off the face of the Earth six months ago. She moved out of her old apartment, and she keeps it like a ghost. She only appears every so often. I was following her for a little bit, until I realize that she's really sharp. So I had to back off her tail."

"How are you keeping tabs now?"

"From a distance, I don't think she made me, but I don't wanna go up to her because of what I found out." Nadine rattled it off. "For the last four years, she went to school in New York, you ever heard of Astor U?"

"Yeah." Reed's girlfriend's baby sister went there.

"So Eden Belova started school when she was eighteen years old, and she was training to be a ballerina. As in prima. She's the real deal. But while she was there?" Nadine sighed. "I did some digging. I went back to New York and I came back to Chicago after asking around. So I definitely can't go up to her now. She had a boyfriend. Christopher Melendez, first generation Mexican American. Solid kid. Straight A's, dean's list, he played soccer, and he got into the school on a scholarship."

And something tells me all roads pointed to him.

"You're not going to like any of this. She started dating him in her sophomore year after they had the same classes. And he's a working class kid. He didn't know who she was. And she never told him."

"How do you know this?" Alexei sat up.

Nadine let out a breath. "Because Chris Melendez was found hanging in his dorm room in his senior year. Around the same time, Eden dropped out."

My blood ran cold.

"Dmitri found out?"

"Or Viktor. One of them found out that their princess that they either plan to marry off to somebody else, or have other plans for her, was messing around with the wrong kid. Chris is dead. His family was devastated. She left school right after that she dropped out. Something that pissed off her family."

Nadine broke off with a breath. "Six months later? She moves out of her apartment. She's still a redhead but I saw the crime scene photos, and the cops labeled it a suicide."

"Except it wasn't."

"No, kid was stellar. Everybody that I spoke to said that they were in love, and that he was the absolute fucking shining star of the team. He was always with her and they were happy. They were making plans for being together after..."

"After..."

Nadine huffed out a breath. "I think someone in the Belova's found out Eden was dating beneath her. And they fixed the problem

143

for her. Everyone I spoke to at Astor who knew Chris? Said he was sunshine. Like the kid walked on water. Good instincts. Level-headed. And check this out? He had defensive wounds when he died."

"So he fights back," Alexei looked grim.

"Exactly," Nadine said. "Sounds like you're Bratva princess is out for blood. Her own blood."

"But then why does she keep going after mine?"

"Because she wants you to do her dirty work—she's one person," Nadine said. "One girl. She can't do it. But she is taking out little people every so often just to get a rise out of you. That's probably why her father and her uncle have no idea what the fuck is going on. That's why they never suspect her."

"But she disappears?" I asked. "Oh wait a fucking second—"

"They think she's throwing a temper tantrum. This is Bratva. They think Eden will come back." Nadine finished.

"And when she does, they will have their kingdom back," Alexei looked at me. "This is more than I thought. I did not know about the boyfriend."

"That's because after Eden left Astor, her father erased all traces of her in the school. His parents suspect that she had something to do with it—but we all know she loved him. And she loved him until he was murdered."

By her family.

She wasn't a princess.

She was an angry fucking girl.

I understood how she felt. I did. Deep down inside I did.

The kind of rage that filled your heart and it flickered every time somebody pissed you off. But she was playing a game that I had mastered long before she lost her crush. And I had no sympathy for her.

I wish I did.

But that didn't excuse what she was doing.

"Nadine, I'm going to kill her when I find her. She's forcing my hand. I don't tolerate that. She's trying to use me as a pawn. I don't even think she understands the game. She's playing." I said. "Her family doesn't know it's her."

"No, but I think they're asking the same questions you are. I just

144

don't think she is their first conclusion because they don't think she's capable of it. Rachel ran the hair you found? It's a match. Its her. She is pissing everyone off."

I blew out a breath.

As sad as her story was, nobody in the underworld cared. And it wasn't that we didn't care about her story, but we all had stories. We all lost things.

Killian lost his soul and his pound of flesh my dad whipped into his skin. Even now he was covered in scars.

Kieran was on drugs and used sex and alcohol to numb out the nightmares of sex trafficking and girls that haunted his mind from his youth.

The things no child should've been exposed to.

My father had tortured me. Burned my skin alive. Flayed into me with knives. I had scars and tattoos and bruises covering my flesh.

Everyone had a story.

Nobody's was worse than the others.

Eden Belova was a twenty-one-year-old with the inability to see the world. And she was forcing my hand.

I was righteously pissed off.

"I need this fucking girl's head." I puffed out. "War over a fucking boyfriend."

"I know," Nadine muttered. She was at least thirty and she got it. "I'm trying to figure out a way to attract her to you. Did you wanna ambush her?"

"I do." But at the right time. "What does Cade say?"

Her boss in Titan Chicago was Cade Rodriguez. He would do it in a heartbeat if it meant reducing a problem.

Ruthless efficiency. Nadine was sly about it.

"Cade wants her off the streets ASAP. She's bad for business. If her only interest is her own, and not the well-being of others, we can't have wild cards roaming around the city."

Cade would only weigh in everything.

"He doesn't want a wild card." Nadine was honest. "He says you have free reign but Rachel and I have eyes on her at all times. We're tagging her."

"Do not kill her. That's mine."

"Yes, sir."

But we needed a way to draw out the wild card.

My eyes landed on Alexei. A plan begin to form in the back of my mind.

"Nadine... how much information does she have about us? She knows about some of the local bars. So she knows where we hang out. Only Downtown though."

Nadine was quiet. "You think she's watching you guys?"

"I think she's working her way around the little guys she thinks I don't see. I've lost three. That's three too many."

"I'll let you know where I find her, what are you thinking?"

I smirked. "I think Alexei and I need to go pay the Bratva princess a visit."

"Ohhh, can I come?"

"Yes. Bring the team."

Whether she liked it or not—Eden Belova was going down.

I couldn't have this shit under my roof.

25

AIDAN

It was later that night, that I woke up.

I couldn't sleep.

I went down to the kitchen, I could smell something lemony. Something zesty. And I knew who was in the kitchen.

Of course she would be there, since neither one of us ever slept like normal people anymore.

I was so tired, though I just didn't give a fuck as I walked in.

I paused at the sight of her, bent over in a green mid-length slip.

In the fridge as she pulled out a stack of desserts. Only she didn't see me until it was too late.

A small scream erupted from her throat and the lemon looking things in her hand almost toppled out.

I moved fast, catching it with one hand, wrapping my arm around her with the other.

Emerald eyes blinked up at me. "You scared me."

"Sorry, I couldn't sleep." I glanced down. "Are you baking again?"

"No," she was breathless and her accent got thicker. "I baked it earlier, it's just my timer went off and they...they're cool now. They have to be eaten...cold...Nisha gave me a recipe..."

Both of us stood there a little too fucking close, her body molded to mine and I could feel the tips of her nipples digging into my body.

I bit back a noise as I stepped away before she could feel my dick. I handed her the dessert tray.

"Did you want some coffee?" Her eyes met mine, and I caught the heat climbing her cheeks. "Water?"

No. I wanted her.

"No."

But I couldn't have her.

My mind was swirling with ninety different things right now. Including a one Sonya who stood there with her soft green robe looking way too comfortable. Way too pleasant.

Like she belonged her and I fucking didn't. I was all too aware I was in softer sweats and a fucking hoodie and we fucking looked like we lived here together.

You do, asshat. You live here.

And she lives here.

Because you volun-told her.

"I'm straight."

I walked over to the open fridge and got out a bottle of water, and some gin.

Because if I was going to be around her? I couldn't do it sober.

I think a month passed since she'd been here.

And we adapted like some weird co-parenting situation with Alexei where he alternated between us.

Turning into my attack dog when I needed him, and then he would go over and he would turn into a complete fucking golden retriever with her.

Eating all his snacks and all the food she made like a fucking vacuum cleaner.

Sonya was going on Nisha's blog from what I saw on an open tablet, and taking recipes from there and trying it out.

I didn't think she left the house much but I also think that she was working full-time on Haven while she was here with Gemma.

They were communicating all the time, but for the most part, her divorce was going smoothly.

The tabloids died down when she wasn't in the city. And overall, her life was a lot better from what I understood.

I poured myself a few shots and took it without thinking my back to Sonya as I inhaled it at the counter. It burned down my throat but the good news was?

I'd go to sleep without wrapping my fist around my cock and imagining Sonya all over me, under me, her lips in my ear in that soft accent whispering my name.

Fuck. This wasn't working. I could still smell her and feel her in the room wary of me.

"How's your day going?"

How's your day going? What the fuck is wrong with you?

"Good. And you?"

"Good."

And cue the awkward tension.

What did I do? How did I talk to a woman I couldn't be with?

I couldn't have her, I could barely speak to her. And now I was talking to her like some estranged wife.

"Nisha is two months away from having the baby."

Now I opened my eyes and half turned to Sonya who was staring at her lemon looking desserts.

"I want to go see her. I was thinking we would all go since the baby would be new to the family. It would be nice for us to be there."

It would be. If Eden *fucking* Belova didn't kill everyone by then.

I nodded. "Yeah, that sounds good."

And cue the awkward tension again.

Her eyes turned to me. "Do you want one? I made them, Nisha sent me a recipe."

I know. She said it already.

But what the fuck? It was already so awkward. You could cut the tension in the room with one of the knives in the butcher block.

"Yeah, sure. Why not?" I said figuring I had two shots already. "What is it?"

"It's lemon posset," she murmured, her accent hitting the t's and she looked almost proud. "It's good, Alexei tried the first set—"

"First set?"

She looked a little embarrassed. "This is my fifth." And then she looked a little nervous plating it up for me. She passed it to me and I saw her hands trembled.

She only did that when she was nervous. I took a few steps back and parked my ass on the island.

"I don't know where the kid gets his appetite from."

Sonya looked down at her lemon whatever it was. It half a lemon skin filled with some cream or something as she explained it. "I wanted to talk to you about Alexei…"

I took a bite without thinking and the flavor of lemon exploded on my taste buds. Rich zesty lemon and cream and sugar. I could devour this. And then some.

Fuck, this shit is good. I think I ate mine in like two bites and then I grabbed some more.

And then she explained to me her theory.

I frowned mid-bite. "You think he's younger than twenty?"

Sonya ducked her head again and nodded before her eyes met mine. "I think he's still a teenager."

I stopped moving.

"How did you meet him?"

I told her. He had tried to rob me. As a teenager.

"He was big for his age, taller too. I couldn't find any paperwork of him so I asked him how old he was and he told me he was fourteen. I had the Titans make him paperwork. He wanted to be Alexei Markovik. So thats what he became."

"Yes, but who is he?" She whispered. "He's got to be nineteen. Doesn't he have family?"

I shook my head. I don't know how to tell her and it didn't feel right to tell her. I almost felt like he was already my family so I didn't really wanna say it out loud.

"I think he was a victim of trafficking. My father dealt that business and I thought maybe he was a repercussion of it. I think they picked him up and he just got lost him on the kids. I think he tried to fight me because he thought that I was my father. But I took him under my wing."

I explained to Sonya his origins. And she frowned deeply.

"I had no idea your father was that cruel."

I did.

Sonya had her demons. I had mine.

"I never thought that he was a teenager though. I knew he was young..." I trailed off.

I just thought he was a growing boy. He always ate like that.

Sometimes he got a little too thin, because he lost the weight really quickly. But once he started eating, he could pack away the entire fridge.

The housekeeper loved him. She had a reason to go grocery shopping all the time. But I just thought it was because of his age.

"I'm not saying it isn't normal he eats so much, but it's how he acts, it's what he does...sometimes when he looks at me, I feel like he's seventeen if not nineteen. I know it's not much of a difference, but it is worth looking into. I think if you can accurately identify how old he is, it'll help you better take care of him. He is like your son after all."

I stiffened as she said it so softly. So casually.

Like it was a fact.

Was he my son? I didn't even know what to say but her eyes met mine now with a slight smile in them. "Do you like your lemons?"

I looked down and somewhere in the middle of our conversation I had three.

"I do. This is good. I never get a chance to sit and eat properly—"

"I know, you should it more often."

"Hmm," a smile curved my lips. "Are you cooking? Cuz you know I burn water."

"I am following all of Nisha's recipes. I did not know her blog was so successful. She says she wants to do recipes and film them from her kitchen. Maybe do a social media page with it. Killian is supportive."

I snorted at that.

"Nisha could kill someone and he would be supportive."

She smiled ruefully. "She says sometimes the baby keeps her up at night and they cook together and she goes to sleep before she can eat any of it." Sonya smiled and a wistful look entered her eyes.

"You and..." I swallowed at the mention of even saying his name. "You two never—"

"No." She was quick and I realized I hit a sore spot. I did. Because she shut down in front of me. "No. We did not."

I didn't say anything else. Because I saw the look all over her face. "What did he do to you?"

It left me in a way I knew I heard my voice get two octaves deeper. I could feel the familiar Fletcher, darkness and shadows edging into my vision. Because she didn't say that word like a woman who didn't want children.

And I saw the way she talked about Nisha's baby.

I saw it in her eyes when she called Alexei my son.

I didn't feel the same way she felt. But I caught patterns.

"He hurt you?"

I knew Michael beat her. I read the fucking paperwork. And I read in between the lines. I knew because I had a mother too. I knew what my father had done, I knew she cheated on him and had Killian, and I didn't know who his fucking father was.

And I knew Kieran was a product of my father asserting himself. Raping Mom. She left him.

Neither of my brother's knew anything.

And nobody knew how much I watched and listened and I waited.

She didn't say a word and that was enough.

Rage flickered in my chest.

"It's good you're here then," I caught myself saying in a low voice. Not to freak her out. "If we ever get back to the city, there won't be much left of your ex-husband."

Her eyes flickered up to meet mine and I saw the way she watched me.

Sonya was quiet. "And you? No lady friends in your life."

That sent the mood in a different direction.

"I wouldn't call them friends."

And I saw the look in her eyes. I did. I smelled jealousy a mile away as her mouth dropped open but I wasn't a fan of hurting her.

"I don't keep women in my life," I said giving her honesty. To my surprise, Sonya handled it well. "I never have. Never will. This isn't a world anyone belongs in."

She frowned a little looking adorably confused. "But you're in it."

"Exactly," I said. "I didn't have a choice. Nobody gave it to me. I took over based on need and stayed here ever since."

At that an unreadable expression filled her face, or at least one that looked more like empathy to me than anything else.

"You never chose this life?"

I shook my head. "But I don't have or know anything else."

She paused. She was watching me sometimes like she did Alexei. As though she was reconfiguring me on where she mentally put me in her brain.

I stood up then uncomfortable in a number of ways.

Verbally sparing with her was always nice, she always called me out of my shit and I like that, but being around her always made me feel unfamiliar with myself.

I knew who I was when I was at work, and I knew who I was when I was around my guys, and I knew who I was in general.

I didn't recognize who I was when I was with her.

I wasn't sure how I felt about him.

Unfamiliar sensations filled me at the sensations of lemon zest, and Sonya, and secrets and lies coming undone.

"I should get some sleep, thank you for the lemon—"

"Possets."

Right. I wasn't gonna pronounce it.

She stood with me and went to open her mouth. Except she never got to finish what she had to say.

The sound of crashing glass filled the air. And I saw emerald eyes widen at me, and I was on her in another second taking her slight form down to the ground.

"Don't move, Sonya."

I was righteously seething as I looked around and saw it wasn't in the kitchen. No, the hallway?

The moment the glass shattered, the alarms went off in the house and I covered Sonya as the house went red.

Rachel had done security in the house. And she had decided to light this bitch up like a motherfucker if anything were to break into it.

The inside sounded like sirens going off. The entire interior lights turning to a flashing red alerting anyone and everything someone was trying to break in.

Big mistake.

"Motherfucker," I swore as my phone rang in the silence. I dropped it somewhere on the floor. "Sonya, don't move, love."

I was going back to where I had been standing earlier crawling through the red light to get to my phone. When I got it I picked up.

"Nadine, get that fucking bitch in my house right now." I roared into the phone over the alarms. There was only one fucking person who would be stupid enough to attack my turf.

This late.

And this eager.

"On it, we're chasing her down! Nope, Josh got her—*Do not kill her Callahan!*"

Someone else muttered they didn't give a fuck. Cade. No doubt.

"Bring me her fucking head. And for the love of God Rachel—"

"I'm sorry! I'm turning it off right now!" And then the lights turned normal, and the fucking awful shrieks died down.

Only for me to huff out a breath and turn to find Sonya still on the floor, eyes wide and clutching her legs to her body looking petrified.

Fuck my life.

As if I needed another reason why I couldn't have someone in my life. Night time break-ins were traumatizing for anyone. Let alone a survivor like her.

"Sonya, love..." I was slowly walking to her and picking her up into my arms. She was shaking so hard she didn't even speak. "I gotcha." She was in my arms looking like a ghost as Alexei burst into the kitchen with his gun.

"What happened?"

I was going to rip this girl limb from limb when I got my hands on her.

"Who do you think?"

"Eden," he breathed out. And then he swore in Russian.

I got it. I felt the same as I cuddled Sonya tight to me while she shook like the frigid temperatures outside.

26

SONYA

I wasn't expecting Aidan to know *who* threw the rock into the house.

I was shaking to my bones. That had been terrifying.

And for him, it just looked like another day. Once again, the permanent annoyed expression was back, and he just looked peeved. Only he could look like it was a minor inconvenience when someone had thrown a rock into his house.

The alarms, combined with the noise had sent me to a bad place and then throwing me off?

The way Alexei barked orders on the phone in Russian and English transforming into someone I did not recognize.

That was not the same Alexei who ate snacks in my bed and watched movies with me like I was his—No. I wasn't his mother. But for a moment with him, it felt like I had a teenager.

Aidan gripped me tighter and I felt his nose in my cheek. "Sonya, breathe for me…" I did. "Are you okay?"

I nodded barely able to function.

Until you had red lights flashing in your face and sirens going off on you, I didn't understand panic of a different kind—I knew panic from Michael, but this was different.

"What—what is that?"

Aidan quickly ran me down what he'd been dealing with on the side of me being here. I blinked as he told me about one angry woman.

"And from what it sounds like—the Titan's in town got her. They're bringing her here."

And then Alexei was moving to the door as an entire team of black clad agents stormed in less than an hour later.

Some of them were wearing plain clothing, but they were all moving around central figures.

I was sitting on his lap feeling heat crest my cheeks as I almost climbed off. But he kept me closer to him as he scowled at the people filling his kitchen.

"Nadine."

He said it to a dark haired woman with sharp features in a high ponytail. Her brown eyes landed on him first, tip tilted and feline in appearance.

And she was flanked on her other side by a man who moved like a predator. Her shadow.

His face was covered up to his nose, but all I could see was his eyes, a piercing blue as he landed on me.

He had hair whiter than Alexei did and the two of them side by side would have been striking enough with the way they looked.

If it weren't for the captive in between them. Flaming red hair, she was tinier than both of them, and her blue eyes were vibrating with fury.

"Boss," Nadine said. "Look what Josh and I caught."

"I caught her," Josh muttered. "You made sure she didn't die."

Nadine rolled her eyes shoving the dark-haired forward. "She's all yours, sir."

"Eden." Aidan muttered as I saw Alexei talking to two others in the back. A taller dark haired man with blue eyes and a brunette next to him on her tablet. "And you guys brought the whole gang."

Nadine's eyes fell on me. "Is this the Mrs?"

Her smile was wide, canines flashing like this was just another Tuesday. But my gaze was more focused on the redhead who was now watching Aiden.

Aidan was focused on Eden as he wound his arm around me. "How did you do it?"

156

I didn't like the way Eden looked at him.

At all.

"I disagreed with your plan," Nadine said to Aidan. "respectfully, I handled it differently. I thought you might get cocky if we let her think she had the upper hand." Nadine nodded to the black haired man behind her with the piercing blue eyes. "Cade agreed."

At the mention of his name, Alexei brought the man forward strapped in black tactical gear and the brunette at his right with her dark eyes watched us.

"Rachel," Aidan greeted the brunette. "You stayed busy."

The brunette smiled all shy. "Surprise." Her eyes flickered to me. "Hello, I'm Rachel. This is Cade."

She motioned to the black haired man next to her looking morbidly upset he was even here. "Don't mind him he's usually grumpy."

It was the man with the black hair—Cade—who looked annoyed down at Eden.

"Do you want to keep her or should we take her with us? I intend to keep her locked up for a while. Her father be damned."

The way he talked? It was like he couldn't give a damn if she lived or died. Because to me I saw someone who dealt with it every single day. He didn't care about Eden. But he answered to Aidan or at least considered Aidan his equal.

I had so many questions.

Aidan looked like he was considering it. Cade didn't look at me. He kept his eyes on Eden and everything else happening. Rachel shot me a pleasant smile again and a finger wave I returned.

Around Eden the two taller agents holding her up were firm about it.

The white haired blonde, Josh looked like he couldn't care less if she lived or died. And Nadine looked more concerned with how the situation was going to unfold.

"She can't stay here," Aidan said calmly watching her. "I'll take a word and then you can do whatever you need to."

Cade tipped his head respectfully as he motioned for Rachel, the girl who I assumed was IT judging by her tablet and shutting off the alarms followed him. Along with several other agents clearing out half of the them.

He clearly ran the team and owned everyone in the room.

Titan Chicago was nothing like the New York team. These guys looked sharper and darker. A blend of something dangerous when they mingled with the O'Hara's.

The other half stayed as Aidan stood.

I felt in the shift in the room that is about to happen.

Something I wouldn't like.

Aidan had given me Eden's rundown.

Everything. I felt for her. I did. I just didn't know that I handle a situation like her.

Aidan stood in front of then and I saw her eyeing him down with hatred in her eyes. In one motion that made me and Nadine flinch, he ripped the duck tape off her mouth.

An animal noise left her as I covered my mouth.

"I fucking hate you." She growled.

He scowled looking annoyed again. *"I don't even know you.* I don't understand why you keep coming around me. You're an idiot." Nadine looked away and Josh smirked. "You're a child. I'm passing you over to Cade and I can handle your fucking father and uncle or whatever the fuck it is."

Eden made a wild noise as I saw her eyes taking him in. "You're a fucking monster!"

And Aidan being Aidan sighed.

"Yes, I know. But so are you."

Aidan looked more annoyed than anything else.

Like he always did. But now I saw it as a sign of him being worried.

"You killed three of my guys, tried to attack me and my woman in my own home, and you wanted to start a war—because *you're a fucking idiot."*

The girl looked righteously livid. Righteously pissed off.

"They killed my boyfriend—"

"My condolences. You've suffered in life. Do you think you're the only one?" Aidan looked righteously bored with her and that had not been the Aidan I saw coming. "You think I go around killing people willy nilly because someone off'd my girlfriend?"

He paused and then he turned to me.

My eyes widened as he looked back at Eden. "Nevermind, Josh let her go."

Josh's blue eyes widened on Aidan but he tipped his head.

Nadine held onto her though and Aidan brushed her away with a flick of his hand and suddenly Eden was in handcuffs standing there facing Aidan.

"You didn't have to kill three people to get your point across," Aidan told her his arms folded over his chest. "I would've killed your father for free if you asked. But you're an idiot. You can't run the Bratva. You can't even break into my house. Rachel has had her little eyes on you for a month. You didn't catch that?"

He looked more disappointed in anything else.

"Look, I know about Chris Melendez. I know—" he broke off. "You didn't have to start a war. And you broke my window pane. Do you have any idea how much money I'm going to bleed your family dry for?"

"I don't give a fuck about them—"

Aidan made a noise. "That's your fucking problem, you stupid bitch—" I thought she might spit on him with the way she looked and Nadine and Josh moved at the same time.

Nadine kicked her legs out and took her to the ground as Eden made a wild noise.

I stood but I was surprised as Alexei came over to my side like a sentinel. He held a hand out to me motioning for me to stop.

Aidan looked more bored than I had ever seen him.

"Josh, take her Downtown. I'll be meeting her father and telling him *everything*. When I am done, nobody will let you into Chicago. You'll have enemies at every door. There is an a place that you will run where no one will know your name. You tried to use me as a fucking pawn." I saw Aidan's rage like an aura around him.

Normally? He came across as light and teasing like Alexei. Harmless. The kind of man I bantered with and made lemon possets for.

Now?

Now he looked like a demon out of hell as he glared at her.

"You threatened my empire? My family? You tried to drag me into war? I have been around longer than you know how to breathe properly. And you thought you would start war in my territory and manipulate *me*?"

Even I glanced down at the island along with Nadine and Josh. Nobody moved. Every single agent was waiting with baited breath.

"Now I'm righteously pissed off my heating bill is going through the roof because some *stupid bitch can't get her life together.*"

Josh and Nadine hauled her up and even I knew he was being cruel. I knew he was cruel.

I had *always* known there was a part of this man that would cut into people for daring to threaten his empire. Aidan did not take threats lightly.

There was a part of him that existed in absolute ruthlessness. Darkness. And I didn't understand him.

I saw Eden's chest rising and falling and the more I looked at her the more I realized how young she was. I felt for her.

She had killed people. For her boyfriend and her love in a misguided attempt to start a war. I couldn't blame her, but I also knew what it cost Aidan. And nowhere.

I didn't know what to do. My instinct was to protect people.

To take care of them.

I didn't know how to step into his world and make a decision or a choice or anything.

What did I do?

I didn't recognize him or Alexei who stood there with a stoic expression. I didn't understand their politics. I didn't understand the way they viewed things and their reality.

Because their reality was so different from mine.

As Nadine took her screaming and kicking out with Josh, Aidan sighed and turned back to us. He looked like a king holding court again.

"Problem solved."

2 7

SONYA

AIDAN CAME TO ME LATER.

After Alexei called people to fix the hole in the hallway windows.

After Nadine and operatives cleared out the house.

I couldn't stop shaking not just from the slight chill, but unlike Reed or even anyone on his team I'd interacted with? These Titans held an edge I couldn't process.

Aidan didn't say a word as he reached for me and I was in his arms letting him carry me upstairs to my room.

"Alexei can take care of it," he was so casual about it as he took me into his room. His voice rumbled in his chest. "Figured you needed a second."

The scent of him invaded my lungs as I breathed it in like a lifeline.

"Is that…is that your world? Is that normal?"

He shrugged lightly looking careful to maintain space as he set me down onto his bed.

"Not always. Usually it's worse because it's not a woman like that doing it."

"What are they going to do to her?"

"Nothing. Probably lock her up until the fight bleeds out. They won't kill her."

"But they will torture her?"

I knew things too. I was Turkish.

"I don't think they need to," he said it so casually, I laid back into the warm blankets that smelled like him for some reason. "I think she's in enough hell on her own without me rubbing it in."

That was true. In Eden Belova, I saw a woman haunted by her grief and unable to process it.

"She does not have a good family," I whispered drawing up his blankets as he sat on the edge of the bed.

"No."

"But you don't have faith in her to change."

What I liked about Aidan is he did not seemed phased by my questioning. Only contemplative as he considered it.

It hung in the air between us like a weight as he shook his head. "No." I thought he wasn't going to say a word. "When you turn that dark? You're not fixable or savable."

Meaning, Eden Belova was going to dig herself into a hole.

And Aidan wasn't going to dig her out. Or save her.

"Sometimes you are cruel."

Now his lips twisted up. "Thank you."

A reluctant laugh left me then. Only he would take it as a compliment. He was not morally gray. He was night. Darkness itself. But he was also kind.

I didn't know how to comprehend both halves of him.

"Your family was cruel to you?"

"That's enough questions for tonight, princess. You gotta get some rest."

"And you?" I don't know why I asked. I felt the air between us shift as he looked over, amber eyes striking on his features.

Sometimes I didn't know how to process how lethal and dangerous he was. How he made me feel. What to do with those emotions. Michale had never made me feel this way.

Never this alive and never this aware of a man in a good way. Aidan—I was aware of.

Like my breath was caught in my throat which worked overtime to get in air.

"What will you do?"

He didn't say a word as he took me in his sheets, his blankets, and snuggled in there with my robe on.

The tension in the room went skyrocketing up.

"I need to go."

Right. Because he had things to do tonight.

Not stay here. Except I didn't want him to go.

Whenever I got Aidan alone with me a strange phenomena happened. I wanted him to stay. To be around him all the time.

Maybe it was the events of the last few weeks, or the fact that he hadn't been around.

Maybe it was the lemons and the sugar rush and then having the house flooded with Titan's that seemed more terrifying than Reed.

I didn't know if I was gaining confidence by living with him in his world or what. But it came out of me easily.

"Will you stay?"

With me.

Stay with me, tonight.

Amber turned on me then, his eyes narrowed. "I don't think it's a good idea for me to be anywhere near you. Especially not here."

"Why not?"

His throat worked, Adam's apple bobbing. "I'm not a nice fuck, Sonya. If that's what you want, since that's what you probably need. I don't know how to…I can't be that person for you. I just know how to be me. And I'm not your type."

I felt the heat crawling up my face as I watched him say those words. *I'm not a nice fuck.*

"You…you are not my type?"

He shook his head, looking away from me almost uncomfortable.

"What is my type?"

Since he knew it so well.

He huffed out a breath. "Not me."

But he was wrong. I knew in my gut—like I knew the back of my hand—he would never hurt me. Not in bed. Not outside of it.

He had a temper that flared from annoyance, but even then he rolled his eyes and walked away. Which was funny to me.

Aidan never struck anyone, and even Eden he looked more

annoyed with her instead of Michael who would've used that moment to push his power onto her.

I was sure he could've. I was sure Aidan could've killed Eden—but he showed her mercy and let her live in her own mind.

"You don't know that." I was surprised by my own confidence now. "You don't know any of that."

Aidan was facing the windows as he calmly said his next words.

"I know he hurt you *enough*." As Aidan said those words I knew what he was saying. "Last time I kissed you, you freaked out. Not your fault. I'm just saying. I know things too. I can't...I can't be the person you need...I'm not...I'm not a blue-blood pedigree man that will give you flowers and take you out on picnics or whatever it is your kind does. I'm not built for that. I'm not a good man."

No, he would give me a crown and a gun and tell me to stand behind him and shoot whatever moved wrong.

And Alexei would back me up.

I got that now. The words 'my kind' lingered in my head. I swallowed with the words I couldn't say in the past but it came easier now.

"My kind held me down and shamed me for nine years for my accent." I didn't know where it came from. "My kind did take me out on picnics with bruises covering my body. Flowers to hide my legs with. Long sleeve clothing so nobody would know."

I took a shaky breath as I felt it emerge from the shadows in my soul, the places Michael carved out and tried to soil.

"My kind spent nine years destroying me. And yet, the man I least saw coming, the man who saw a problem in my life and did something about it—is the one man who also happens to be a known criminal."

I was beginning to think every single thing I knew about my reality was wrong. Every single aspect of my life was twisted.

I'd certainly learned living here.

"Maybe I do not want flowers or picnics anymore." My breathing caught in my lungs as Aidan turned to me a little warily. Like he wasn't believing me. "Maybe you do not know what I want because I'm still figuring it out too. But I know one thing—I don't want my kind."

I was beginning to think I wanted something else.

Maybe it wasn't enough to be a doormat for people on paper who were legal and good and clean. On paper. But they committed the most heinous of crimes.

Aidan didn't hide who he was.

And nobody liked it—as Killian said, they could fuck off.

"What do you want?"

I felt so many words flutter to the surface.

Only one sentence came out of my mouth.

"I want you to stay here tonight."

With me.

I stayed still as he moved not breathing as his lips hovered over mine. "And you'll...you'll tell me...you'll..."

I didn't think he could stutter.

"You'll say something if I freak you out?"

I'm not a good man.

No. He was the best. And I did want him.

"I will."

I didn't stop him as his lips came stamping over mine and my entire body sighed.

Finally.

28

AIDAN

I WASN'T A GENTLEMAN.

Not even close.

And I never claimed to me.

But I took her down to the bed immediately tearing off the blankets she had and coming down on her in an instant. I was starving for her.

Not once did I stop kissing her. Not fucking once.

I felt hungry for the taste of her. Soft and sweet lemons and sugar. She tasted like a possibility that *was* real.

The kind that made you feel loved and accepted in your own ways.

This was wrong.

So fucking wrong.

Sonya wasn't a fling. She wasn't the kind of woman you fucked once and left. Or twice. Or left at all.

I was committing a grave sin. And yet I couldn't get myself to stop as I made out with her like a wild teenager finally getting to kiss his crush.

Acutely, I was aware Sonya might freak out, but I couldn't stop myself from fitting myself over her, my cock rock hard now, lengthening and pressing into her stomach. I braced myself on my elbows making out with her.

Tentatively, Sonya's hand's elegant, soft and curious slip up my arms like she was learning me and testing me.

She was so soft under me and still, healthier than she had been when she'd first gotten here. All that eating with Alexei must've caught on because I felt her curves under my body.

Her fingers curled into the collar of my hoodie. "You can take this off?"

I could. She didn't have to ask twice. I tugged it off, getting up on my knees and baring my entire chest to her. Her eyes went wider at the lights on my tattoos on my chest and my scars.

"Are those…" she looked at them. But I wasn't here for that.

"Want some help?"

I motioned to her robe.

She nodded but her fingers were clutching the fabric closer. "I haven't…I don't know…"

"It's okay, we'll just go slow." For her. Not for me. I didn't need it. But she did and I wasn't a total dipshit.

The silk parted and I swallowed realizing she was in a delicate slip underneath it.

"I—" she was struggling and covering herself and somehow I wasn't surprised.

"It's okay," I dipped my head not stopping now kissing my way down her neck, tasting her skin, finding her pulse and latching onto it feeling her hands falling away. A soft moan left her as I worked even lower.

Sonya tasted like sugar and something warmer, something just her. The moment my tongue circled her nipples she almost came off the bed.

I lifted my head up. "Good?"

Her eyes were closed as she frantically shook her head. I ducked my head and hid my grin.

And did it again loving the way she moaned as I used it to tug her slip down. Over her arms, and lower until I got to panties. Scraps of nothing.

My fingers working until it got to her heat. Fucckkk. I was going to lose my shit if I kept going.

A soft moan escaped her and shot straight into my cock. All of the rational thoughts in my head went out the window.

Using my mouth and tongue on her nipples, I worked my fingers against her pussy.

I looked up to watch her expression as she stiffened a little.

Oh, I fucking her shit ex-husband never gave a fuck about her.

But I would.

"*Aidan.*"

Her fingers tangled in my hair as licked her lips watching me then. My eyes locked with hers as I felt her clenching around the tips of my fingers and I hadn't even put them in yet.

"Fuck," I whispered over her nipple. "Let me feel you, look at me… there you go." I held her eyes on me. Green on amber as I slowly gentle pressed.

Sonya closed her eyes then and tipped her head as I went deeper, further, her body opening letting me in.

Holy…*shit.*

A softer noise left her mouth as she arched into and I pressed curling my fingers inside of her. Her nails dug into my scalp and I hissed.

"Sorry," she whispered looking out of it. "This is new…am I doing it wrong?"

Shitshitshitshitshit.

"No, you're doing great, love."

Wait…a thought just occurred to me in that moment. No rational thought should've existed but one did now…

"Have you ever…" *No. Don't even ask. You think Mikkey cared?* "This your first time?"

Sonya understood off the bat.

She'd never had an orgasm. I would bet money on it.

In my head, I had already dreamed of dismembering Michael Devereaux slowly and painfully. Excruciatingly accurately.

But none so more than right now.

Right now?

I would dig my fucking knives into his skin for what he did to her.

I should've killed him in New York. She doesn't need a divorce if he's dead.

I could do this. No thoughts of murder. Just her. Just her tiny tight little pussy squeezing around my fingertips and driving me over the edge as I curled it inside of her.

Sonya said something in her language that sounded highly complimentary.

I felt myself smile a little. "Good?"

She nodded. "Good."

"Now let go for me."

I dipped my head and captured her nipple again as I began stroking her from the inside, rubbing against that spot and sucking.

Moans left her as she clenched around me again and again, tighter and tighter, like she couldn't help herself.

And didn't that satiate all my demons. I felt nothing but hunger as I kept going away of how fucking hot she was right now.

In my head, I was memorizing every sound, every little touch, everything she did—because I'd be damned if I forgot it when I didn't have her.

I pushed that thought aside of never having Sonya again.

"Let me have it," I whispered darkly into her skin, against her throat. "I can feel it."

"Aidan—" That's how I wanted her to say my name, desperation and need mingling into one word—me.

I rose up over her, bracing my arm over her head and sealing my mouth over hers. My fingers curled inside of her and rubbed that spot.

"Right fucking there isn't it?"

A broken ragged cry left her as she bucked up. "Aidan, please..."

"I know, is that what you needed?" I kept going keeping my pressure steady as I felt her clench harder. "Let go. I know, that's scary isn't it? But you trust me. And when you do fall apart, I'll be right here the entire time."

"Oh...god..."

"There it is. Come for me, baby."

She shattered. Just like that. Oh. Fuck. Me.

She was gorgeous crying out, bucking her hips as I held her steady and low as she came. Her walls clenched harder and faster and I worked her through it making out with her like a fucking teenager.

169

As she kissed me, I felt her cheeks wet and I stopped slowly breaking off to notice her eyes watering.

"Intense?"

She nodded, almost looking embarrassed. I felt a light smile curl my lips. Masculine satisfaction, predatory pleasure, and all of my demons were pleased. She was perfect.

I was still contemplating murder in the back of my mind, but for right now? She was my primary focus.

I slowly slid my fingers out of her, drawing them into my mouth. I closed my eyes over the taste of her as she made a small noise.

"We're not done yet, princess. Not even close."

I was just getting started.

29

SONYA

SEX WAS DIFFERENT.

Especially when you wanted it.

My body was humming with the aftershocks of my orgasm as I came down. I was buzzing.

I had never felt like this with Michael.

And as Aidan took off his sweats and rolled on top of me again, I knew I'd never be the same once he was done. His straining erection even in the dimly lit room seemed more imposing than ever.

"There is more," I whispered feeling my heart thundering in my chest.

His chuckle was low as he covered my body moving in a way that let me know he wanted me as well. "I hope so. Are you on anything? I have condoms."

And just like that all of my joy was zapped out of me.

I stilled feeling my blood run cold.

Say it.

No, this isn't the right time.

But if you don't tell him, he will never know.

But what if he judges me.

It does not matter, his is not yours—he is just this moment.

What if he thinks less of me?

What if he doesn't want kids?

What if he does?

"Sonya." I snapped back to reality to Aidan brushing my hair back. "Where did you just go? Was it him?"

I didn't even realize how hard I was breathing in and out, or that I was panicking, as the fear in me flickered and faded away. I was focused on amber eyes on me.

"I cannot have children."

That's what came out of my mouth.

Instead of my choosing to lie to him. He had never lied to me.

It felt wrong to tell him something and lead him on.

"I cannot have them ever. I tried for years…"

And failed.

It had become the number one failure of my entire life. Not being able to be a mother. That was the excuse and everybody used, even though everything in my life had gone wrong even before that.

Amber eyes blinked in confusion. His lips parted and I could see him struggling with himself like he didn't know what to say.

But because he was Aidan, he didn't say anything. He didn't have to.

He just dropped his lips over mine and kissed me as I felt the head of him pressing between my open legs. In his kisses, I felt something softer, tender, more of an ache that satiated me inside and out than anything else.

My body braced for the pain, for the sheer agony of it all—and it never came.

Instead a delicious stretch filled me as Aidan kissed me the entire time he worked himself into me. Slow. Steady. Enough to make me want to scream a little with the pressure.

Michael never felt like this. Like every single molecule of my body was attuned to him.

I felt fuller than I ever had been and more pleasure than I thought I could survive. This was intense and all in ways I never saw coming or expected.

"Still good?" His voice was underlaid with a tension that made me clench. "Fuck. I'm trying here—I am."

I knew.

I didn't know how to take much more of this. This already seemed too intense for me. Every nerve ending felt electric. Every bit of me felt raw and exposed, torn between pleasure and sweet aching sensations.

I could feel every part of him, all of him in me, and I felt my eyes watering, as he kissed me. Noises left me as he drew out slowly and I thought it was over. I did.

Sometimes that what happened with Michael.

But Aidan seemed to stay forever.

"Sonya—"

"I'm okay." I was dying. I wasn't okay. "This is too much for me."

Amber eyes flickered up to mine. "What?"

"This is a lot," I held onto his broad shoulders. "You are a lot."

His smile was tight. "You say the nicest things."

But as he shifted his weight an electric sensation went through me.

A noise left me at that and my fingertips dug into his shoulders tighter. I needed something then. Something more. Even if it felt like I wouldn't make it.

Aidan pulled out slowly, slowly, and when he moved back into me —I wanted to scream.

"Oh that's different," my teeth unclenched and a moan slipped out. One after another.

Dark pleasure spilled from me as he kept going. The muscles on his back flexing as he stamped his lips over mine and I screamed a little as he picked up the pace.

"Fuck, you feel so good," he growled. "Hold onto me, baby."

I whimpered as I did and I felt his strokes change as he slammed into me then and the moment he did, it lit up somewhere so electric in me I couldn't control my scream.

"That's my fucking spot," he was all animal now and I felt him do it again and again as I held on trying to stifle my screams. "There you go."

His voice was dark sin in my ears as I lost it, I bit down on his shoulder to keep my screams in as he drove deeper.

I didn't know it could feel this good. With Aidan I just focused on his scent, his eyes, everything about him was different. It wasn't anything from my past.

And I was so close. I was. I was right there—and then it happened. Like it always did. I tensed.

"Aidan," I sobbed. "I can't—I'm scared."

He didn't stop moving, instead he slowed his thrusts down to long and slow strokes that were determined to draw out every ounce of my pleasure by the sensations they stirred in me.

"Why's that?" His rumble in my ear made me clench tighter.

I whimpered at the intensity of my emotions. "It's never good…"

"It can be." He kept going and a ragged moan left me again. "It can be, just trust me." And then he reached down, lifting one of my legs higher as he thrust in.

A cry left me as he did it again and again and I couldn't stop it, feeling like an animal with how desperately I kissed him. The moment my tongue thrust into his mouth he only went harder. I thought I needed gentle and soft. I thought I needed lovemaking.

This was not that and somehow it was.

Aidan was everywhere, all around me, inside of me—and moving with the intent to make me lose it. The sensations were so sharp—I exploded.

An electric shiver went through me at the animal noise coming from me. With every thrust I felt another burst of pleasure and it was endless. I was shaking so hard, he held me down as I came and came and came.

Until it felt endless. Until I felt Aidan groan and shudder as he seemed to swell and heat filled me.

I kept kissing him like my life depended on it. Hungrily, desperately, needing him closer, closer until he couldn't leave me.

My breathing calmed down slowly as he broke off, amber eyes burning so bright on me and I realized my vision was blurring.

He swore softly brushing my hair back and kissing me all over, anywhere he could reach.

Before either one of us could open our mouths I heard a knock at the door and both of us froze, Aidan's mouth at my neck stilling.

"Sonya!" Alexei called. "Are you asleep? I cannot find boss anywhere."

Aidan groaned low and I stifled a chuckle that turned into a squeal and me trying to hide, the moment the door cracked open.

Aidan swore viciously. *"Alexei, I will disown you!"*

I heard swearing in Russian as the door closed with a slam. Aidan groaned as I held him tight laughter bubbling in my throat.

I heard the sound of his feet shuffling away.

"Goodnight!"

The giggles left me easily. One after the other.

Aidan shook his head ruefully. "He's never gonna let me live it down." I felt easy and light laughter leave me. "This is what it's like having kids."

At that my laughter died a little. "It doesn't…upset you?"

He frowned. "That you can't have kids?" I knew it was sudden after that but his comment, even after what we just did—it definitely left a mark.

"No," Aidan looked confused as to why it would. "Your self worth is never based on you being a mother. You being Sonya is enough to me. Whether you had kids or not—it wasn't going to make me like you more or less. You're you. That's the only thing I was looking at this entire time."

And he didn't know what those words did for me. How it made a firework explode inside of my chest as he said it.

"You like me for me?"

He shot me a dry look as he nipped my lips. "I'm still inside of you, princess. You think I do that cuz I don't?"

Another light laugh bubbled up.

"Why are you like this?"

"Why are you like this?" He said it as he kissed me though and my laughter died out into low moans.

Because he had no clue what he had done for me in that moment. Making me feel more seen and more loved than I had been my entire life.

I was falling in love with this imperfectly complicated man and I didn't know how to stop it nor did I want to.

30

AIDAN

I figured once or twice wouldn't be enough.

No.

It wasn't usually.

But the amount of times we were all over each other. I wasn't going to get any work done.

Nothing. I took her everywhere. In the library bent over the bookshelves. Things crashing to the ground around us not giving a fuck. In the kitchen one late night, wrapped around her while she tried to bake and failed.

Because of me.

I relished it covering her nipples in whatever jams or sauces she made and letting her lick it off me. Sex changed Sonya.

"You look different," I whispered one night covered in something like cream and sugar and raspberry jam as I laid my head on her chest panting.

"I feel different. Better," Sonya smiled down at me when I stood. "You are messy."

"Says you." I lifted her into my arms. "I'm so glad Alexei had radar now."

She giggled as I carried her out of there to shower together. I did everything with her.

She brought me breakfast in the mornings to my office, and I shamelessly made out with her unable to stop reaching for her.

After that first night?

I felt like Sonya and I were wrapped around each other all the fucking time. I couldn't explain it. It was completely out of my character to search for her in everything I did.

But she'd been living here for weeks now. Turning into months and I was…I was growing used to it.

"*Askim, iyi misin?*" Sonya breezed in one afternoon with food in her hand. "I brought you something, you haven't eaten all day."

Sonya had gotten comfortable in my home.

"What does that mean?"

"Are you okay?"

I looked at the clock. It was two in the afternoon. "I haven't eaten yet?" I didn't remember.

She set down a sandwich, some chips, some juice. "Dinner is in the oven, I am making steak and potatoes something Alexei wanted."

"Why does Alexei get to choose dinner and I don't?" I asked easily taking her into my lap, like I had done it my entire life.

Before Sonya walked in, I'd been trying to figure out how to manage the Belova's and now?

All thoughts evaporated from my head like mist leaving me with a soft and warm emerald eyed brunette in my lap.

She was smiling at me brushing my hair back.

"Because you do not eat real food, you eat snacks." But Sonya was smiling as she said it. "We eat real food, and you just eat what we eat."

"You always look at me like that," I murmured, her touch feeling more soothing than anything else I felt. "I eat real food."

"Like what?"

Like I was her sunlight. Like she was—I swallowed hard unable to let myself think of it.

I forgot sometimes she was quiet on her feet and a stay at home wife. Not mine though.

But a man could dream.

The idea of Sonya being mine—and no one else's—shouldn't have filled me with possessive pleasure but it did.

It did.

It soothed every part of me that ever imagined her with someone else.

I shook my head unable to even formulate the words as my chest expanded and filled with unfamiliar emotions.

"I don't know."

"*Askim*, you must eat something. And then after we can spend time together, hm?"

I was possessed by the spirit of whatever was seeping out of Sonya's skin because I felt nothing but peace around her. Nothing but warmth and good things as she rubbed my chest.

"*Come.*"

She motioned for me to take a break and I did. I kept her on my lap and she filled me in about Haven and how Gemma devoured working on her project enough to start launching it.

"They said they has small problems, but little things Gemma enjoyed fixing. She hired a smaller team..."

As she spoke about her passion project, her eyes lit up. Her accent got so thick, she almost didn't speak English, intermingling her native tongue with English.

And she laughed in a way that I found myself grinning with her. She was contagious. Infectious.

I didn't even recognize who the fuck I was turning into.

I felt like I was fucking teenager around her figuring out women again. Especially this one who got under my skin and now was lodged there.

She was all consuming in a way that made it impossible for me to imagine a world that I could go backwards to. I didn't understand it.

Maybe because she accepted all my scars, my wounds, my traumas and my past? She didn't judge me for it. Merely accepted it with a curiosity that I often admired. I didn't judge her either. And I realized mutual respect was a two-way street with her.

In the past, I would've thought that with someone with her background, I would've already gotten bored. Or I would've been irritated that she didn't understand my life and she demanded me to be different.

The biggest reason why I felt at peace with her was because she didn't even do that. Not once said she asked me to change.

She adapted to everything that I was.

She was gentle, where I was not, she was calm where I had chaos, she was innocent, and I was wicked. And yet, every time I was in her, she met me at every step, pleading with me to make love to her. To fuck her. To take her.

To make her mine.

In some sick world? She was. She was mine. All consuming. Angelic. Soft, lush, vibrant and mine.

She chatted happily and I found myself devouring the second sandwich as quickly as I had the first with Sonya making sure I drank something in between.

Yet another tick to add to the mental checklist in my head of the things I liked about her.

I never thought I was the kind of man who could be this.

Was this how Killian felt?

"Askim," Sonya brushed my lips with her fingertips. "Are you still hungry?"

I thought about it. I was. I was starving. For so much. I just didn't know how to tell her how she made me feel.

The initial agreement was that this was temporary. It was temporary for her to come here, and ride out all of the terrible things happening.

Her divorce was proceeding now. Pending by the looks of it. I knew the stage it was at now that it had gone back and forth and Liam Sullivan had filled me in that it was now in the system.

He had been successfully fielding off any slander attempts on Sonya. So if and when she did go back to New York? Not only would I absolutely decimate her ex...I realized she'd leave me too.

And I didn't know how I felt about it.

"Askim?"

Right. She asked me a question.

"I am. Is there more?"

She smiled wide on me. "Yes, I will be back."

I didn't want her to leave my sight for a second so I followed her down to my kitchen where she seemed to know where everything was.

Like it was her home too.

I WAS PLAYING HOUSE IN MY OWN HOME.

Alexei seemed more relaxed than ever spending time with Sonya.

I did catch that little shit having movie nights with Sonya. No wonder he looked so tired, the two of them stayed up watching—

"You two watch rom-coms together? What the fuck is happening to my life?"

Sonya shushed me eating popcorn. "This one just came out." I looked over and found Alexei with the same under-eye masks on his face and a headband to pull his hair back as he sat there with Sonya looking the same.

What the fuck was happening in my house?

"Sit," Sonya said motioning to her other side. I was beginning to realize, I would never turn her down. It was impossible. She was turning out to be the one weakness I did have.

Crawling in with the two of them until the three of us were leaning against the headboard of my bed—felt like a surreal dream.

I don't know who I am right now.

My entire life, everything had been planned out for me. Everything had been given to me just because. I had never really given a choice. Not in the food that I ate, not in my life, not in my secrets, not in my darkness.

Sonya...she felt like something I wanted...for the first fucking time—I wanted.

I wanted to sit with her between me and Alexei. With the two of them looking way too comfortable.

Sonya passed me the damn basket of snacks.

"Hmm." She made a noise motioning to it and I looked down at it realizing she was giving me a choice. Again.

I felt unfamiliar sensations in my chest.

It kept swimming up over and over again threatening to choke me a little with the tightening of my chest. I thought I was having a little heart attack.

I forced myself to take a few bites of the salty and sweet mix I found.

Halfway through the movie I was lost. I had no idea what was happening. One of the characters magically turned into another animal and I was done.

"This movie makes no fucking sense."

"Shh."

"Shh."

I smirked popping a few of the candies into my mouth in Sonya's hand. She leaned her head against my shoulder and for just one fucking moment—one fucking moment—I imagined this was real.

All of this was real.

Aidan O'Hara had a family by his choice.

He had a wife.

He had a son.

He had a little world to himself.

And I realized why Sonya scared the shit out of me.

Because it wasn't a dream.

It was happening. And I knew deep down it wasn't forever.

But I wanted it to be.

31

SONYA

AND SO WE ALL FELL INTO A LITTLE ROUTINE.

One where Alexei stayed with me in the mornings making crois-sants and coffee. Every other day I was in the kitchen cooking with him from Nisha's blog.

Today he sat perched on the counter licking the brownie batter off a spoon. "Mamochka, do you think you will make this all the time?"

I laughed easily. "If you want, if your father doesn't disagree to you eating ninety pounds of brownies."

"No, he does not mind," Alexei said looking regally pretty as he kept going.

"Don't eat raw batter like that, darling. Just a little. It'll be done in twenty minutes."

I rolled the last of the croissants and popped them into the oven with his help as we tidied up the kitchen.

"Alexei, where's the update for the Belova's?"

I knew he was coming here. The air shifted just enough for me to feel him, his footsteps almost silent for a man his size.

"I'm getting it—"

"Are you getting it before or after you eat everything?" He grum-bled as he walked up to me and I felt his arm around me as he pressed his lips to my temple.

The gesture so easy and affectionate I watched him carefully. Aidan moved around me to grab coffee.

"Please tell me those bake quickly," he stared at the croissants in a familiar position to Alexei who grumbled about it not being fair to him if Aidan got some first.

I pressed my lips together holding back my laughter.

"There is enough for both of you," the laughter bubbled in my throat either way. "Alexei, what did I say about sneaking in chocolates?"

He was too quick for me as he moved around me and Aidan, dropping a quick kiss to my cheeks that had Aidan scowling before he left.

"One of these days," Aidan sighed. "One of these fucking days."

"Don't you dare," I pursed my lips to him so he could kiss me again. "We are finally alone and I'd like kisses for my hard work."

His smile was dark. "Hmm, you don't say?"

"I made all this," I motioned to breakfast. Only to stop when I saw how much of it was gone. "Well…some of it now."

Aidan's eyes glittered as he kissed me again, while I inhaled his cologne into my lungs and calming down from it.

"You know, I still have time before I have to head down to Titan."

"Do you?" I wiped my hands clean from washing them, feeling my body react instantly. I looped around my arms around his neck. "How much time?"

Aidan eyed his watch and then the kitchen door he walked over and locked deftly.

"For you? I've got time, princess."

I was in his arms a second later with him hauling up my dress.

It was a little strange for me to adjust to Aidan's home.

I fell into a rhythm more comfortable than my own. As someone trained to be a housewife, I found myself finding more comfort here than I ever had.

Floor to ceiling windows letting in some sunlight while the entire house ran hotter now in the Autumn.

Chicago was cold, but I found myself loving the O'Hara mansion.

My coffee pot I purchased on the counter, pots of herbs and plants I had now in the space from Alexei. Now I had recipes printed on the fridge.

My home with Michael had been sterile.

A space where I constantly had to make myself smaller, invisible, and constantly was cut down for being a human being.

My space with Aidan? All of it felt like I was welcome here.

Aidan made me feel like my existence was a breath of fresh air, I was something golden, and he and Alexei wanted me here all th time.

Today I was making *manti*, Turkish dumplings I thought Alexei would enjoy. Whenever I made Turkish food at home for my own comfort, Michael would find a way to complain about my rice being 'too seasoned' for him. And only monkeys ate with their hands.

My people.

Not his.

Michael never failed to remind me every single day I was an outsider. Here? Every single morning I woke up to Aidan moving over me, his tongue moving inside of my body or his length stretching me open and making love to me.

Love.

That's what this house had.

I would come downstairs to find Alexei waiting for me with a smile and I'd kiss his cheek before the two of us busied ourselves.

Now? When I cooked, when I did anything for the boys I imagined this was my life. That this wasn't temporary and I wasn't getting divorced. In my imagination I was free.

Aidan was my husband. Alexei was my son. The one who cuddled up to me and watched romantic comedies in secret while his father grumbled beside me as he ate his snacks.

I finished making the manti and setting them aside for the boys when they got home.

My little family that I didn't want to leave. Ever.

And it didn't take long. By the time I was out of the shower, I heard their footsteps, Aidan shouting at something Alexei did and his laughter.

I emerged in my pajamas to Aidan's grin on me.

"Princess, sorry we took so long. This one wanted to bring you something."

I laughed as Alexei held up an enormous stash of cilantro.

"That is perfect." I kissed his cheek as I led them into the kitchen where Alexei made a noise. "I can chop some up for your dumplings, hm?"

Alexei said something in Russian I didn't understand and Aidan groaned.

"This looks great, baby," he kissed my temple again and the two of them were off as I laughed at them.

Even as my heart clenched. Michael would judge me for everything. Maybe it felt like a relief to be accepted for all that I was. Scars, bruises, culture, spices, and even my decor.

Alexei hung up the evil eye beads in the doorway of the house. There was a mosaic lamp in Aidan's study. And I watched the two of them grumbling to each other and sitting down while I brought them something to drink.

Some part of me had to admit—I liked being Aidan's.

I liked being Aidan's so much I wish I had never been Michaels.

I COULDN'T THINK.

I was just *feeling*.

Aidan's mouth ate at mine long and slow and his tongue matched his fingers gently teasing my sensitized pussy. My body was arching and gently writhing, all for him.

I was a mess.

And I'd woken up this morning with his tongue all over me.

"*Aidan*."

"You're so beautiful like this," he was whispering over my gasps. "So fucking beautiful."

"Let me," I was saying. "Let me."

I worked him in my grip, stroking his impossibly hard length.

When I wrapped my fist around his length, his groan mixed with mine, and I panted as he thrust into my hand.

I worked him twisting my fist at the tip and he groaned hard. "Goddamn, baby."

Aidan dipped his head groaning around my breast sucking as I worked him. I moaned and went harder realizing his plan. I gasped as he sucked harder.

"Lick your palm."

I flushed realizing what he was asking, his fingers trailing lower until two of them dipped in me. I moaned loudly as we both worked on each other.

There was no way I could walk away from him.

Not this.

Not his kisses.

I fisted his length harder and stroked him until I felt his shoulders bunch, his hips buck, his cock swelled impossibly lengthening and growing almost as the first squirts of his orgasm hit my legs.

Over and over he came and came until my thighs were covered by him. His fingers curling inside of me and I cried out feeling my own orgasm flood around him.

"Easy," he came up, and stamped his mouth over mine. "I have you. I always gotcha."

Nobody had ever kissed me the way Aidan kissed me. Hot. Commanding. Dominating. Until I melted into the sheets.

"We should always wake up like this," I whispered.

"We do," he grinned looking boyishly young. "I might get addicted to you."

"I am already addicted to you."

His smile was softer. "That's not so bad, is it?"

"No, not bad at all."

He kissed me again and again until I felt him moving over me.

"Again?"

"Princess, you keep kissing me like that, I won't ever leave the bed."

32

AIDAN

"Where are we going?" Sonya whispered as I covered her eyes.

I felt like a fucking teenager with her, giddy with excitement, and all around happiness as I led her into the ballet studio.

It was early one morning when I knew there wasn't a class open that I took her there.

We had an hour and I figured she might like it. Nestled Downtown, this tiny place often did classes for children and sometimes adults. It was among a few of the buildings I owned on this street, but I thought she might like it.

Sonya had told me Michael had hated her dancing.

And she had loved it years ago. I wanted her to heal and love it again. So I got us some time and an empty studio.

"Ready?"

"Yes."

I dropped my hand.

Her eyes, emerald and shimmering with laughter went wide as she looked around. *"Allah'm, bu ne?"*

I didn't need a translator for that.

"This is a dance studio, we have an hour, but I wanted to bring you somewhere you could enjoy. You've been in Chicago long enough, I thought you might wanna come somewhere that makes you happy. Again." I motioned around us, the long mirrors, the dimmer lights, and the barre equipment to the side. "They do classes here all the time if you ever wanted to start back up again."

She turned with joy in her eyes and she was in my arms a second later.

There was something liberating about being with someone like her. Someone who wasn't afraid to be close to me, so close that I could smell her perfume on her. Lush green ripe pears and the scent after it rained.

I could inhale her into my lungs all day and never get tired of it.

"*Askim*," she murmured into my coat. "Thank you."

Her slender form released me then looking around with a child-like glee.

"Now you know why I asked you to dress comfy." I motioned to her outfit of leggings and one of my hoodies. She looked comfy. But she took it off leaving her in an emerald green bra matching her eyes that made my dick suddenly throb.

Sweet. Fucking. Christ. I wasn't ever going to get enough of this woman.

"Askim, how do we—" She looked around for the speakers and I went over to try and help her. Once we figured out how to work it and connect her phone to it? Sonya squealed a little. "I have not danced in forever."

I knew.

Walking to one of the mirrors, I slid it open to get to the costume closet on the other side. I knew they had one of these here. It was one of the reasons why I picked this place. "Have you seen this? They have accessories."

Sonya came over eyes wide as she plucked up a few things, some shimmering, some like a tutu.

"This is amazing." She kept fluttering and kissing me with excitement. "I am nervous."

"Don't be, shit I'll do it with you."

Her laughter rang out musically in the room and I grinned. She was fucking infectious. She eyed me with a curious expression. "You do not care if I just—"

"If you just dance?" My hand found her waist tugging her close to me loving how beautiful and adorable she was. "Nah, I'm not much of a dancer, princess. But I'll watch you any day."

She turned a shade of blush only she could.

"I can't fucking believe you existed in New York," I whispered looking at her olive skin, peach tinted cheeks, dark emerald eyes. "If I had known you were real, I would've snatched you up a long time ago."

"Hm," she pouted at me. "Maybe. If I let you."

I laughed then as she pushed away. *Who* was this fucking woman? Sparks ignited inside of me, thousands of light fragments peppering my skin making my chest expand with warmth.

Sonya laughed as she darted to the speakers leaving me a little dazed staring after her.

And she turned the music on low something with strings and percussion and drums that sounded nothing like ballet music and I was salivating already at the sight of her.

Long-limbed grace as she wiggled out of her leggings, the sunlight catching her hair and curves.

"I didn't realize—" I sounded like a dying man. I cleared my throat. "What are you—"

"Putting on a costume." She smiled over her shoulder, eyes twinkling with mischief, and I thought initially she'd grabbed scarves.

They were *not* scarves.

No, somehow Sonya had grabbed the worst imitation of pants known to mankind. Completely see-through, covered in jewels, and I knew that it was fake, but against her skin?

"You look like a princess."

Out of my dirtiest fantasies.

Shit. I had brought her to this place for her to have a great time.

Not for me to have a better time watching this.

She laughed at my expression as she tucked some of the fabric into her bras and I leaned against the wall needing a second.

I swore softly. "You look..."

She looked ethereal, beautiful in every way possible. Sonya's laughter echoed in the room. "You know, I didn't just train in ballet."

"No?" It was a wheeze.

She shook her head looking mischievous tugging me to her as she approached me with a sway in her hips.

"I was also a belly dancer once from when I was a girl, but my parents did not know. It was not respectable for a woman to know this." her lips grazed my ear. "I show you?"

Yes. A thousand times. *Yes.*

I stood there stumped as my Sonya now blossoming with newfound confidence and wonder in her moved away from me turning the music up.

Sonya moved like nothing I had ever seen before in real life.

She laughed and with a wide grin on her face and her eyes twinkling she began to move, her fingers in graceful arches, her body moving in a way that seemed fluid. I swallowed a little. She laughed.

"I have not done this in forever." She turned to me tugging me to her. "You accept my culture."

Yeah. "I accept everything about you," I wrapped my arms around her as she swayed to the music with me.

I'd dropped my coat and shirt earlier leaving me in a plain t-shirt. Next to her? I looked like a limp rag.

"I accept it all. Not just this, but everything you bring into my home."

"Like the *manti*," she teased me, eyes twinkling.

"Those dumplings are fucking fantastic," I dropped my mouth over hers unable to stop, kissing her and pressing my dick into her. "This is your fault."

She giggled between my kisses and I felt my lips tug up unable to stop. I didn't understand what was happening to me with her.

But it was more than that. Sonya hung these evil eye beads around my office door like that would be good for me. Alexei was learning some words with her. She laughed and spoke in her language more often. My kitchen smelled incredible.

I did accept her culture. "I accept all of it. All of you."

Because she also accepted all of mine.

Even the parts I didn't like.

Her eyes shimmered up at me as I said it. And I caught the heat in them as she watched me.

"You don't care I cannot have children?"

190

"No, I don't think it makes you less of you."

Her breathing hitched as her eyes watched me with lush green wonder in them.

My hands moved her hips as the music carried on around us. "We don't have much time here, princess." I clocked about thirty minutes before we had to leave.

"Hmm," she murmured into my chest. "Not enough time?"

"Not nearly enough for what I wanna do with you...unless..." I wasn't even finishing my sentence before she turned off the music and I moved making sure the door was locked.

She was in my arms a second later with me turning her around to face the mirrors.

She gasped at the sight of my arms around her barely clad body. "We should take this off." Sonya motioned to her outfit.

"I couldn't agree more."

My hands were all over until she was gloriously naked in front of me. All tanned and golden lean lines. Hair flowing over my arm.

"We have twenty-five minutes, princess."

"Hurry," she panted as I palmed her nipples rosy tipped and hard while I shoved my pants down, and palmed my dick. Rock hard and throbbing for her, I pressed her angling her body, her hips back as I panted.

My eyes felt hazy with lust and anticipation locking onto hers as I groaned. "I know you can take me, princess. Spread your thighs a little wider."

"Aidan—" she whimpered, her hands gripped my wrists. One arm banded around her, under her breasts plumping them up, and my other one reached around to find her clit as I pressed into her further.

"There you go, baby. There you fucking go..."

I groaned closing my eyes for a second relishing every single second of her adjusting. Her soft whimpers filled my ears.

Her lips parted a little as she moaned pushing her hips back and seating me in deeper. Deeper. Until finally—fucking finally—I was balls deep in her. Our eyes met in the mirror, but Sonya turned her head to me. "*Askim*," she pursed her lips.

"Want kisses?"

I smiled into her lips sealing my mouth over hers and I began moving. I groaned at how wet she was.

"I think you like almost getting caught."

An animal noise left her as she pushed back on me. "More, please."

I could do that. I held her tight to me as I fucked in. "You love this, don't you?" I growled into her ear as I watched her breasts bouncing, her cheeks flushed as I pounded deep into her. "You love me."

"Yes," she whispered biting her lip and holding onto me as she closed her eyes. "Aidan, *yesyesyesyesIloveyou.*"

I felt the moment she exploded clapping her hand over her mouth and crying out, the electric sensations shot me through and I gripped onto her giving myself over at that.

Fuck, she was wet hot heat and I was losing it. Pulsing in her as I came harder than I ever had. Just from the sound of that alone.

I was insane. I was losing my shit.

And yet I inhaled the scent of her into my lungs as I came and came inside of her.

I love you.

She said it.

She loves me.

I told myself it was just the heat of the moment. Thats all it was.

But I saw the way Sonya softened in my arms after, like she completely trusted me, and she *loved* me.

She leaned into my touch, cuddled me tighter to her, and kissed me as I looked down at my watch. "Shit, five minutes."

Sonya squeaked as I rushed to put my hoodie on her and do her sweats up as I practically carried her out of there.

I was telling myself my heart was hammering because of narrow escape—and not because this beautiful, stunning, incredible woman —had picked me.

33

AIDAN

"Who is Gwendolyn?"

I stiffened at the mention of my teenage crush.

I kept that shit to myself.

Which meant one of my brother's had talked.

Sonya blinked up at me with lush emerald eyes from my bathtub where she was scrubbing me down with whatever flowery pear scented body wash she used. Lemons, pears, something expensive.

She was lathering it all over me and I was having a great time.

A naked tanned Sonya on my lap kissing my face every few seconds as she scrubbed?

I was in heaven.

Until she said that.

"Uhh, nobody." I don't know why I said it. I hid all parts of myself from everyone. Including—especially—that one. The part of myself I rarely talked about. Unless Lucas brought up the board game *The Domain*. Then it was a wrap.

"Askim," she narrowed her eyes on me. "You like another woman and you do not think I will ask."

I felt heat on my cheeks. "Sonya, she's fictional. Who told you—Kieran?"

"Killian." She laughed in my lap at my face. "I see. I did not know you liked fantasy movies."

"I don't usually advertise it on my mafia social profile."

Her laughter was musical in the bathroom. "You think I look like her?"

Oh. Fuck. Me.

"A little, just enough. I was eleven when the movie series came out," I might as well come clean to Sonya. "I was young and baby sitting Kieran one night. Killian was already asleep and we didn't have cable. We had like five channels. One of them was this one that played movies and they were playing reruns of Lords of Nightshade."

Her eyes softened on me as I told her I had stayed up watching the movies and I finished one and had been obsessed with the series.

The fantasy of dragons, faraway lands, and kings and queens and —I broke off.

"I thought if the television was this portal, I would take my brothers to this land and keep them there. Earn an honest living."

Her eyes blinked a few times as I caught the emotion in them.

"You wanted to be normal?"

I didn't know why that shit made me emotional. It shouldn't have. But then again nobody knew me and what I wanted.

"I guess I did. Once."

Until life came at me fast.

"You don't know the things my father did." I did know that Lara was friends with Sonya. She mentioned her girlfriends sometimes and Alisha, Reed's girlfriend came up with Lara. I knew they had photos together. My father was extremely well connected, and then I came up in the world, I didn't realize how many connections he had.

"There is so much shit, he pulled. I had to pull my family out of that. Which wasn't easy."

She nodded as she used some of the water to clean me up. The soap bubbles popping, the water becoming less hot than before letting me know we were both turning to prunes.

Emerald eyes watched me as I told her. "There's a few people in this world of mine that were victims of my father's crimes. I still pay for that."

"Like who?"

I shook my head. "I like you, princess. But I don't talk names."

She frowned at me mockingly. "Fine, keep your secrets." Her chest bobbed a little in the water as she rose up over me and turned laying on my chest then. As she laid back her toes turned on the spout to let more hot water run.

"When I got old enough to run this business, the first thing Gabriel recommended I do is buy legitimate properties. I don't know if you know him. But he's solid." I explained to Sonya what I had done to drag my family into prosperity. Kicking and screaming. "I used the real estate to maintain my territorial control so that I could slowly start converting illegal fronts to legal ones. Your buddy Lucas helped."

She gasped, turning in my arms again. "Lucas knows!"

I grinned at her expression. "Most of the Chicago properties belonged to his father, Charles. My father and his were solid. Until they weren't."

I didn't know how to tell her that not only had we built strategic alliances, but Gabriel being former CIA taught us intelligence networks were much more powerful.

"I learned as I got older the right information can open the right doors and while violence is necessary—it isn't always the answer. In turn, Gabriel took Killian and Kieran, and he took care of them at Titan."

"That's why Killian worked with Gabriel."

"He's still second-in-command if he wanted it. But—"

"He still kills people."

I shrugged. "Reed kills the most people. You just don't see it."

Her eyes went so wide as I said it casually. "Reed is…"

"Reed might be the CEO, but he didn't get there by being a nice guy," I told her. "Everything you see about Titan on the outside is a mirage. It's real. But it isn't. Gabriel knew better than to trust the Intelligence community. I don't know what happened to him, but I know that people have fucked him over in the past. Gabriel woke up one day and decided that being a criminal was better than being an honest man."

And thus Titan Security, the O'Hara family, and even the Devereaux's had straightened out.

"It is all connected?" Sonya whispered. "Everything. Everyone."

I nodded. "Gabriel thought it was smarter to create a network. This way, there isn't a singular weakness. Everything is spread out in a way where everyone covers for each other. Take Killian and Kieran. Both of them if anything happened to me could cover for me."

As I said it her eyes widened on me.

"Because you are in danger?"

"Technically," I kept my voice low. "Everyone's really in danger. What if alien's invaded tomorrow?"

"*Askim.*" She gave me that stern look that I thought was hot as shit as she shoved me gently. I grinned at her expression. "That was not funny."

"I'm sorry, princess."

"Your life being threatened is not funny." She added her brows drawn more now.

Maybe. But that was my reality.

"I'm sorry," I whispered dropping my voice and inching closer. "I can apologize to you if you want…" I trailed my fingers up her thighs and felt a smug smile curve my lips as her breathing hitched. The scene of citrus and pears and something wonderfully her filled my lungs. "Make it up to you."

I slid my fingers lower and lower.

"I love that you trust me this much," I openly admitted it. "There you go spread your legs a little wider for me."

"Of course I trust you." Sonya gasped as I lifted her gently, easily over my cock. As she slid down we both groaned. Her eyes shuttered then as she whimpered. "*Aidan.*"

I loved the way she said my name as her fingers held onto my arms for support. "I can feel you around me, you take me so well, love."

Only when she fully seated on me did I lean back. Spreading her legs a little with mine until she had to rest on me. My hands moved to her nipples, finding them tight and hard like diamonds.

"Just feel me," I groaned my lips grazing her ear. "There you go, such a good girl for me."

She leaned back as I thrust up into her the sound of rushing water drowning out her moans.

Her slick heat, clenching and pulsing around me had me closing my eyes. Desire rushing over me as I ground deeper and Sonya cried out.

"You take me so well," my voice was dark in her ear as she moved her hips down to take more of me. I rocked up to meet every little grind. "I never wanna leave you, you were made for me, princess."

Sonya whimpered, her mouth turning down as I felt her getting closer.

"Right there?" I rolled her nipples tighter, thrusting my hips up feeling her shatter. "That's my fucking girl, let me have it. Keep coming for me."

Sonya's legs closed and it made her even tighter as I groaned into her skin, my orgasm taking over, my arms wrapping around her tighter to keep her closer until it felt like we were one person.

It took me long moments to come to and that was only because Sonya made an errant noise.

"Aidan," she gasped. "Wait—" she flicked her toes out and turned off the water motioning to the tub.

"Oh shit." The water had rose with both of us to the lip and was about to spill over.

"Don't move." She reached tugged the damn drain chord up and the sounds of water draining out filled the room. Sonya made a noise of relief as she sat back.

Laughter bubbled up in my throat mingling with hers in the room.

And some of those moments with her—I swore I didn't recognize who I was anymore.

34

SONYA

NOBODY HAD EVER TOLD ME THAT IF IT WAS POSSIBLE FOR BAD SEX TO tear you down—it was possible for good sex to lift you up.

That is how I felt with Aidan.

I was hungry for him. Grabbing him and feeling like a criminal walking into his study only for him to take one look at me and the two of us to be all over each other.

Sneaking around this house like we were hiding our relationship when it was no secret we were together.

In the bedroom, the kitchen, the study, the office—everywhere.

"You are very good at this," I whispered to him one evening when I'd sat on his lap naked in his office. Riding him slowly enough to drive him crazy.

"Not so bad yourself, princess."

I wrinkled my nose stopping my hips feeling him pulse in me as he groaned low.

"You call me this to insult me?"

"No," he brushed my hair back and I was aware of how powerful I felt despite being naked on his lap while he wore his clothes. "I call you that because that's how I see you. Like in another life you had your crown and your castle...like a princess."

I smiled aware of how silly and young he made me feel. Even

though we were the same age and I felt a world apart from him—he still made me feel like I was a young woman falling in love again.

My second chance.

"Oh? And I suppose that makes you the King of another land coming to take me away?"

I kissed his laughter over and over.

"Nah, I'm definitely the pirate king coming to steal you."

I laughed with him as he lifted me up without breaking contact and set me on his desk. "To take you." His voice dropped in my ear. "To fuck you."

I moaned as he began to move and I lost track of everything.

I didn't even know it could feel this good, I was grabbing at his shirt as he lifted me into his arms slamming me down on him so hard I came right there.

I was shaking as he continued. Long moments later Aidan groaned and followed me. He held me tight to him as he panted.

"I think I have an addiction."

"Me too." I agreed.

Our laughter filled our kisses and I realized part of it was the truth.

"Can we go to bed?"

"Yeah, we can go to bed."

I was falling for Aidan. It happened so slowly and built so much I didn't even see it coming.

"I WANNA TAKE YOU OUT," AIDAN MURMURED ONE EVENING. "ON A real date. Not pizza."

"But pizza is good."

"Pizza is grounds for warfare here. I wanna take you somewhere else. Come on."

And so we were off.

I had never been on dates except with him. But New York City where he had come to win back Nisha for Killian did not really count.

"Where are we going?" I asked him bundled up in a coat and scarf and a hat. "It is so cold here."

He grinned looking handsome in the night. "I found something I thought you'd like."

And he took me in a cab to somewhere I did not expect. I knew the moment I knew what it was.

"You brought me to a night market?"

The moment we turned the corner, strings of lights that criss-crossed all around us, with lanterns illuminated stalls that filled the air with familiar spices and sounds that brought me back to my home.

It had been forever since I had been home.

There was nothing there for me anymore. Vendors that called out in different languages. Steam rose from countless pots and grills. And I could smell all of the spices mixing with meat and dough and wonderful sweets.

"Askim!"

Aidan's laughter filled the air behind me as I sped off to the stalls with excitement. "This is amazing."

I looked at him feeling my heart was sputtering with excitement, my hands shaking with it. I was vibrating as I turned over my shoulder to find him grinning. His dimples in place as he laughed.

"I come here sometimes, I don't bring anyone though. It's good here, nobody knows me and I'm just another guy trying out new things."

I didn't recognize him. He was so different from the man that I had met months ago.

But then again, I didn't recognize myself. Something about removing myself from my problem in New York and coming to Chicago had really helped me.

I felt parts of me that were sore and aching heal over as though being here was putting a Band-Aid on it.

Not only had my shoulder healed in the time I had been here.

My heart felt whole again.

Around him.

"You want to show me your favorites?"

His eyes shimmered in the lantern's lighting almost boyish in his happiness. That's what I saw in him.

Over the last few weeks that we have been together, I saw him looking younger. Among the lanterns and food stalls, he looked like a younger man having a good time.

I didn't think he did most of the time. Nor did he take care of yourself properly. And as we wandered through the market, I found myself memorizing every inch of him. Every single bit of him.

Aidan was healing in his darkness.

He was healing me. Inside and out. He was teaching me new things every single day about sex and love and my body, encouraging me in the best of ways.

"Here, try this first, scallion pancakes are good but only with that sauce..." and we sat down to try all types of dumplings and crispy, pancakes and skewers of grilled meat.

I was surprised because I didn't see him as the kind of man who did this.

He shrugged when I asked him. "Sometimes I get bored." It was such an innocuous statement that I couldn't stop myself from laughing at him.

They had a Turkish vendor he motioned me to and I almost moaned and died a little at the taste of home.

"When I was little? I would eat this all the time..." I motioned to the *lahmcun*, a meat seasoned flat pizza.

"You're gonna hate me but I put sauce on it."

I gasped. "Blasphemy."

Aidan laughed easily and I was so distracted, I didn't see the two figures walking by us. I caught the eyes on me first and I turned my head.

A brunette with dark eyes blinked at us in her dark coat. A wide smile stretched her lips. "*Heyyyyy*, Aidan. Aidan's lady friend who lives with him. Sonya, right?"

Aidan's smile dipped as he turned and to my surprise right behind the familiar brunette was a familiar dark haired gentleman looking left and right scanning as he approached us. His amber eyes shifted as he took them in.

"Rachel." Aidan greeted her without any chill in his voice unlike his eyes flattening out when he saw the other figure behind her in his dark trench coat. "Cade."

The Chicago Titans.

Cade as ever looked more composed than his counterpart Rachel, who grinned at us openly. "Ohhhh, that looks so good. Cade, we should try some. We haven't even started yet…"

She was tiny compared to him, smaller than me, and I didn't think they were together, but they were certainly close friends. He didn't touch her and kept his distance. Just coworkers out for dinner.

"O'Hara," Cade dipped his head to Aidan and then me. "Rachel, don't breathe down their throat. He's having dinner. Leave him alone."

Rachel pouted at me. And then up at Cade who scowled. A moment of silence passed.

"No." He issued. He looked at Aidan. "My apologies. This isn't about work. She was hungry so we came to get some food."

Aidan tipped his head like he got it but I noticed his shoulders tensing.

He hadn't done anything about Eden.

He said he was letting her simmer. "A few months of a locked box should straighten her out."

I thought he was being cruel to her.

But Aidan said if she wanted a piece of their world—she had learn like all of them did. Especially since her father knew about her and he was livid. Right now, tensions were tight and I could see the stress on his shoulders.

As Cade plucked an eager eyed Rachel away, the two Titans blending into the crowd like wraiths.

It was still a little unsettling.

"They are different from the ones in New York."

Aidan nodded. "They get trained differently. Reed plucks people out of one team into other teams. If they don't fit on the New York team some of them get sent here. I think Nadine was one of the few they liked for the New York team, but her and Rachel and Josh work really well together in Chicago."

"And Cade?"

He was quiet for a moment. "He's their lead. He has to be that way."

I could see in his eyes that he was haunted by something. Something in him had changed and he was slowly becoming the Aidan who was stoic and cold around me.

The one who shut down and shut me out.

But I could see him slipping away, and I didn't like it at all. I didn't want him just to be the cold and controlled version of him who always kept everybody at arms.

Over time, as I had gotten to know him, I realized how much depth that he had and how much he hid from everybody around him.

He was funny and he made me laugh all the time—this closet nerd with hopes and dreams beyond what he did. I didn't know Aidan wanted to go to college years ago. I didn't know he wanted another life. And couldn't have it.

Ever.

I saw a different side to him. And I didn't want to see him fading despite the chill in the air? The heat of the tent and our bodies close together eating food—I didn't want to lose him.

I held up a soup dumpling to his lips. "*Askim*, take a bite for me."

He blinked as though he was waking up from a dream. And he looked at me with a surprised look, like he was wondering why I was here. And it ached. It did.

"Hm?" I held the dumpling to his lips and he hesitantly gently blew on it and bit into it.

"Mmm, that's good."

A small smile lit his lips as I passed him a mango lassi, I had snagged from an Indian vendor.

"It's okay," I nudged him. "This isn't work. It was temporary. You can breathe again." My hand moved over his heart, over his coat and rubbed it there. "It's okay."

And it was. It was slow, but he did calm down, and we walked through the market. I don't know what it was, maybe it was the cold or just the good company, but I ended up eating more than night than I ever had.

"I am so full!" I giggled. "I gained like twenty pounds with you now."

He grinned back. "Looks good on you."

I kissed him under a streetlamp feeling all the world like a woman who didn't have a past or a future doing anything.

In the time that I was spending with him with everything being handled with everything else in my life, I got to just breathe.

And for a moment, I imagined this being my new home and just continuing what I had been doing for so long—from Chicago.

For a moment kissing Aidan under the lamps and moonlights and lanterns, I felt like anything was possible.

We headed home early into the morning. And it was in our room as he took a shower and cleaned up, and I sat in my towel wrapped around me my phone dinged.

I looked down feeling the rush of heat and cold mingling on my skin.

I had never felt so cozy.

My eyes dropped to the text message this late.

I knew better than to read messages this late night because no good news came after midnight.

Killian.

> Nisha thinks she's going into labor.
>
> It's been on and off for a day now. But the baby's coming soon.

I waited until Aidan finished his shower and got dressed.

I showed him the text messages after and he frowned down at it.

When his eyes meant mine, I knew that he was thinking the same thing.

"We have to go back to New York."

35

SONYA

Helping Nisha meant helping Killian who was laying on the bed with her holding her with an anguished look in his eyes.

If there was anyone who loved his wife—it was him. At some point they had gotten married after she'd gone back to him.

That did not surprise me.

Killian didn't seem like the kind of person to let her walk away.

But now, I got to see another side of him after meeting him on the occasion back when he'd come to get Nisha's things and help her settle in with him.

He cradled her to his chest as she breathed through another contraction, crying a little, his other hand on her belly while he kissed her.

I privately looked away, aware he looked like he was trying to absorb her through his skin.

"It's all right, luv," he murmured. "I have you. It's okay, I have you…"

I didn't even think he heard me. "She's going to be okay, I made her some hot tea, do you need anything?"

He shook his head and focused solely on her while I buzzed around, grabbing towels, getting him water.

He didn't let me move his jacket from the chair closest to him and Nisha.

Instead he just motioned me away to the other side of the room when the nurse bustled in. Her entire face turned to a grimace.

"Father's shouldn't be on the bed with her."

What?

Killian didn't move save for brushing Nisha's inky hair back on the bed while she shook in his arms.

I turned to the nurse, ready to protect both of them.

"Pardon?"

"Yeah, he can't be on the bed with her, it causes complications."

For who? "For who?"

Maybe being with Aidan and having love and support had given me a backbone but I felt irritated at the sound of her voice alone let alone her walking into a room with a pregnant woman—and her first words being of criticism.

I felt his anger churning through me. Aidan would absolutely ruin this woman.

"As far as I am concerned, father's are allowed in the room and in her space," I shot back. "He's allowed to be here as per hospital policy. And she's in pain—"

"Yes, I can see her—"

"Then act like that—"

"Miss, if you keep acting out—"

"*Call security then*, and I will tell them a nurse is actively harassing a father and a pregnant mother who happens to be his wife."

Her mouth turned down and her eyes, snake-like and laser-focused on me, made my skin crawl.

And she rolled her eyes and I wanted to stab her a little.

Just then, I felt bloodthirsty.

She looks like Mum. She looks like my family.

Even if she wasn't, and the conclusion wasn't rational or logical, but I associated her to my mother.

And to me, that was a strength.

It was like a warning signal in my brain, telling me what I was being prepared for.

Her eyes glanced over Killian and Nisha with barely concealed disgust for some reason and it made my blood boil. Nisha was

206

shaking and crying quietly. And Killian looked like he'd rather take it all on himself.

"Is there a problem here?" I repeated myself.

And I swore the nurse muttered. "Dramatic."

At Nisha.

While pregnant.

In labor.

I was trying to summon the strength to calm down. *Askim, I am turning into you.*

"I beg your pardon?"

Part of me could not even fathom, that this was a real interaction. I was having with a healthcare provider.

I felt Killian stir and the energy in the room shift slowly.

"He can't be on the bed, and you need to stop being dramatic—I can call security in here in another second."

"Don't touch Nisha," I stepped in between her and Killian and this garbage nurse. "I didn't know there was a requirement on you being a mean person to be a nurse—"

"I can have you detained and taken in by the police—"

"Over mine and Aidan's dead bodies yes—"

Did she not realize the head of security for this particular hospital was currently in the bed with his wife?

Or was she just an entitled idiot like every single mean maternity nurse I know?

I really didn't understand why maternity nurses in the States were so cruel when internationally a woman could receive state of the art care.

I felt the temperature dip as Nisha whimpered in pain. A low moan left her.

"Baby..."

I turned to find her knuckles white on Killian's arm as she closed her eyes in pain.

Nisha was in active labor while this idiotic woman held her up. Rage filled me.

Killian hadn't looked up as he murmured something to her, his head lifting slightly for me to see how predatory dark his eyes were.

Good. Lord.

He's going to kill someone.

But the nurse went on.

"I need to check her," she said roughly ignoring everything else but what she wanted as she reached for Nisha I saw Killian's head snap. Faster than I thought possible.

I didn't see him move.

I didn't even see it coming when his hand reached into the jacket he had told me not to touch.

And I hadn't realized how close I had gotten to him. I was standing in front of Nisha and closer to Killian than before and I usually kept my distance since he didn't like people touching him.

The metallic *click* of a gun cocked through the air and I froze, my spine turning into iron.

He tucked Nisha's face into his neck as I swallowed.

The air in the room turned frigid as he locked wild eyes with the nurse. My eyes darted to her to find her jaw open.

"Get. *Out*." His canines barred a little as he said the words with lethal precision and I knew that look.

That was the same look Aidan gave Michael.

"*Now*."

He hid Nisha's face further as her white-knuckles gripped his arm.

The nurse horrified, scurried out of the room swearing about calling the cops and security and I knew eventually she'd run into someone who would fire her.

I texted Reed quickly as I heard Killian tuck the gun away and turn back to Nisha, his entire expression melted into heartbroken worry.

"Easy, luv. I have you...I have both of you I know...I know I have her..."

I felt like I almost imagined what I saw.

But I knew I hadn't. He was willing to protect everything that meant anything to him.

I realized why I was falling in love with his family and his brother.

Because they were showing me, where Michael had used violence to control and belittle me—the O'Hara's used violence to protect. To defend their loves one.

And the only thing Killian cared about was in his arms right now.

I rushed outside to get another doctor and texted Reed rapidly.

Finally, we made some headway when another female doctor came.

"Hi, I'm Dr. Radcliffe," she took one look at Nisha and stepped in.

And finally, hours later, Kiara O'Hara was eight pounds of crying baby when she'd come into the world with a full head of inky hair and bright amber eyes.

Those eyes slowly opened to stop crying only when Nisha had held her.

"It's okay," Nisha had soothed her shaking wildly. "I know, baby. I know. Mama's gotcha now. Oh, you're so sweet…"

And she'd taken her daughter into her arms with Killian's help.

Nisha was trembling, there was blood—so much blood—and all I saw was my vision blurring.

His hands supporting Nisha's shaking ones and Kiara had stopped crying immediately as Nisha cuddled her. Amber eyes blinked up at both of them.

And I was done for.

It was hard to not break down a little watching a little dream I had for myself.

One day in my next life, I'll be a mom.

In a world where I wasn't defective.

One day I would wake up on a Sunday morning with my husband still asleep and I would make chocolate chip pancakes in my kitchen.

One day I would fill up bowls full of Halloween treats in front of my house that my husband decorated for kids to come to.

One day I would be someone's wife and be happier than I ever could be.

That day would never happen for me.

Not in this lifetime at least.

Nisha whispered to Killian. "She has *your* eyes."

"Aidan and Kieran's more like it."

At the mention of a baby having Aidan's eyes I drank her in. And my heart? The pieces and fragments of it coated in what fragile film it was—shattered. Jagged edges of it hitting the floor as I wiped my eyes.

She had Aidan's eyes. The O'Hara's eyes.

She had a full tuft of inky hair like Killian though, who didn't resemble his brothers too much. And my heart snapped a little as my stomach ached. No, not my stomach, deeper than that. Somewhere it felt like my insides had been ripped out.

I'd *never* get to experience this with Aidan.

Defective.

Defective.

Defective.

Maybe if you weren't so broken Michael wouldn't have hurt you.

Really Sonya? Crying about rape?

It's just rape? He's your husband.

He can do whatever he wants to you.

He can do whatever he wants to you.

It's just rape.

It's just rape.

Calm yourself the fuck down. You're being so dramatic. So what he hit you once? He's your husband.

Who else is supposed to hit you?

Be a good girl.

Be a good girl.

Be a good girl.

Shut up Sonya

Stop talking Sonya

Nobody cares what you have to say.

I didn't even realize how hard I was shaking.

How hard my fingers rattled on my skirt.

I could only do this, live in this moment, through them and my heart ached a little like it was bleeding raw. No.

I wasn't bleeding raw.

I was that girl again. The one Michael held down.

The one where I felt the searing agony of what it felt like when a man did not care what he did to you.

Nobody cared when you were a man's punching bag.

They only cared if you showed up dead.

And even then they'd forget about you.

I was shaking so hard I couldn't stop.

Oh God.

What was wrong with me?

What was so wrong with me that I couldn't be happy for a mother and her baby?

Defective girl. Look at you. Being so fucking selfish. You ruined your marriage. This is your fault. If I were you I would be grateful anyone ever wanted me. He's your husband. Who else will sleep with you?

It's not rape. It's not rape. It's not rape.

Michaels boots. On my throat. On my stomach.

I can feel it.

I exhaled. Harder.

Killian had just looked overwhelmed down at the little lady blinking up at both of them.

"She's cold," he murmured gruffly.

"I have a warmer blanket," I offered quickly snapping back into reality, moving on auto pilot. *Defective.*

The midwives worked around us with the doctor. I tucked it around Nisha as she was cleaned up.

Defective.

She hadn't stopped shivering as they took Kiara who continued to wail the moment she was out of her mother's arms.

Defective.

"Oh, I feel so bad right now, I don't want to let her go," Nisha had held onto Killian who was helping the doctor's with his wife.

"I got her," he spoke to someone and taken care of Nisha. "It's all good, luv. Look at me, she'll be right back."

And I had followed to make sure Kiara was good before bringing her back to Nisha who was now comfortably on the bed, with Killian soothing her.

That will never be yours. You should never have gotten divorced from Michael. What's a little marital sex? So what he was rough with you? You deserved it.

You probably said something to deserve it.

Nobody just hurts their wife.

You are the problem.

Defective girl.

Defective.

I was losing my mind.

Now? An hour passed and I was holding a heated blanket at Nisha's side. She had been shaking for the last hour while I gave her electrolytes and something warm.

And then she slowly dozed exhausted.

I was kind of processing what kind of a man the O'Hara brother was while grappling with my mother's voice. His entire personality despite being intense, had softened tremendously around his daughter.

And it was like his energy in the room was now dispelling my mother's voice. Before when he'd been focused on Nisha—I hadn't felt it.

The more I watched him with his daughter, the more it scared my mother's voice away.

I was witnessing a man who loved his wife.

I was witnessing what a wife being taken care of looked like.

I had never been that wife.

Ten hours had completely wrung Nisha and Killian out, but he stood there holding Kiara like he was alive with energy now.

Part of me was still trying to comprehend the jacket on the chair near him. Always vigilant. Always alert to any threat to him and his wife and now his baby.

I still felt the adrenaline coursing through me and now baby Kiara was in her bassinet the hospital had wrapped in a blanket.

Killian had held her initially for long moments soothing her with his voice.

"She recognizes me," he murmured. "I talked to her all the time when Nisha was pregnant with her...I heard, I read that she could hear me..." he looked more emotional and in wonder than me at her.

I nodded feeling like all I could do was cry.

She made a noise in his arms of discomfort and a soothing noise left his lips. He pressed his lips over and over to her cheeks as she breathed. Kiara pouted up at him, pursing her lips a little.

His entire expression melted. "Oh, little luv. Daddy's got plenty of kisses for you."

I didn't know when Aidan had become my whole heart—but the truth was I loved him. I loved his family.

Would he still want me one day when he looked at Kiara and saw that she was something he wanted?

Kiara settled in his arms and I saw him blinking his emotions back. Killian took deep breaths as he sat back with her looking down at his wife.

"She fell asleep," I murmured looking down at Nisha. "She's just cold, I need to get her something warmer to eat."

She was my primary focus as I let him hold Kiara.

He nodded brokenly looking down at her staring at him like she couldn't get enough of him. Whenever he looked away she made a noise and he turned right back.

"I'm right here, little luv."

I saw him getting emotional more than once that night. And that was before I went out to tell the boys—they had a little lady in the family.

Who had one lineup of protective Uncles for her.

And the moment I did bring Aidan back?

I knew something was off about him.

And my worst fears came to life.

Did he want children? Did he want this? Did he look at Kiara and see a future he would never have like I did?

I wondered if it was watching his younger brother, living his life and having a child and having a wife if that's what he wanted.

And just like that she was back.

The voices in my head.

You're not good enough.

Maybe he beats you because you failed him as a woman.

You don't deserve to be loved the same way a woman who has children can be loved.

My mother's voice wasn't just triggering.

It was going to drive me insane. I could feel her breathing over my ear, her cackle. I could hear her.

Her inability to empathize with me leaving me cold.

I watched Aidan watching Kiara with softness and I felt like less than a doormat. I felt beneath everything in that moment.

In that moment, Nisha was a success.

And I was a failure as a woman.

The familiar sensation crested inside of me of insecurity and being a letdown when I saw the way he watched Kiara.

I could never give him that.

Give him a *Kiara*.

I almost missed the sensation for a second, when I was focused on Nisha who was fast asleep after days of false labor, then real labor—but now?

It was the equivalent of my mother slapping me and telling me to move on.

A husband who beats you is all you deserve.

Because you are not worthy of being a woman.

I couldn't breathe as Aidan spoke to Killian in low tones.

Nisha had passed out after snuggling with her baby and Killian had been nothing but emotional at the sight of them.

I got to see him by her side through everything and right now?

Kiara was tucked into her little bassinet they had and he looked like he'd never leave.

His white t-shirt was soaked with sweat from both him and Nisha. Some of her blood. I didn't realize how many tattoos he had, but he had more than his brothers.

For the last ten hours he was the best husband in the entire world helping his wife through all of it.

The boys—Kieran and Alexei—got a chance to look at her and congratulate their brother.

Now, with Kiara asleep, it was just me and Aidan in the room with his eyes glancing over Kiara softly. I felt like a ghost.

Like I was a wanderer in the desert unable to find any kind of salvation. My eyes searched Aidan who looked as lost as I felt.

Why?

Why did he look like that? He was watching Killian with an expression I had never on his face.

Killian spoke as he finished his coffee. "Nisha and I wanted to ask you something."

I thought he was talking to me, but he was talking to both of us.

"We want you two to be her godparents."

I didn't even know how to form words as he said it. Aidan looked just as stumped as both of us looked at Killian.

He picked up another cup of coffee as he blinked back his emotions. "Nisha and I talked about it even before you guys came out here. She needs people that are going to be there for her if anything would happen to us, but people that are gonna love her as much as we love her. And you helped Nisha," he glanced at me before turning to his brother. "And you helped me. We thought you two would be perfect for her."

Aidan looked like he didn't know what to say so I said it for him. "We would love to."

I wasn't going to say no.

Being a godmother was as close as I was going to get to having a baby. As close as I could get.

Watching Killian with Nisha all night, into the early morning? It was as close to motherhood as I would ever get.

I wasn't envious. Not watching her. Not feeling her squeezing my hand and Killian's. Not at all.

But maybe I could adopt a baby?

Naturally, there were always children who needed homes. Maybe Haven could be a safe space for everyone.

I had seen panic in people's eyes before and then I saw the dread in Killian's holding her in pain.

Killian shot me a relieved smile and he looked over at his brother. "Thank you."

Aidan tipped his head and I saw his emotions hidden in his eyes.

I knew out of both of his brother's, he talked about Killian differently. He was hard on Kieran because Kieran was the family clown.

Killian was his favorite. I could tell.

And right now? I could tell this meant the world to him.

"I'd love to," Aidan found his words as he looked down at her. "She's got our eyes."

Killian's smile was soft. "She does."

"But she looks like Nisha more—" Aidan started.

"Thank fuck," Killian whispered.

The brother's smiled and I felt my lips twitch at their humor as Nisha stirred then making a noise. "Baby—"

"I'm here," Killian was moving so fast nearly dropping his coffee moving over her.

I was at her side in an instant turning on her heating pad which I missed had turned off. She was probably cold. It had turned off and I adjusted her blankets, warming her up.

"I'll get her a few more things," I murmured to him as he looked down at her pale skin with worry. "She'll be hungry when she wakes up."

And I saw Aidan over Killian's shoulder looking down at Kiara with a look in his eyes I saw in him before.

It was the same look he had when he watched Nadine take Eden away. The same look in them when he felt resigned over something.

He was making decisions. I could see it.

We talked about his desire to make unilateral decisions based off of not wanting any vulnerability and wanting to control everything around him.

The only thing was, I was worried about what decisions he was making.

Especially right now when he was watching his goddaughter.

Because in my gut as my stomach twisted, I just knew none of them could be good.

Not when it came to Aidan.

36

AIDAN

Nothing prepared me for the sight of Killian absolutely fucking distraught.

Absolutely nothing.

Alexei was on our heels as we rushed to the Titan hospital.

I had called Kieran to show up for them. And when I got to the hospital he was outside their door.

"Don't do it," his amber eyes flashed, his chocolate hair a mess on his head. "He's an absolute monster right now. He isn't letting anyone go near her. Perla is treating a patient tonight and Nisha's been crying the entire time. He's a wreck. An angry one."

Sonya paled a little. "Let me go," she looked at us. "I can be there for her. And you guys can calm him down."

Kieran shook his head, amber eyes concerned, but I just waved him off.

"Killian won't hurt her, he won't—it's all good." I knew Killian. He was going to kill anyone who went near her.

Besides, if there was anyone who knew what to do it was Sonya.

"It's all good," I reassured Kieran who looked at me haggard.

"It's not good," he muttered. "I've never seen him like that."

"Well, he's terrified of something hurting Nisha and now he gets to witness it in real time for hours."

Killian had texted Sonya that Nisha had been in and out of labor pains for two days before coming to the hospital. Not quite there. Not quite ready.

And now? By the way Sonya rushed into help them?

It was clearly hitting the fan.

None of us were prepared for this. This was not an occurrence that was a reality in my world, but now that it was, I had no idea what to do.

Alexei looked just as pale next to me.

"What do we do?" He asked me. Kieran looked at me as well for answers. I had no clue. There was no manual on this.

"I'll go talk to the doctor and figure it out, you two go get some coffee for everyone and food, it can't hurt."

Both of them were off, and I knew they were good friends having got along since they were kids.

I went to find a lady doctor to help me understand what the fuck I needed. But before I could go, my phone rang.

"Askim," Sonya sounded breathless. "Can you go and get me some things from the store? For Nisha? She is in pain but I know a few things that may help…"

And then Sonya rattled off a list I frowned down at.

Herbs. Supplements. A heating pad…

I kept going as she said. "This will be good. Please hurry and bring it to me."

And I was off. Forget the doctor. I trusted Sonya more.

While the boys were grabbing whatever meal it was and lots of coffee, I went the nearest pharmacy in a cab and I ended up picking up a bunch of stuff.

When I came back to the hospital, Kieran and Alexei were sitting outside quietly drinking their coffees while I knocked on the door.

Sonya poked her head out and I heard the sound of Nisha's muffled scream. Both of our eyes widened as she snatched the bags and rushed back inside.

It was endless.

All three of us sat outside like useless fucks. Unable to do anything. Halfway through Sonya walked outside in scrubs oddly enough and red-faced. She walked over to me and Kieran wordlessly handed her coffee she chugged on.

"How is it going?"

"It's good," she smiled a little. "The tea is helping and I think the herbs also will be good for her. She said she had spicy food and she went into labor—" I blinked a little, not even understanding how that was a thing. But what the fuck did I know about women?

I got the feeling Kieran and Alexei were just as confused as me as Sonya continued. "I left them in there to have a moment but your brother does not want to leave her."

Rather than looking upset, I saw respect in her eyes.

"He is very good to her. I ask him if he wants a break, but he says he won't leave her."

"That sounds like him."

She nodded blinking back her emotion. "I go back now." And she didn't think twice and neither did I as she kissed me soundly before going back to the room.

When I turned back both of the boys were staring at me.

Alexei with a smug smile.

Kieran with his jaw on the floor.

"You too? I fucking knew when you kidnapped her ass—I should've fucking know."

"Not a word," I growled. "Killian is having a baby. We are not doing this—"

"Why not?" Kieran shot back. "You're dating Sonya. I should've fucking known when you all but carted her out." He swore sitting back looking stunned at me. "You, my big brother, felled by the elven lady crush you have."

I blinked. "How the fuck did you know about—"

"What was her name?" Kieran continued like I hadn't said a word. "The mage from those movies you liked? Guinevere."

Gwendolyn.

Gwendolyn Fairchild, the light mage and an elf from the land of Solaris.

She became the high priestess and diety in the final movie and I had been rooting for her to be single.

Secretly. I didn't know Kieran even knew about my obsession with the Lords of Nightshade Series.

It was a thing. Or it had been.

I did have a crush on Gwendolyn when I was a teenager. I hid all of that shit so nobody fucking knew.

Of course, Kieran's sneaky ass would find it.

Sonya did look like that.

"Shut up, or I will tell everyone you know and like about your collectibles under your bed. They're still there, idiot."

Kieran shut up about his toys right then.

He leaned back with a scowl. "Soul sucking vampire."

"Idiotic man-child."

Alexei sat between us perturbed by our dynamic as always.

Five hours later, Sonya came back out all smiles.

"Congratulations," she said to us. "You have a new baby in the family." All three of us were waiting with baited breath as Sonya took her phone out. "You can see her after they take care of her, but her name is Kiara."

Sonya showed me a photo of a bundle of...baby...it was a baby wrapped in Nisha's arms.

I couldn't see my brother's face, but I saw Killian's tattoos with his arm braced under hers. Like he was helping her hold up his kid.

He'd been there for her the entire time—I never expected Killian to leave her when she needed him the most.

Something shifted in me realizing he was a dad.

Killian was a fucking father.

I felt a grin stretch my lips at her teary eyed smile.

Kieran was grinning ear to ear with Alexei who looked stunned and happy. It was real now for them.

"Killian's a fucking dad," Kieran whispered. "Holy shit."

"He is," Sonya looked so proud, happy and exhausted in one smile. "You can all go see her in a little bit, but I think right now they need a minute." Her eyes met mine. "*Askim.*"

She was in my arms a moment later resting her head on my shoulders as I inhaled and exhaled the scent of her and antiseptic and ninety other things like herbs and chemicals.

"How is he?" I asked her rubbing her back.

"I don't think he is ever letting Kiara out of his sight," she laughed low into my chest. "He is very much in love."

And the craziest part was, I realized so was I watching Kieran and Alexei grin at the photo of Kiara and Sonya slowly dozing in my lap.

I was falling in love.

And then something akin to dread filled me whole.

37

SONYA

That night he came home with me and Alexei leaving Killian at the hospital with Nisha.

My fingers felt colder as I sat there unsure, and insecure in my own skin. My mother's voice was in my head. She was insulting me. She was pointing at Nisha saying she was better than me.

My anxiety was spiraling out of control and Aidan looked deep in thought for once as he rode the car home with me.

I wasn't imagining the yearning he had held in his eyes when he looked at Kiara and then Killian.

I knew he raised Killian from a little boy and I imagined it might've been pivotal to witness Killian becoming a father. My insecurities were going to eat me alive and it felt like every swallow, there was glass in my throat.

Once he realizes I will never be Nisha, he's not going to want me.

No. Stop it.

He's tired. You're overthinking this.

Kieran had volunteered to stay wanting to be around Kiara for a bit longer than everyone else.

We'd retired to our rooms and I could tell by the set of his shoulders, the way his eyes looked. I didn't think twice about moving to him, running my hands through his hair.

It wasn't like him to be this way. Not when I knew he was delighted about Kiara.

"*Askim*, what is it?"

"Nothing, just exhausted," he pulled me closer to him and wrapped his arms around me.

"Tell me." I knew something was bothering him.

Please help me.

I think I'm drowning and I don't know how to swim through this.

Please tell me you love me even though I'm not perfect.

Tell me you still need me.

I didn't say a word, my insecurities crawling into my throat and lodging tight there.

"I need you." The relief that shot through me was undeniable. "I need you, princess."

His fingers moved to undo my robe, his lips met my skin at my collarbone.

"Tell me you locked the door."

I was already all over him, desperation warring with my desire.

"Yes."

Tell me you still need me.

Tell me you love me in spite of my flaws.

38

AIDAN

I NEVER CRIED.

I never hurt.

Not once in my life.

Until her.

Did I like Sonya?

No.

I fucking loved this woman.

When I looked at Kiara tonight, all I kept seeing was something that I would never have.

A life I couldn't give Sonya. Because of my own life.

I did raise Killian.

And watching him tonight, holding his daughter something inside of me completely shattered.

I saw nothing but peace in his eyes and nothing but happiness on his face.

The way he looked at his wife I knew more than anything else in the world I could never be him.

And I could never give up my seat on my throne because I would never let him sit on this one.

I would never let him worry about his next breath. About his daughter. And now I had even more to protect.

Now I had even more concerns.

And Sonya?

Sonya deserved so much better than a fucking scumbag like me.

Someone who couldn't go out in public with her without hiding his face in case someone decided to recognize me and kill me.

Someone who wasn't a fucking monster.

Someone who didn't have hands and an empire that was covered in blood.

Someone without a criminal record who could adopt a kid for her.

Someone who could raise the kid with her.

Someone who would be there for her if she ever went through that.

I couldn't give her a home.

I could only give her problems, politics, the fear looming over my head. And paranoia.

And I fucking hated myself.

"I need you," I whispered to her. I needed her since the hospital. The moment I saw Kiara, I wanted to ask Sonya if she was okay and the words were stuck in my mouth.

Because I saw the sheer longing in Sonya's eyes as she watched Kiara.

And I could *never* give her that.

I was such a fucking failure.

I heard my father's laughter in my head.

Sonya was my safe haven.

Sonya was everything I could've ever imagined and then some.

And I couldn't have her.

My eyes blurred as I kissed my way down her body, breasts trembling with her breath as I licked and sucked until I spread her legs open. Eating at her pussy like it was my personal fucking temple. Sonya was and always would be—the one woman I'd ever fucking loved.

I let her into my house. Into my life.

And she didn't meet my expectation, she set every single one for the future.

She moaned into the dark shadows of the room as I ate at her knowing where to make her shake and tremble. The way her fingers

225

twisted into my shoulders, my hair, tugging until I hit that spot that made her come apart.

Sonya sobbed as I ate at her hungrily.

It wasn't until she came apart that I took advantage of her pleasure, rising up to bury myself so deep we both gasped.

"*Aidan.*"

"Say my name again," I growled. "Say it."

I began to drive us both insane with long slow strokes designed to draw out her pleasure and let me see her at her most vulnerable. Open, whimpering and begging for me to let her come.

And my heart cracked open as those green eyes watched me, like the flow of the galaxy was in them. Nobody had eyes like that.

Nobody ever looked at me like her.

Like she loved me. Like I was a man worth having, worth saving, worth any of it. I pushed deeper into her loving the way she gasped.

A broken noise left her.

"Better?"

A fuck drunk Sonya was a dream.

Her eyes low-lidded and soft moans leaving her. I kissed her deeper, further and I couldn't stop kissing her. Because Sonya was every ounce of goodness in me I didn't have.

I didn't want to be a good man.

I just wanted to be her man.

Tonight I didn't wanna fuck her.

I wanted to make love to Sonya because I knew deep down it was the last night I would ever have her.

She came apart and I drove deep burying myself so tightly I couldn't think anymore.

"*Askim,*" she whimpered. Her love. Sonya's arms wrapped around me holding me so tight I didn't know how to breathe around the sensation.

Always hers.

Sonya trusted me not to break her. And I was going to anyway.

And didn't that make me the biggest fucking monster in her life.

39

SONYA

I<small>T WAS ONLY AFTER</small> K<small>ILLIAN HAD GONE HOME WITH</small> N<small>ISHA FROM THE</small> hospital, days later, that I felt the shift.

I was in my kitchen. And Aidan walked in.

I took one look at his face and I felt my heart splinter.

My mother's voice was back.

I told you. How could anyone love you?

Why would anyone ever love you?

You are not a lovable girl.

You deserved Michael.

You don't deserve to be loved.

Because I saw it in his eyes, Aidan had made another decision without *me*. Unilateral.

I *knew* his amber eyes. Had memorized every tiny little micro expression on his face, learned languages of his body.

I'd mapped out every tattoo and every scar on him. Whether he knew it or not—I knew his soul and loved it.

I loved him.

I did.

But right now? I saw what was coming from him and I knew whatever he said next was going to devastate me.

I just knew it.

And it was already breaking me.

Aidan and Alexei had come to my townhouse. Kieran went back to his apartment because he lived in the city.

Aidan had been shuttered after seeing off Kiara. And right now when he sat at my kitchen island I felt my breathing cease. My body went still.

He wouldn't even look at me.

He'd kissed me in this kitchen months ago. Now it felt like years ago.

"What is it?" I stayed where I was wrapped in my sweater. I couldn't get the chill out from under my skin and when I went to sleep he had been busy on his phone or laptop.

He was pulling away from me and I didn't understand why.

"Your paperwork is going through smoothly enough. So is your restraining order. It's in place. I talked to Kieran to come and stay with you here, when you need him—" and then it was like a sledge-hammer to my chest.

That hurt more than Michael had.

Because I knew what he was saying before he even finished.

I knew exactly what he was implying.

I knew. I heard his words like we were underwater and it was coming through slowly but painfully. Shards of glass trapped in my throat as my stomach turned. It twisted deeper.

"I need to go back." He wouldn't look at me. "I don't belong here."

I swallowed as I felt the way my chest ached, the pain blooming in it as I realized what he was doing.

Yes, you do.

You belong with me.

You are mine.

"You're...leaving." I whispered it feeling myself snapping in two. I was trying to memorize every inch of his dark hair, amber eyes, long lashes, and cheekbones carved from marble.

I was trying to take in the shoulders I hugged and the kisses I loved.

I was trying not to snap into pieces.

"I am."

It was final.

He...he made a choice...without me. Again.

"When?" I couldn't even speak as I blinked back my tears. It hot was and it stung every part of me.

"In the morning."

I nodded trying to blink back my emotions and failing. And he had made this choice without me. Without my input or my say or anything.

But I remembered one memory I had. Just one.

Those memory I had of calling my Mom. I remember asking her for help and I remember in that moment learning, what devastation felt like having people make choices for you without your input.

Without your happiness being considered. Without what *you* wanted.

Because it was never about me.

This was about him.

It hurt so bad I felt like I was swallowing shards of glass as I dumbly nodded and I numbed out.

"Do not come back. Ever."

I saw his throat work as his eyes finally looked at me in shock. And I didn't pause to feel it.

I felt nothing but ache.

I shut down like a plant in the darkness and I walked away feeling his eyes on me the entire time I went to my room.

Locked the door.

And felt myself snapping.

I snapped.

In that moment I never wanted to scream so much in my life.

At my family for selling me off to a man who tortured me.

At Michael for abusing me for years.

At every single woman around me who knew letting it happen and only two men stepping in. Andrei motivated by his love for Talia.

And Lucas motivated by his desire to be different than the horrible people in his family.

And then finally, at how I had been fighting for my autonomy for so long. My right to make choices.

And he had made the most important one for me.

I couldn't forgive him.

I walked to the back of my walk-in closet. Locking myself in there.

Further back where I held all my evening gowns.

And I buried my face into one of them and screamed and screamed and screamed.

I couldn't stop it if I tried.

And I kept going. I kept screaming grateful the door was locked.

Grateful he wasn't going to hear me in a townhouse this big as I ripped the dresses out. Off the racks.

The jewelry off the stand. I

was tearing at my bags and shrieking at the top of my lungs.

And none of it mattered—

Because nobody heard you screaming in a gilded cage.

Even one of your own making.

40

SONYA

"You good?"

"Kieran, this is the fifteenth time you've asked me this," I muttered. "If you ask me again I will stab you."

"Okay. Sorry."

At the way he said it I felt bad, but I was juggling a few things that day to be gentle.

Maybe I was also a little mad at his brother.

No, I *definitely* think that I was mad at his brother. The oldest O'Hara had been taking up my thoughts.

After losing Michael, I didn't think or know how love felt…Aidan had been the first time I had…and heartbreak hurt.

The day after my meltdown I woke up and Aidan had been gone with Alexei in tow. Instead, I found Kieran appearing at my door telling me he would be my guard.

With his easy smile, I took into account that maybe Kieran might not know.

I had taken in a cup of coffee and sat there for a moment feeling myself splintering to pieces while Kieran ate breakfast texting Nisha between bites.

The two of them got along well and it always broke my heart when he referred to me as his sister.

Like I was Aidan's. So I was his family.

That's what he called Nisha.

"Hey sis, how's the baby?"

He was talking to her while I juggled my work at Haven.

I was drowning in my own sorrows but I found when I refocused my energy it didn't hurt as much as it could've.

I truly thought Michael what was the worst kind of heartbreak I could've gone through.

But I realized it didn't even hold a candle to actually falling in love with somebody.

Through Aidan I learned that what I thought was living was a lie. I had lived with him. And I was learning that loving someone and losing them hurt more than anything else in the world.

Actually *feeling* loved and then having it completely ripped out of your hands.

By a unilateral choice.

Now? I felt like I was shattering to pieces.

He wanted the world to think he didn't have a heart. He wanted the world to think that he was cold, a dark king in his castle of shadows, and I had gone into it, and I had seen him for who he was. Been a part of his darkness because it had been the most kindness I had ever experienced.

And I loved him for who he was.

Not the cold and cruel king—but as a man. A man made up of layers that I had thought I was unraveling.

I had come to the conclusion that I did fall for him. I used to think that love had to be gentle, but now it was learning to breathe again.

But he did not *like* me.

Because I didn't think that when you love somebody, you made them feel like this.

I refocused my gaze at the sound of Kieran's laughter on my emails. "I need Valentina to come over today, can you handle yourself?"

"Who is that?" His brow rose.

"My new assistant hopefully, she goes to Astor U and takes classes online," I explained it to Kieran who stiffened.

"She goes to Astor?"

I nodded. "She's a senior I believe, and she wants to do this for me and work at Haven. So I'm having her come over. Do you want to give us some privacy?"

"No," he frowned. "What if she tries to hurt you?"

"Why would she try to hurt me?" I raised my brow now. "Not everyone is a murderer, Kieran."

"Not everyone can be," he smirked at my expression. "I'll vet Valentina with you."

Since I had been gone, Gemma had been working miracles. She had coordinated with Alisha and Lara her best friends to figure everything out.

Obviously, I checked in with all of it, but everybody was finishing up training in the groups that they had hired.

The security systems were state of the art, every piece had been catalog and insured

And Haven didn't have anyone staying in it right now.

Gemma had hired the staff, done the background checks and was now just finalizing everything.

For some reason Liam did not work at Titan anymore.

That was news for me.

Instead I had a new IT specialist helping me. Lucas's wife Evie Devereaux had a host of people who worked under her and this one came from her since Reed figured he could move it to Evie.

Kieran stayed with me now since another round of paperwork had come through from my attorneys to Michael's attorneys, and we were just about finishing up. It would be processing for a few months after this.

It should have been a relief.

Only for me? It was a week into my grief. And I didn't see a way through it.

A text had popped up on my phone from Adam Whittaker, that I least suspected. He was dating Lucy Devereaux, Lucas's little sister. Technically, that made both of the Devereaux family members Eleanor's relatives.

But Lucy wanted to visit Haven for something.

I met Lucy and Adam downstairs and she was nothing like her brother. Besides being blonde, she was much shorter than Adams six feet even height. Shorter than me with curves encased in jeans and a coat, all blonde curls and bright baby blue eyes. The snow from outside on her long lashes and those blues bat up at me.

"Hi," her small was all teeth when she saw me and Adam gave me a resigned grin. "Nice to meet you."

I found myself reluctantly smiling down at her.

"Lucy's excited about seeing the painting," Adam held his arm around her. "Just seeing it."

"Yeah." She agreed with that smile. "I completely forgot Aunt Eleanor had that painting."

I didn't really know why Lucy wanted to see the painting in Eleanor's bedroom. But I took her there anyway.

Everything in the house was already insured by the Nash group.

And if anything were to happen, they had a security team that would go out and take care of it and find it.

That being said, I didn't think it would hurt for Lucy to see the painting that was in the room.

It was an odd request but anything to distract me from my heart-break was welcome.

"I believe at one point it belonged to your family so please have a look around." I didn't know what it was about Lucy but her smile was infectious as we walked up the stairs.

She had childlike energy about her and her intensity, and Adam looked like he was just used to her whirlwind energy.

"I didn't know you were dating Lucy Devereaux," I commented with a teasing smile. "I was wondering why I liked you so much when I met you."

Adam turned red as Lucy practically bounced in his side.

When Lucy got to Eleanor's room she was almost careening off the walls with excitement and Adam had his arm around her waist as they walked in.

"Nononono, Bunny, don't run—"

"Oh my god, it's real!" She squealed zooming off to it as Adam sighed. "I don't know why I ever forgot that Eleanor had this." Her blue eyes bat up at me. "Tell me nobody else knows you have this painting?"

"Why?" I was confused, but Adam seemed to understand a little bit more, smiling at her enthusiasm as she glanced up at me. "Just the housekeeping staff, Gemma, the insurance company..." I drifted off. Quite a few people knew.

Lucy's eyes narrowed. "Not to give you unsolicited advice, but I think that you should put this painting somewhere safe that isn't this bedroom. I can't believe Aunt Eleanor had it out in the open this entire time, but this painting is worth two hundred and fifty million dollars. And with all of your guests coming in and out of the house, I think it might be important for you to put this in a handful of other antiques in this house somewhere safer. Somewhere not in your home."

My jaw dropped as Lucy explained, Adam had told her about Haven.

When they had come back from their vacation, she had done some research on the house and she found a list of red flag items for me to move out of the house and into a safe.

I would need to reach out to Nash Group since I had no idea.

Lucy pulled out her phone. "I actually did the math on some of the antiques in this house? That vase right there is three million."

She pointed to one by my beside.

"I'm pretty sure it was owned by a President's wife. No clue how Eleanor got it...Unless she was fucking him." She looked up at me with an apologetic look. "If I didn't know any better I'd think Eleanor was a thief in *her* past life."

Lucy paused and snuck a look at Adam whose jaw fell open. He paled a little.

"It might run in the family, Bunny."

I didn't know what he was talking about.

"Sonya, I made a list of all the cool shit Aunt Eleanor had..." And I felt overwhelmed as Adam as I sat there while Lucy rattled it off.

I needed to update Nash group and ask them to send some of their security guys over.

Lucy took photos of the painting before she left citing it was for research purposes. Adam would start at Haven as soon as the doctor Gemma had hired, Vera Sinclaire started.

"Come on, Bunny." Adam motioned for Lucy to take his hand.

"Coming, Doc. Thanks Sonya!"

I went back into the kitchen to find Kieran. "Alls good, shall we go over and see Kiara?"

He looked delighted. "It's great seeing Killian as a dad now, he's gotta watch his temper all the time."

I grinned at his mischievous smile. Both he and Aidan had similar smiles to me. But Killian looked different from his brothers which I assumed came from his mother.

"Do not provoke your brother, something tells me he'll just tell Nisha and me to hold Kiara while he whips you back into shape."

Kieran had chocolate hair, but he had Aidan's eyes.

I saw his brother whenever I glanced his way even if his personality was completely unlike his brothers.

He was much more playful and easy-going. He kept me laughing with stories about how much more paranoia Killian had now that he was baby proofing his entire home.

"You should've seen it before Nisha, it was his bat cave and now it's covered in pink."

I laughed. "I do believe that. He's different from you and Aidan."

"How's big bro doing?" Kieran parked right into the garage inside of Killian's building as he was laughing over something that I had said. "If Aidan doesn't marry you I'm pretty sure Alexei would since he's in love with you."

At the mention of that my chest tightened and it felt like I swallowed glass.

"I wouldn't know," I answered honestly. "We don't keep in touch since left."

The silence that followed, I could hear a pin drop in it in the parking lot. His smile dropped, and his eyes went wide.

"What?" Gone was the smile and sunshine that he normally had. And in his place was somebody else. "What do you mean—you two—you..."

In any other situation, I would've found him stumbling over his words funny. But right now I didn't really wanna talk about it.

"Wait," Kieran paused like he hit a wall. "No. No, he wouldn't be so fucking stupid. Are you fucking kidding me? That's why he has me guarding you?"

I was trying not to snap at the seams.

"If it's all right with you? I'd rather just go see Kiara and come home, hmm?"

I didn't gauge his expression and instead, I just walked away. I really did want to see Nisha and spend some time with her and the baby.

Right now, I was making my own choices and one of them?

Was to not focus on the man I would never see again.

Even if his family was in my life, I didn't really want to ever see him again because that was my choice.

If he was going to be making unilateral choices without me, then I could make them without him.

Upstairs in Killian's penthouse, I found a haggard Killian at the door.

"Sorry, we just put Kiara down for bed. Nisha's in the bathroom exhausted. I gotta clean her up."

Kieran and I looked around the kitchen.

"I'm guessing the nanny and mid-wife aren't here?" Kieran asked looking at the bottles and wipes and napkins.

"No," Killian rushed off as he said. "Nisha and I wanted some peace and quiet for a few days. I'll be back I gotta help her."

"Umm," I stopped him. "Why don't you let me help her, and Kieran can help you?"

He paused and took a deep breath, his hair sticking up in multiple directions. "Are you sure? She needs a bunch of—"

"I got it, I promise. I've done plenty of research."

Even if I couldn't have any didn't mean I didn't know.

Killian looked ready to argue until Kieran put his arm around his shoulder and I realized Killian always looked taller than his brother's but they were the same height. "Let's go, we need to sit you down and put some food in you."

I dropped my coat on one of the barstools of the island and went and knocked on the door to Nisha's bedroom.

"Baby?" She called out. But I poked my head in.

"It's me, can I come in?"

She looked relieved to see me. "Hi, please tell me you convinced Killian to sit down?" Her voice was a fierce whisper.

I laughed lightly figuring that was what the new dad needed.

"Hovering?" I whispered back.

"He's protective. But so am I. He's afraid if he steps away from her something will happen." She motioned to the bassinet where Kiara was fast asleep. "I'm going to pump. Let's go to the nursery."

"She's not staying there?"

Nisha looked at me resigned. "Neither one of us want to sleep without her."

I nodded like I understood. In a way I did. I wouldn't want to leave her little self alone either.

"Killian is in love with her, and he's been great," Nisha whispered walking out with a few contraptions on a little pink cart.

When we got to the nursery done up with elephants and all sorts of shades of cream and pink Nisha and I got comfortable.

"I bet Kieran's stuffing his face," I said lightly.

"No doubt while Killian is asleep on the couch."

Nisha smiled though as she said it. "He's been so good, Reed gave him a break from Titan to just be with us and he's been loving it. I think he says he'll go back but not the same as he was prior to leaving. So less assignments. More training."

"That's better for you and her."

"It is and I'd feel safer too," she hooked herself up to the pump as she said it and I averted my gaze feeling slightly awkward wondering if she knew. Did she know Aidan left? Did Killian know?

Did he feel sorry for me?

My own mind was whirling as Nisha said. "How's Aidan? How are you two doing? I feel like Alexei is like your kid and I was about to ask you about your son for some reason."

I froze. I didn't even breathe.

Alexei is like your kid...

I blinked rapidly not wanting to bawl like a baby in front of Nisha but that one hurt. That one hurt more.

Because it wasn't just about losing Aidan.

It was about losing cooking moments, movie nights, and even him finding comfort in me all the time. It was losing Alexei that made me close my eyes and breathe through my nose.

"What?" Nisha rapidly blinked like she couldn't process that.

I turned away to not show her how close I was to breaking.

"Aidan is in Chicago."

Silence filled the room.

"For good?"

I tipped my head not looking at her feeling myself shattering and I didn't shatter in public. I never shattered in public. Or in front of people.

"Oh my God," she whispered. And I heard the sound of machines and tubes and the sound stopping as she unclamped herself and adjusted her towel. "Come here."

I was in her arms breaking down not realizing how badly I needed this.

Nisha held me tighter as I snapped.

41

AIDAN

ALEXEI WASN'T SPEAKING TO ME ANYMORE.

I mean, he was.

But in grunts and frustrated growls like a wounded animal.

No more Russian proverbs came from him.

Instead he just looked pissed off.

He rarely interacted with me after we left New York and even tossed my duffle at my feet and walked off to the town car. Devlin looked a little shook at the kid who didn't look at anyone. He pulled up his mask, put on his ear plugs and blasted weird rock music the entire way home.

And once in the mansion he stormed off before the car even pulled over.

"What did you do to him?" Devlin's entire expression went blank at the look in my mine.

"Fill me in on the Belova's." It's all I gave him.

I didn't know how to talk to Alexei. And I could feel him staring at me with his judgmental side eye—his silent accusations digging into my side like thorns. He was back to eating like a raccoon in a trash can, and every time I walked into the kitchen, he just walked out pissed.

Even if I didn't tell him anything, he knew when we didn't come back with her.

He knew.

He wasn't a fool.

But his judgment was worse than anything he could've told me.

I was the one walking in on him and Sonya having their moments together. His head on her shoulder. Cooking with her. The two of them spending so much time together and I never really got jealous. Mostly because Alexei was a part of me. And naturally he'd become a part of Sonya.

I didn't expect him to get as attached as I had.

And me? I felt like I had ripped my heart open and left it in New York.

With her.

Sonya.

After spending a lifetime, becoming everybody else's monsters, she was the first person in my life who saw past everything in my darkness and chose to stay.

Control was how I survived, but now I was beginning to reconsider it. Enough.

Because I kept seeing her stuff everywhere.

I kept seeing her baking supplies everywhere, the bowls of limes and lemons still sitting on my counter.

Her scented candles of eucalyptus to calm everyone down where everywhere, lush hydrangeas that she had ordered for the house because Sonya insisted they gave it personality, and even in my old room, my sheets still smelled like her.

The scent of lush perfume and ripe lemons that clung to her skin were now all over me. It was the only thing I had a of hers left.

I didn't know what to do.

I gave trust piece by piece and Sonya tore it out from me all at once—leaving me raw and exposed. Bleeding from the inside out with a wound I didn't know what to fucking do with.

The fact that she had gone through so much, but she turned into something beautiful, she responded to my violence with healing, she challenged me with everything she did, and she didn't demand that I change.

That was the biggest reason *why* I liked her.

And Alexei was livid with me.

241

Because in a way Sonya had always teased me about being his adoptive father. Alexei saw her like a mother.

I got that now.

He was furious with me taking her away from him. Bringing him back, tearing him away from her. Only now he was back in his cold house and it no longer really felt like a home with her. Not without her baking and cooking and trying to call us downstairs to come eat.

Did I realize that we were both survivors?

Absolutely.

Did I realize that she complimented me in every single way shape and form? That she filled my cracks with her light?

Absolutely.

Did I realize that if I wanted her and if I wanted to be with her, I couldn't do it without asking her to give up everything she wanted or me give up my reality of an empire soaked in blood?

Absolutely.

In order for me to be with her, I couldn't ask her to give up everything that she loved.

But I couldn't give up this world.

If I walked away, it would create a power of vacuum in Chicago that even the Titans couldn't fill.

I didn't want to give up my power.

And I couldn't ask her to give up hers.

If I left or something happened to me, the next in line was Killian and after seeing Kiara, I would never leave my spot.

I took one look at her, and I knew exactly why I did what I did. And I made my choices.

I wasn't happy with them.

But I realized I didn't have to be happy with choices. I had to make them for the bigger picture. The greater good.

Even if it meant being heartbroken temporarily, just like any kind of pain it would pass and it would heal. At least that's why I told myself while I laid in my bed inhaling her scent.

Nobody smelled like she did.

It was like the rainforest after a storm, lush green, ripe pears, and something else. Something her.

Her perfume bottle was a green vial and it sat on my dresser. One of those old school ones that she pumped and sprayed on her. I knew because everything she touched smelled like that.

And while Alexei wasn't speaking to me I decided to distract myself with everything else going on in my life.

I couldn't just sit there and do nothing.

Every time I got up to do something though, I couldn't focus on it.

I didn't want to do anything. I just wanted her.

I wanted her to run her fingers through my hair and laugh and tell me I didn't eat enough today. Like a fucking pussy.

After a lifetime of starvation of every kind, it felt like a cruel twist of fate to feel like I had been meant to find my way back to her.

I was a fool for ever thinking that I could have a happily ever after like Killian could. Sonya felt better than anything I had ever felt.

She felt like home. And without her, I was an empty shell, a body waiting for it's heart to come back.

But that wasn't going to happen.

My house was going to stay empty.

I fucking hated it here now.

Cade was juggling so many jobs out of Chicago, which left me to deal with one tiny little problem that I had neglected. One tiny little redhead that was getting on my ever loving ne

Time flew by and now a few weeks of jail time in Titan Downtown, Eden Belova had become weaker.

Malleable.

I needed to pay her father a visit. And I needed to figure out what the fuck to do with her.

Without Alexei, I went down to the Titan's tower Downtown.

I met up with Nadine in her usually black, her hair pulled up into a long braid.

"You look like shit." Dark eyes roamed over me as she said it.

"Our prisoner is better?"

Nadine filled me in.

Overtime I realized over the last couple of weeks that Eden was just as much of a victim as anybody else.

It didn't justify her actions, but I think that a shitty upbringing and a shitty life led to shitty choices.

Especially when I realized that she didn't really have anybody to guide her.

Over the last couple of days, I thought I was losing my mind when I kept imagining Sonya's voice in my head giving me advice over things.

But she wasn't here right now as a heavy metal door shut behind me and I descended into the basement of Titan tower. The cold concrete walls pressed in on me and there was nothing but fluorescent lights flickering overhead. It wasn't a normal prison.

Not exactly. I mean, they rarely kept people down here, the only reason I wanted Eden down here was because she needed to chill the fuck out. Literally.

The temperature down here was frigid.

She was sitting in her cot with her knees drawn up to her chest. She had a blanket. But that was about all that I saw in the room. In all white, the baggy fabric made her look even smaller than five feet two inches tall. She was swallowed by it.

Somewhere in my chest, it clenched seeing her because I had known that she had seen the worst that humanity had to offer her.

Pretty sure she found Chris in his dorm room after he died. Her head lifted up when she saw someone was there flickering over Nadine and then to me.

Those blue eyes of hers hardened on me.

She was defiant I'd give her that.

But I didn't come here to bullshit.

"Chris was the first time you felt something other than your life." That's what I started with. "Why did you think starting a war with me would ever make you the head of your father's syndicate?"

She didn't answer me for a moment just watched me with haunted eyes.

"I didn't," her voice was low. This is why I kept her here. To thaw it out. Weeks and weeks couldn't keep her angry forever and I hated to admit it—but sometimes tough love was the way forward. "You're the idiot that assumed that."

A humorous chuckle escaped to my lips. She had another thing coming if she thought she could piss me off. I was already missing my heart.

The cavern of ice that was my soul wasn't going to need anything else.

"You didn't answer the question."

"I thought you'd kill all of them."

"And you what? Find Chris again? He's dead."

As soon as I said she erupted launching herself at the doors.

"You watch your fucking mouth."

Nadine stood there with a stoic face, but I saw the tension in her shoulders.

"Christopher Melendez is dead." I said it calmly. "No amount of you scheming or manipulating anyone will bring him back. Your father is out for blood. Yours. You should know your kind has no loyalty they'll eat their own if they can."

Nadine's voice cut through the air. "Joshua is Russian. He went to your father's den and talked to him. Your father had no idea who Christopher was. The only person who did was Viktor. Your father knows we picked you up. He isn't pleased with either one of you."

And just like that Eden paled. "What?"

"He didn't know about your Chris. Which means your father never put the hit out. That was Viktor. Said he was getting rid of a problem not trying to create one."

Nadine and I talked about this.

That was a thing about being young, you always assumed the worst.

Sonya would take her in.

Sonya would give her therapy and let her heal and set her free.

Sonya would call her a broken bird like herself and let her heal.

But Sonya wasn't here right now.

"That being said," I said finding my voice as I took out my gun.

Through the bars I set it down on the floor. I watched her eyes through the steel bars. Icy blue and colliding with my fire I saw angry heat in her eyes.

"You can kill yourself if you feel like it, either way, you're a dead woman walking when you leave this place. I kept you alive to get the answers I needed while I was gone. Now that you have your answers, and you know what your uncle did, you can decide whatever it is that you wanna do with your life."

I let that sink in as she watched the gun warily.

"Nadine here has crawled her way to the top. She's a woman in a male-dominated world. Her boss can be a dick, and for the most part, ninety-nine percent of Chicago relies on her and—"

"Toronto."

"*Toronto*," I would never forget Nadine was Canadian too.

"She's living proof that strengthen power do not have to come at the cost of your soul. You don't have to dig yourself any deeper than you already have. When you leave this prison, your father's men are gonna come after you. Your uncle will be taking over for the Belova's. I can't interfere with their power. It's not my place. He won't touch anything of mine if he knows better. Which by the looks of it, he does."

Viktor wasn't a fool.

But he wasn't a fan of being ousted by his niece.

I was right, they were sexist. When Josh had told her father, he didn't even care. Why would they? If anything the words Josh had used were that Dmitri Belova thought his daughter was spoiled goods.

Eden took the gun and I saw Nadine move so fast I didn't even have to blink.

If she killed me she knew they'd take her out.

If she killed herself she remove herself as a problem.

She aimed the gun at me.

I waited.

In a hairbreadth Eden turned the gun on herself to her head. She shot me a look of pure defiance before pulling the trigger.

Nothing happened.

She did it again and I saw the moment she realized what I knew.

The gun was never loaded.

But I know her choice.

She'd rather die than live again.

And that was precisely the problem. Eden operated from a place of wanting to die rather than wanting to live.

So she didn't care who she took out, she was going with them.

I couldn't have that.

"Leader's don't give up because they lose things. I lose things every single day. I have lost my entire past and future in one blow. I didn't have a choice. I made it my empire because I had none." At the horror in her eyes I smirked. "Losing Chris is not the end. It's the beginning. You thought I'd be dumb enough to give you a loaded gun? I've been in the game for a long time, and you don't phase me. You never have."

I blew out another breath. "I can't fucking believe I'm saying this." I looked at Nadine's dark eyes. "What do you do with her?"

Nadine looked at me like she was physically nauseous. "Cade won't ever make her a Titan."

Yeah. I knew that. Cade had strict rules.

He made Reed look polite.

"I'm not asking you to make her a Titan."

"But you're asking me to train her."

I shrugged. "It's not going to be me." I would kill her.

Alexei would take one look at a Belova in our house and pack his bags and leave for Sonya in the evening. I could see him doing it too.

Eden looked between us wondering what the fuck was going on.

"You can train her," I told Nadine who looked like she'd swallowed a bucket of nails.

"And make her into what?"

I shook my head. "Not this." I motioned to the girl in the prison. "You either try or Viktor gets his hands on her."

I turned back to Eden as Nadine muttered. "I'll think about it. I don't like putting a gun in Russian Barbie's hands."

Eden scowled at Nadine.

"This is a blank slate," I told her. "You fuck up?"

"And you kill me. Got it."

"Exactly."

Nadine opened up her cell and if I thought she'd attack me I was wrong.

For the first time since I've met her, she looked at me with something other than hatred. And then I realized one thing, Sonya was right all along.

The kid didn't anything but a chance. An opportunity.

And I'd just given it to her.

247

I should've felt warmth or something as Nadine frowned down at her.

Instead I just wished I had Sonya to go home to, so I could tell her about my day. The hollow ache in my chest was a yearning for the woman that I could not have. I wish with every fucking fiber of my being that I had her to go home too.

But I didn't have her.

Tell her how she made me better man.

But there was no Sonya.

There was no way for me to walk through the door and see her smiling at me, hear her laughter as she led me into the kitchen because she made something that she was proud of. Feel her arms around me while I was eating as she poured me a glass of something to drink.

Not anymore. Now?

There was only one angry teenage son I had.

My phone pinged when I left Titan tower to a text from Kieran.

> You stupid ass punk bitch. You broke up with
> Sonya?

I sighed.

I should've seen that coming. He was always ready to call us out on our bullshit. Too bad I wasn't in the mood.

> What do you want?

Instead of answering me? He called.

And like a little bitch, I answered. Because I was a glutton for punishment and maybe I needed to fight.

His voice was tight with anger.

"I wanna know why you ended it with her? You know about her husband, you know everything that happened to her, and you still chose to do what you did? What the fuck was the point of you taking out Chicago? Why would you do something like that?"

I wasn't going to get a word in I could tell.

Everything he said was true.

"She's funny and beautiful and kind and wonderful and she smells

248

like a goddamn department store. She's richer than you and literally the best woman you could find if not the only woman. Why the fuck would you Break up with her, two days after Killian had his baby? I told Killian and he's just as pissed off. Sonya's been crying—" my chest tightened at that.

I conceded to everything that he said. Everything that he said was true. She was the funniest. She was so beautiful. It hurt my eyes to look at her because she was everything I had ever wanted. She did smell absolutely fucking incredible. I would know because I slept with her blankets.

She was better than me and every single way shape and form.

And that's why I made the choice choices that I did.

But I never expected him to understand.

The one thing that did hit me was knowing she had been crying.

I didn't wanna upset her.

I didn't want to ruin her life.

Kieran was going off on me for once and

I waited for him to finish. I didn't feel a thing and the chill of the winter air was getting worse.

It was maybe a singular digit today outside. But inside of it being outside inside of me, it felt even worse.

"Sure," I said conversationally getting into my *Roadster* SUV. "I'll just leave and go get Sonya tomorrow. And tell you what? You can come to Chicago and take over for me while I do it."

I was met with silence.

I felt a mean grin curl my lips as red hot fury filled my chest with menace.

"What's the matter Kieran?" I mocked him twisting my verbal knife deeper into his soul. "You don't want it? I could've sworn this summer you came to me and you asked me to leave. Actually, no, you asked me a few years ago and I said we would see. And then instead of asking me this summer you just took enough drugs to funnel your own cartel and then blacked out so many times that Killian had to come and rescue you and clean you up from your fucking mess."

I knew all about Kieran's drug problems.

His addictions. His private sex club he had opened *De Nuit* where he acted out all of his depraved fantasies.

He might've been smiles and sunshine on the outside but we both knew he was a fucking dark demon like me on the inside. He was my brother I knew him better than anybody.

Kieran wasn't fooling anybody.

"Killian was the one who talked to me about letting you loose and so I did." That was what happened. "But see if he hadn't? You would be the next one after me. Killian took that position. The one that nobody wanted."

Because nobody actually wanted to be me.

"And now? He's got a baby girl. And you wouldn't want him to come to Chicago would you? Could you even imagine Nisha fearing for her life? What do you think Killian would do if the entire Chicago criminal underground found out that he had a baby girl? Do you have any idea how much money would go for her head?"

Because I did.

Of course I factored that into my decision.

Just because I had power, the Titans, a reputation? It didn't make me immune. It didn't make me all powerful.

I knew very fucking well if Killian came to Chicago with Kiara, she was the most vulnerable person in the family. The next one was Nisha. In New York? It was his empire. Nobody would touch him.

But if Killian led Chicago? The primary target would be his daughter. He knew it too. He didn't have to say anything to me. I could see it all over his eyes when he had her. He couldn't look away.

And I saw the dread he felt when I was around.

Like he prayed I would stay put.

I would.

"You don't get to point a finger at me about anything. *We can't all be spoiled like you—*"

"*Aidan—*"

"*We can't all run from our fucking problems.*"

He went silent.

"I live the life that I do so that you get to have your *fucking choices. The sheer fucking gall of you to call me and berate me on mine when you're a fucking drug addict with a sex addiction is mind boggling to me.*"

Sonya was right.

I was cruel.

And without her?

I couldn't stop it.

"I let you go and all you've done is fuck your way through New York, you hit on your *former* charge who by the fucking way is related to Reed Whittaker, your fucking boss. And I know *exactly why* you think you can call me up and talk to me however the fuck you want. And it's the same fucking shit that lands you in trouble all the time. I am the only person in charge of anything in this family. I am God. *I am everything under the sun that lets you live your fucking life.*"

I was lashing out and I knew it was wrong. I did.

But I couldn't stop it. Not anymore.

"You forget your place in this family? Call me when you figure your own shit out. Unless you plan on taking over all of Chicago and stop running from your fucking life—*you don't get to say shit to me. I am the only reason you are what you are. Because I allowed it. Do not call me unless my girlfriend is in danger.*"

I hung up feeling so the rage red hot burning in me as a growl left me. I didn't even realize what I was saying.

I was livid. I was. I was angry that my son wasn't talking to me. Couldn't even stand to be in the same room as me. Like I was my father.

I was angry that I lost my wife and I couldn't have her because of my life. That I would never get to build a life with her or wake up to her, making cinnamon rolls in the morning and fall asleep to her scent every single night.

I was angry that I was never given a choice as to whether or not I wanted it. At the path that have been laid out, before I could even understand what that path meant.

I was angry that I had to put Gwendolyn Fairchild into a shoebox into my closet, and pretend like that part of me had never happened.

That I couldn't just be a regular fucking person.

Like there was never a part of me that just wanted to go to school like a normal person.

I was angry that at twenty-four years old I had been given an empire of blood and been told that I had to figure it out.

I was angry that every single day of my life, I was snapping into

251

somebody that I didn't recognize in somebody that I wasn't proud of and somebody that I didn't want to be.

And I was angry at the fact that I got to look at Kiara and I got to know that I would never have anything as soft and precious in my life as Killian.

It was enough resolve for me to decide that I would never give up anything in Chicago as long as I breathed—I would protect Kiara and Nisha and Killian with my fucking life.

Killian had it the worst.

Now, he had an entire world that he deserved.

And Kieran?

Out of all of us, he was the most free. And he chose to do nothing with his freedom. He was a Titan because that was a part of his deal.

That was it.

He had a choice.

Killian made a choice.

The truth was?

The only reason I took away everybody's choices and I made them myself was because I didn't trust anyone to make the right ones.

Because nobody had ever made the right ones with me.

Nobody but her.

And now, sitting in my car, consumed by the fire hot rage that had been building in me since I first came into contact with this world, I felt like I was scum. Because I had let go of the one fucking good thing in my life, thinking that I could push her away and protect everybody in return.

All because, I knew deep down, without her, I was just another monster in the city full of them.

And the worst part was, I didn't have a choice to be anything else.

42

SONYA

"THIS IS CHEDDAR."

Kieran dropped an enormous orange and white cat into my lap.

"His previous owner said that he got too big for them so they gave him up. I didn't name him. I just kept his old name because I didn't wanna keep changing it for him. Pretty sure the guys traumatized already."

I blinked down at the forty pound cat on my lap purring like a sewing machine.

The city was covered in a blanket of frost outside, and it had started snowing.

The year was almost over.

And I couldn't believe that I had started this year filing for divorce. It was halfway through.

The adorable ball of fluff felt like a sack of potatoes on my lap. "He's so adorable."

"I know, he's like a giant puff. I love him, but he's really gotta workout more. I was trying to hide his snacks in his toys, but he just gets frustrated."

I laughed as Kieran told me his plights with his adopted cat.

He was coming over more often now and bringing croissant over. Over the last few weeks, I did feel a little bit better. Everything still ache but over time? I did heal.

I spent a lot of time with Kiara and Nisha.

I didn't know how healing it would be to be around a child, but it showed me that the love that I have been given, was not meant to be conditional.

Loving Kiara and being her godmother and being able to be there for her, it meant the world to me.

I had already purchased so many toys for her Killian had moved all her things into a different room and now she had a nursery.

The first couple of weeks, neither one of her parents had wanted her out of their bedroom. But now they felt like they could let her go a little bit more.

Kieran never did bring up Aidan but I saw him acting a little different around me. Like he felt guilty over the last few weeks.

He brought me flowers and snacks and cookies.

He was always there for me. But I just distracted myself with the incoming folks at Haven. It felt really good to finally get it off the ground.

Months and months of Gemma's hard work, and just me giving her some sense of direction. But it all came together.

It felt good to finally have something open for women and children to come to get refuge.

We documented everything, and it was open to pretty much everybody of any social class.

We just marked off the first floor completely, and everybody had it signed rooms and clean clothes.

I felt nothing but accomplishment going there.

For the last couple of weeks, I had just felt like I was laying in bed, emotionally coping with losing a marriage that had gone nowhere.

And then losing our relationship that I thought was gonna go everywhere.

Seeing Haven and seeing people think me and seeing the cluster of individuals working all throughout the shelter, it really made me feel accomplishment for the first time in my life.

There was nothing else that could have made me feel anything.

But that moment, that's when I really felt it.

Walking through the hallways and feeling people thinking me, just knowing that you know, Gemma and I had worked really hard to get this off the ground. For the weeks that I had been a haze of heartbreak and sadness, I had finally found my purpose and my calling.

Now I had a choice on whatever I wanted to do. I didn't have to choose to be upset about anything. I could just choose to be happy.

I could choose to sit in my townhouse in the evenings and eat pizza and watch television. Without anyone. Sometimes Kieran.

But for the first time in a long time, I felt a possibility. And I felt like I didn't get to choose a lot of things in my love life, but I got to choose everything else.

I knew that if I saw him again, it would absolutely break me, but that was the unique part about him being in Chicago and me being in New York, I could choose if and when I ever saw him.

I could choose it all.

And even if he didn't care about my choices?

I did. I cared.

Somewhere in the middle of my heartbreak and my disappointment and my morning, the end of so many things, I didn't realize how many things had started. Good relationships, good people, I needed to check in with all of my friends.

From what Lucy had told me, Lucas was now married with a baby girl. And Talia would've had her son too.

Gemma and her bodyguard Nathan were a couple. And life was moving on without me.

I would have to keep moving forward with or without him.

"I gotta run downstairs I think that's our pizza," Kieran said with a smile that didn't meet his eyes.

I held onto Cheddar on my lap dozing now when the bell rung just as Kieran left. My spine stiffened.

Kieran wouldn't knock.

A loud slam echoed in the hallway. Male voices. *Kieran?*

I wanted to run and help him I did—but after my lessons I had learned?

I knew better. Now? I knew better.

I bit back a scream quickly setting Cheddar down. I wasn't going to scream. And Cheddar wasn't here to protect me. Kieran was gone, but I knew to text him. I wasn't the same girl anymore who panicked.

Now? I just bolted into action.

I rushed into the kitchen to grab a knife. At this point I understand why Aiden felt so annoyed rather than angry when these things happened.

The townhouse doors have a security alarm on them.

Not if I activated them first.

I hit the alarm on my phone and similar to Aidan's penthouse?

The lights flashed red for a nanosecond and a shrill alarm rang out in the townhouse. My fear for Kieran's well being and my own security was paramount.

Cheddar lost his mind.

Meowing all throughout the house as I ran to the security cameras to find two men running away.

Kieran's long lean form firing his gun reminding me he wasn't just happy go lucky. Not at all. Kieran moved like a lean predator with lethal grace shooting until I heard them die out.

It took twenty minutes for him to run back to me.

"Sonya!"

His arms wrapped around me as black SUVs converged on my street.

At this point, my neighbor's lights had turned on, and I felt a little bit embarrassed. But I held onto him tightly as I realized the alarm had activated a sector of Titan Security.

"I already talked to one of them," Kieran told the man who approached us. "He said he was hired by Michael Devereaux to scare her—"

The other man looked grim and I felt my blood run cold as Kieran held me tight to his side.

I breathed out panting in fear as Kieran rubbed my back.

"Bro, Aidan's gonna fucking kill him."

43

AIDAN

I was going to fucking kill Michael Devereaux.

I was notified about her alarms. Her security cameras. And Kieran who texted me not to freak out.

I did freak out.

Several times while rushing out of the house. Barely human on the plane and snapping at everyone.

My blood was turning to ice and the same feeling I had after finding her broken on her floor months ago, was the same I felt now. Except it was amplified because now I loved her. I loved her. I loved her so much. And I knew that.

I wanted her back like nothing else in the world.

Nothing was going to keep me from her.

In that woman, I knew, I knew that the best days of my life had been with her, and I wouldn't ever want anything else, but her. I would trade it all for her. I would do whatever it took.

Long distance, traveling back-and-forth to see her, splitting holidays in my priorities. And that's the moment that I felt like a fucking idiot.

That's the moment that I realize how fucking stupid I was.

That's the moment that it occurred to me that I had made a choice without asking her what she wanted out of it. If she wanted to end it. If she wanted to be with me long distance. If she wanted to spend the rest of our lives with me in Chicago and her in New York and us splitting our time. Or she would come stay with me parts of the year and I would come stay with her. Because I would've made it work.

For her?

In that moment, sitting on the plane, I knew that I would do everything. And I would've done it all.

I would've caught her and I would've told her that I would never let her go.

I was such a fucking moron.

Sonya was the purest thing despite her darkness, and even if I was ankles deep in blood? The truth was?

I wanted her so fucking much, to affirm she was alive and well and I could breathe in her scent.

I felt like I couldn't talk to anybody because I was gonna snap.

Alexei looked grim next to me no doubt worried about whatever condition he might find her in.

He was attached to her to the hip. At this point?

If he told me that he was gonna start moving in with her, I wouldn't even be surprised anymore.

The most he had said to me since we'd rushed out of the house was just all about coordination.

I couldn't even breathe.

Not until I got to her.

The drive to her place felt never-ending, and the moment we both stormed out, Alexei tore off into the house. "Sonya!"

When I burst through the door, I caught a glimpse of her wide emerald eyes before he lifted her into his arms.

Letting me stand there like a helpless idiot watching him hug her. Burying his neck into her throat. And inhaling her in.

I saw her hug him back, her slender arms around him as he lifted her off the floor.

And I stood there like an open mouthed idiot as he turned her away, my hands clenching, unclenching.

My heart bottoming out into my stomach like I had been dropped off a roller coaster.

I didn't even know what to do with myself.

I had left her. She'd been in danger. And now my son was hugging her like she was his lifeline.

I felt my eyes stinging.

No fucking way I was gonna pussy out and start crying because Alexei was hugging Sonya.

"Hey," I didn't even hear Kieran moving to close the door and his amber eyes landed on me with a softer look in them. I hadn't talked to him since I cursed him out. Not until now.

I blinked back my emotions shutting them down as I watched Alexei holding her like she was everything.

And she was.

She had been.

In a few months, she has stayed with me, she turned my cold mansion into a home. She cooked for him and she gave him a family. And he'd been starving for more than just food.

Sonya had given him a sense of stability, and he loved her so much he hadn't spoken to me the entire time I fucked up with her.

Clearly taken her side over mine.

Now, I stood there like a moronic ass.

"She's okay," I cleared my throat feeling like I had swallowed a bucket of nails. Gruff. Unable to put one word in front of another. Like an idiot. I couldn't even think what the sound of her in the air, and she was so far away. I couldn't even breathe around her.

She looks beautiful.

"She's good, I caught 'em. It's all good—"

"It's not good." I looked at them feeling that rage return. "Her son of a bitch ex-husband sent them."

Kieran didn't look phased. "I got some of the guys to get him. He's in Titan Midtown."

I raised a brow as Kieran smirked. "What? You think I'd let it rock? He's scared out of his mind when Landon got a hold of him."

Landon was one of Killian's guys out in New York.

I glanced back at Alexei holding her. What did I say? What did I do? I broke up with her. Broke up my family. I didn't think that I deserved it, and I was such a fucking idiot that I didn't realize I had it the whole time. I had it.

If I had trusted her, we would've just made it work.

We would've made it work.

I had no right to her. *None.*

I felt my throat as Alexei finally set her down and I heard him say. "Sonya, I stay with you. I miss you."

It was like a gunshot to the chest. Kieran's eyes widened on Alexei before masking his expression completely.

And I turned away feeling my chest aching like someone shot me. I wasn't welcome here. I knew that. She didn't look at me. She didn't say a word to me. Like I didn't exist.

Why would she?

I fucked her over. I broke up *my* family.

I was just like my father.

I grit out the words. "I'll go to Midtown."

I didn't bother looking at anyone as I left feeling like I ripped my heart out for a second time.

I couldn't see as I got into the car.

Couldn't breathe outside of the aching blooming in my chest at the mess of my own making.

44

AIDAN

I found Michael in Midtown.

Sitting tied to a chair with one of the guards in the room moving aside from me. He already had two bruises blossoming on his face no doubt coming from trying to talk back to us. But nothing was going to save him anymore.

"You know, the last time I was here, I completely forgot to kill you." I said feeling like I was swallowing glass still from seeing Sonya in Alexei's arms. "But now? I won't."

Midtown was where Reed brought people he didn't like or felt annoyed with. When he did? They usually left in a cast or a bodybag.

Now?

Michael would be the latter.

I took my knife and I moved so fucking fast I cut the ropes hauled him up and slammed my fist into his face. The crack of bone was so satisfying, I had to grin.

"You stupid fucking piece of shit."

I think I channeled every ounce of rage I had felt for the last eight years into every single hit I laid into him. And every animal noise that left him, I remembered that he held my woman down. He raped her. He tortured her for years.

I remembered all of it.

And I was going to do the same to him.

261

With interest.

I grabbed his hair yanking his head back to find him grimacing at me. *"You fucked that stupid bitch so now you want to protect her?"*

Oh. Man. It was like the more he taunted me, the more he catered to all of my demons. And I knew he was a stupid fuck because he didn't realize who he was talking to.

Guys like that would never learn.

I was gonna have a *blast*.

I moved so fast he didn't even see it as I shoved the knife deep into his gut as he howled.

"You know what Mikey?" I growled. "I think we're gonna take a walk. And I think we're gonna have a great time while we do. Nine fucking years, was it? Don't worry. By the time I'm done with you? You're gonna wish you killed yourself first."

Savoring his scream was one way to put how it made me feel. I went after him with everything I had. Until I couldn't even recognize him. But he was still alive and he was still breathing.

"Get up."

I didn't even recognize my voice. But he couldn't, I dragged him by his ripped up clothing to the stairs. I could feel his blood all over. Reed might have a bit of a mess to clean up but he would send his guys over.

At this rate the guard quickly moved out of my way no doubt alerting his boss.

When I dragged Michael Devereaux up the stairs I heard every part of his body hitting each and every single step as he threw up blood.

"Messy stuff, isn't it? Murder. Makes me wonder how Lucas turned out fucking normal with the shit show your family is."

He grumbled something and I didn't understand him.

I just heard her name.

I rolled my eyes and shot out one of his kneecaps to his animal screams.

"There you fucking go, every single time you say *my* wife's name, I will take out another joint."

At the words I said I saw him look up at him with confusion and I grinned. "You wanna know something Mikey? Bet you and your tiny rapey little dick didn't think Sonya would end up with me, did you?"

I realized Michael had relished constantly belittling her. Constantly making her feel less then. Constantly dragging her down and her ego and her self-esteem unable to fathom how this incredible woman would make him look bad all the time.

So he spent his life shitting on her, so that he could feel better about himself with his family.

"I wanna know something, Mikey. I wanna know where you got the fucking gall to go after my wife." She wasn't mine.

But in theory?

She was.

She had never stopped being mine.

I dragged him to the snow covered rooftop of Titan Tower.

At over fifteen hundred feet tall, I felt the chill in the air cut through my face. It was dark and cold and I felt nothing as I dragged his body out to the snow.

Blood everywhere. I took out another kneecap.

"That was because I was bored and I just wanted to hear you scream."

I kicked him in both of them.

And a wicked grin lit my face. "Did you listen to Sonya scream? Is that why you did what you did? How many times did you hold her down and make her scream?"

I tipped my head curiously aware of feeling an operative emerge onto the rooftop with me.

"Did you count?" I asked Michael who was a mess on the floor in front of me. "Or should I count?"

I kept going. Shooting at his kneecaps until my gun was empty. I filled it with another round as he screamed.

"Nononono, you sick fuck. You don't get to die. You don't get to leave." I hauled him up to stand knowing he couldn't. "You don't get to hurt my girl for nine years and hunt her down like she was the animal—" I grinned. "Oh, Mikey. Did you think I'd let you get away? I'm only just getting started."

I took out a cigarette from my pocket, lighting it up.

"Sonya told me about the time you threw her down a flight of stairs." I smirked. "Wanna see how that feels?"

～

HE ONLY LASTED TWO HOURS.

And that was because if I threw him off the ledge he'd splatter Down below and hit some innocent pedestrian. And then the commissioner would ask me why his body was littering the streets.

So I just kept throwing Michael Devereaux down the stairs until he couldn't move.

But he was still breathing.

I would drag him to the top and start again.

I smoked through a pack of cigarettes and kept going.

Nine years of hell. Nine years of fucking up her life.

Her fears. Her insecurities. Of ruining her.

If I had met her another life, I would've just asked her out taking her out to get pizza and just asked her to get married.

If I met her another life, she would've been mine. Not his.

And in a way, even if she was, I had fucked up so bad that she wasn't.

I waited until his breathing got shallow in the cold. The sun came up in the horizon as he shuddered on the rooftop bleeding out so much, the entire rooftop was covered in it.

Including me.

I looked down at him putting out the next cigarette into his skin.

"I saw your footprint on her ribs," I whispered. "I saw everything. I read all her documents. Every medical report. You know what's really nice about being *dead? Dead men don't need to get divorced.*"

Dead men also didn't rape.

I had never felt more alive when I watched the last breath leave him.

It must've made me a sick fuck.

Maybe.

Or just a man who knew that the most important thing in his life had been threatened time and time again.

Now?

I was simply upholding my family name.

Finishing my cigarette I stared down at Michael's pathetic body. I felt the operative behind me move. The entire time I wasn't really paying much attention to him because I knew he wasn't gonna stop me.

But the last person I expected to sit with me was my brother.

Kieran sat down next to me staring at Michael's body.

I was so out of it I didn't even know it was him. His face was unreadable as he looked down at Michael.

"I came because I didn't know what you'd do."

I motioned to Michael with a smile on my face feeling myself covered in his blood.

I probably looked a little demonic right now.

"Now you do."

Kieran nodded not looking away from Michael.

"Now I do."

Silence descended as the sun came up on the horizon and I leaned back against whatever the fuck I was sitting on now.

It had been years since I watched the sunrise. A lifetime.

The last time had been me waiting in line in front of a bookstore to get the final book of the Lords of Nightshade series.

I had waited there since midnight. I had saved all my money to get it.

"The last time I saw the sunrise was because I waited for the midnight release of the last book of the Nightshade series," I admitted. "I waited all night. I got it signed and everything."

Kieran made a noise. "I remember, you couldn't stop talking about it. Killian thought you were weird."

I snorted. "Killian is weird."

He was also a dad. To the sweetest little ball of dinner rolls with her little pink bow headband Nisha sent me photos of. She had our eyes. Our family's legacy.

One she would never know was this.

My eyes stung with the way my chest tightened as I looked down at my bloodstained hands. *Never this*.

I laughed a little without any humor at how young I'd been. The things I wanted then.

The things that had been taken from me.

I tipped my head back trying to not snap into pieces at the knowledge that I had to go back to Chicago.

Back to my hell.

And I realized in that moment—I never wanted it.

Not one bit of it.

Gabriel had handed it to me years ago. Right now? I just wanted to curl up into Sonya and stay there forever.

Except I didn't have her either. I blinked back my emotions.

Kieran let out a shaky breath, the air in front of us turning to fog.

"I want to take your place in Chicago."

I stopped breathing and I turned my head to him feeling like I was dreaming.

"What—"

"*I'm* taking your place in Chicago," his eyes the carbon copy of mine met me head on. "I am the new you. You're not going back. Not anymore."

He was dead serious.

"Why?" I shook my head in disbelief. "You walked away."

"Because I thought it would make me feel better. I fucking hated Cormac as much as you two, but you two—Killian—he had it worse than me. You're not the only one who yelled at me. Killian ripped into me a couple of months ago. When I told Nisha about our family." Kieran looked off into the sunrise, the rays making his eyes glow eerily.

"I have fucked up a lot," he said softly, his throat worked with emotions I could only imagine as he continued. "All I do is fuck up. I have done that. I gave De Nuit to Teo since it's more his than mine. And I have nothing here…"

"What happened to your girl?"

He had a crush on Alisha's sister. For the life of me I couldn't remember the girls name.

He shook his head. "She's with someone." At my silence he glanced over with a humorless smile. "She's with Teo's younger brother."

"No shit. The assassin?"

He nodded. "That one."

"Hm, and Reed was chill?"

Kieran shrugged. "You butchered Michael."

This was true.

He blew out a breath. "I thought about what you said. Just because I'm twenty-three, doesn't mean that I can just fuck around and do whatever the fuck I want. You were taking over everything at my age. You did all of this. I can do it. I can lead. I can be the new you. I don't have Kiara. I don't have Sonya, but I have everything you taught me."

He leaned forward on his knees looking out into the sunrise as it rose over us.

"I think I need to stop running away from things and face my problems head on."

I didn't know what to say. For years? I had choices made for me. Years of never really been given a say. Kieran left, Killian settled, and there was me. Solitary. Alone.

Leading something I didn't want.

And now he was offering to take it off my shoulders. The weight that lifted off my chest was unspeakable. I couldn't fucking process it right now. I couldn't believe it.

No fucking way he wanted it. It was all I had ever known—and yet the prospect of figuring it out, any of my next steps, with Sonya was the most enticing thing in the world.

This was the most mature I'd ever seen Kieran.

"You want to be me?"

He nodded looking at me. "And you just be a stay at a home dad with Sonya."

I felt my heart clench at those words as I looked down at Michael bleeding into the snow. "I fucked up with her."

"You just brutally tortured and murdered her rapist—I think she'll forgive you for whatever you did."

I looked over at Kieran narrowing my eyes.

"You can't have Alexei."

Kieran snorted. "I tell you I wanna take over the family business and all you can say is I'm not keeping Alexei?"

"I need to apologize to Sonya."

"Yeah, about that…you might wanna clean up first."

45

SONYA

ALEXEI HAD FALLEN ASLEEP NEXT TO ME IN MY GUEST ROOM SOMETIME during the night from me rubbing his platinum blonde hair back.

The sun was coming up now and I needed to go to sleep.

Or do something with my life that didn't involve thinking about me ignoring Alexei's parent.

It was late when Alexei had crawled in like a little boy and stayed there with me asking me questions with childhood curiosity.

I was honestly under the impression that he was maybe eighteen. I needed to ask Adam or Reed on how I found out his age because he was adorably young.

You are doing good now?

You want to eat something?

Did you miss me, Sonya? I missed you.

I only cried after he fell asleep.

I had missed him.

In the short time that I had been with him, I had adopted him like he was my son too.

And it had hurt not having him following me around with obvious delight. He'd gotten attached to me and texted me every single day he was in Chicago.

Now, he was asleep like a kid and I slowly got out of the bed to tuck him in and leave him there under the heated blankets.

The townhouse was quiet and at some point Kieran had left to do God only knows what. Aidan had been in front of him.

I felt his presence then. Of course I felt it. I just couldn't look at him without snapping in half and Alexei had held my body so tight I thought it might snap.

Now? I padded outside my halls carefully turning down the lights in the room and walk down to my floor from the guest rooms.

The three story townhouse initially had been imposing, but now with the white walls and lush green hydrangeas I got in? I felt more at home.

Not quite, but we were getting there.

I heard a little ding of the bell letting me know Kieran was back as I padded downstairs.

Yawning I called out. "Kieran, you are back?"

I walked into the foyer expecting his lean and limber self holding coffee and donuts or something like he usually did.

But I felt like I hit a wall at the sight of Aidan dressed in sweats and a hoodie. His inky hair frosting a little from the chill outside as he blinked at me slowly like I was a dream he had.

I felt the weight in my chest like a sinking sensation as I rubbed my eyes feeling the weight of the last few weeks in full force.

I didn't know what to say to him.

What did it matter?

He didn't care.

My chest rose and fell as he stood there having closed my door and set his coat down.

We both stood there and the first words out of my mouth that felt pathetic were. "What are you doing here?"

"I came to see you."

"Why?"

He blinked like it hurt *him* for me to ask the question. It hurt *me* to ask.

"I fucked up." His voice cut through the air. "I'm sorry."

Amber eyes watched me from a distance. A few feet and yet it felt like eons between us.

"I'm sorry for not asking you what you wanted. For making a decision without you."

He cleared his throat looking a lot like Alexei when I caught him snatching up treats that hadn't cooled yet.

Like father, like son.

The thought almost made me snap in half.

"I should've asked you, should've checked in and told you how I felt after seeing Kiara. After seeing Killian—" he broke off explaining it to me. Everything.

His thoughts.

His mindset.

His entire shift. How he realized he might not have that when he already had with me and Alexei.

I blinked back my emotions as someone who thought she'd never have children to have a son sleeping upstairs and Kiara as my goddaughter.

Aidan explained it to me brokenly as he cleared his throat.

And then his eyes rimmed in red looked at me as he said. "I love you. I have for a long time. You're the one woman in my life who challenges me every step of the way and makes me consider and reconsider. You are everything I could've asked for and then some. Everything I am not and it is everything I love you for."

He cleared his throat again and I wondered if he was getting sick. With how wet his hair was he just might be.

I blinked back several times unable to stop feeling this way.

This wasn't my life.

This wasn't after weeks and weeks of him not being here. Of him leaving me after finding out about Kiara. Or when he'd taken me to Chicago at the very beginning of...us.

I felt my throat closing in.

"I tried to pretend like I made the right choice. I tried to pretend like if I stayed away from you or if I didn't think about you, I could just go back to my old life and pretend like this one never happened."

He exhaled as those amber eyes met mine.

"But I couldn't. The moment Kieran told me about Michael I ran here as fast as I could because my only thought that has ever consumed me is if you were okay. And I realized in that fucking plane ride over—that I fucked up. All I had to do was tell you how I felt, tell you everything—and work it out with you. Because you didn't want to break up."

I hadn't.

I hadn't wanted to break up at all.

But he had.

And even with my emotions running high from last night, I could see it for what it was. I did believe him.

I did love him. "I love you too."

His expression broke as I said it. Because I understand that moment, I was giving him something that he had never had either. Something that I had never had. Love and acceptance.

And even still I held out a little. It was everything I had ever wanted and wrapped up in a little bow. It just wasn't his first time doing this to me.

I could see on his face he realized when I didn't run to him or hug him he knew something was still wrong.

"But…" he drifted off.

"But this is not the first time you did this—"

"I'm sorry, love—"

"I know. Me too. You can stay here if you need to. The guest rooms are ready upstairs. But I need time too…when do you have to leave again?"

He blinked back his emotions as his chest shuddered. "I don't."

"What?"

"I don't have to leave. Not anymore. I mean…I think I gotta go and get my stuff and pack with Alexei, but I'm done…I'm…out."

Now I was confused. "What do you mean—" He explained it to me. "Kieran is—" Kieran was…taking his place. "Can he do that? He just goes and he—"

"He's family. So yeah. And he is trained. He is actually better than Killian. He just chooses not to do it because he doesn't want it to be our father's legacy. But he doesn't mind it being mine." Aidan explained it to me that Kieran had wanted to leave it for so long until he realized—

"The only way for you to be here in New York with me—"

"Is to leave it for good and be here with you."

Now I was moving, stumbling over my slippers as I was in his arms a second later, my body sinking against his muscles as he practically lifted me into his arms. *"Askim. You left?"*

I couldn't believe what he said. It was his entire world. He liked what he did. He was good at...*everything*.

My question was muffled into his neck as I inhaled the clean scent of an unfamiliar soap. "You don't smell like you."

Instead of responding he groaned as he buried his head into my skin at my pulse. "You smell amazing."

I clung to him breathing in and out realizing he was freezing cold. I didn't know who was shaking harder.

"You left."

"I did...I'm sorry, baby. I shouldn't have done that."

"Yes...you did mess up."

I held my breath a little for what I was about to say.

"I like you and I love you, but I do not forgive you for what you did."

I felt him stiffen under me. I was serious about this.

"I don't trust that you will not continue to make your decisions without me sometimes. And that is scary. I asked you to not do that and consider me. I'm scared next time you will do it again."

"I won't—" his voice was breaking. "I fucking promise I will defer to you from now on."

I pulled back a little, just a little because he didn't let me go at all. My eyes locked with his amber ones and I realized how emotional he was.

"You promise."

"I promise."

"No, you agree too easily. I don't trust this. But you still have to explain how you are leaving. Where you are staying."

Obviously with me.

To my surprise a smile broke out on his lips. "You would say that."

"Is true, you always agree quickly." But I smiled as I said it missing him and feeling my heart swell as I took him in.

"You are freezing. What happened to the Michael situation last night?"

"Uhh," he looked a little away a little uneasy and I knew when

272

those eyes of his were lying or trying to keep things from me. "About that…you don't have to worry about him anymore."

"What did you do, you murderer?"

To my surprise, he grinned wider then. "Fuck, I missed you."

He stamped his lips over mine before I could ask another question.

46

AIDAN

"She's sharp," Nadine said to me on the phone as I checked in about Eden.

Over the next few days, I filled in Kieran on everything he needed to know.

"Eden Belova," Kieran repeated in Sonya's townhouse with us crowded around her kitchen island.

Killian had shown up with Nisha and the baby who Nisha was currently feeding in a guest room, so he sat alone with us.

Alexei was at Sonya's right hand drinking coffee and I just filled in Killian. On everything.

He looked contemplative more than anything else.

"Got it." Kieran said. "One psycho Russian-American girl to check on. Devlin is solid for a right hand. Anything else?"

I asked Alexei or Nadine who had nothing.

Nisha walked in holding Kiara in a bunny suit, the ears flopping over her ear. Her eyes lit up on Killian and she turned so Kiara could blink up at us.

"Daddy."

I watched my younger brother melt. He melted as he took her out of Nisha's arms immediately.

"Did you miss me, little luv?" He nuzzled her kissing her all over as he walked away.

274

Nisha smiled after them before coming to the island. "Oh, is that bread fresh? That would be so good with some butter…"

"Gnocchi?"

"Gnocchi."

"You look upset," Sonya murmured in bed as she blinked up at me later that night. I closed my eyes at the feel of her naked body against mine.

"I think Kieran is still running," I openly admitted it. "He said he didn't have much in New York. I think he took on Chicago because he wants to start over."

"You are worried?"

"Not worried he won't be able to do the job, but that he thinks because of Killian and me—he has to do this or he has to start over." But then again. "I am relieved either way."

Sonya rose up above me looking beautiful with her tousled hair and warm eyes on me.

"But you still want to go with him and help him."

I sighed. "I do."

"Then go." She murmured. "Go take care of him, I'll be here. I will let you take Alexei."

"But I just got back."

"Yes, but this is important to you and he needs to learn. Maybe you can show him and help him for a few weeks and then come back home to me."

"Fuck, I do love the sound of that."

But I didn't want to leave, I might as well though. I talked to Killian and he wasn't going anywhere with Nisha having the baby. She was a few weeks old and Nisha had a nanny to help.

"Unless, she stays with Sonya—" Killian broke off as his eyes met mine. "I don't wanna leave Kiara for a day let alone a few weeks."

Nobody was obsessed with their kid like he was.

He held onto Kiara whenever he could but I had yet to approach the idea of kids on my own. With him.

With Aidan.

EPILOGUE

"ASKIM?"

I peered into the bedroom to find Aidan laying in bed with Kiara on his bare chest. She curled in scrunching herself up like a ball. And my heart absolutely melted.

His smile was shy and soft. "Killian warned me she likes this, I don't know what to do, I don't think I can move though."

I pressed my lips together to not explode at the sight of this enormous man laying here with her.

"She's asleep finally."

"She is like a tiny little ball."

I didn't know how Nisha and Killian did it.

She needed to be fed every hour it felt like, burped, changed, and cuddled. She needed cuddles and it was quickly evident she preferred Aidan's deeper voice to mine.

Kiara had his eyes.

And he blinked down at her with such tenderness.

"She's so small. She barely fits in my hands."

I covered my mouth as we shared a laugh. I went to lay down next to him.

We had talked about not having children—we did have Alexei—but looking at her, interacting with her, I did want kids.

I yearned for them even if I knew I hadn't had children with Michael.

"Killian says she pouts in her sleep," I motioned to her lips. "Look, there she goes."

Nisha and Killian did come back by the end of the night in their pajamas looking disheveled and Aidan smirked at me.

A red-faced Nisha took Kiara in her carrier as Killian helped her.

I sighed as they left feeling emptier after she did.

Turning over my shoulder, I found Aidan watching me carefully. "You ever think about kids?"

I was honest.

"All the time."

He nodded slowly as he watched me his mouth turning down in a way that let me know he was deep in thought.

"You ever think about going to see someone about that?"

He shrugged. "Wouldn't hurt to make sure it's not you that was the problem and it was Michael."

That would make sense.

AIDAN AND I HAD CONTACTED CLINIC AFTER CLINIC UNTIL WE FOUND one to work with that seemed better.

I sat there with him as the doctor came around and did some tests. I was so nervous, he pulled me into his lap holding me tighter as I waited.

For good news. Bad news.

Anything at all.

I had explained as much as possible to the female doctor who I felt familiar anxiety and shame around.

"Mrs. O'Hara—" she began. And I didn't even correct her as Aidan tightened his grip on me. "You said you were with your previous partner for nine years?"

"Just about, yes."

"And you are sure, you were never able to conceive?"

"Yes," I was frowning now. "I never…"

The doctor's eyes hardened a little on me. "Did he take you to specialists who said you can't?"

I nodded feeling Aidan shift a little as though expecting her to say something awful.

"Well, I can promise you one thing, your husband was wrong. And so were the two male doctors you saw." Her eyes met mine directly. "I don't know if he deliberately lied to you or they didn't do you any justice. Because you're not infertile. Actually, you're pregnant."

What?

"What?" I breathed.

Aidan went still under me.

The doctor grinned wide passing me the ultrasound images she had. "You're pregnant. Very much so. You're eight weeks along. With twins."

My jaw dropped as my eyes widened so much so I thought I was going to explode.

"H-how?" He wheezed. "Holy—"

I heard laughter from the doctor as I looked down at a blurry ultrasound photo in shock.

"You were never the problem. Congratulations on your babies. In a few weeks you can come back and find out if you're having boys or girls."

"Oh my gosh…"

"You've been pregnant this entire time."

As the doctor left us there to process our shock with a prescription for prenatal I sat there unable to do anything but watch Aidan's shock turn into a laugh.

"Shiiit," he laughed. "You're pregnant."

"I was *never* the problem," I whispered.

"*We* are having a baby. No, of course you're not a problem—"

"*Babies.*"

And then together I didn't know who moved first as I hugged him so tight I felt my spine was going to snap.

"*Babies,*" he breathed. "Holy fucking shit, I'm about to be a dad."

Laughter burst out of my chest.

"We're about to be parents. *Again.* Alexei has siblings."

Aidan's grin was wide. "He's gonna lose his mind."

278

"We have to tell Killian—"

"*He's* gonna lose his mind—"

"*We have to tell Kieran—*"

"*Fuck me.*"

Our laughter mingled with our excitement.

Aidan pulled back from kissing me once more. "Wanna get married?"

I smacked his chest playfully. "This is how you ask me?"

"No, I swear I wanna make it fancy, but do you want to? I hate surprises."

I laughed. "Aidan!"

"I'm serious, princess. I gotta know."

I couldn't stop laughing. "Yes, you silly man. I will marry you. Now, what am I going to do with you?"

"Hold my hand if we find out we're having girls."

I laughed even harder out of the clinic.

AIDAN'S EPILOGUE

"One more, daddy."

I laughed as I did another push up, and the two girls on my back toppled over onto the bed giggling. Sonya laughed walking in while putting away her jacket.

"Up to no good the three of you?" She teased.

"Mama!"

My twins, Selin and Kiraz had tunnel vision for Sonya who was coming home from Haven and changing into pajamas, while I got the job of staying home with my daughters.

Turns out, Sonya wasn't barren or infertile. But one particular scum bag was.

Did I tell Sonya I killed her ex-husband?

Sure.

But did I tell how?

Absolutely *not*.

Instead I cuddled Selin who turned back to me for kisses while Sonya picked up Kiraz.

"Daddy!"

I turned my head as two girls ran up to me with squeals their faces covered in face paint.

"Girls, what did you guys do?"

Selin and Kiraz, my four year old daughter's ran at me full force their brunette waves flying as they tackled me into the grass giggling.

I caught both of them in my arms to goofy smiles and kisses. Covering me in face paint and laughter.

"Daddy, I'm a fox!"

Sonya came laughing behind them, Alexei with his face painted too. *"You three all got your face painted?"*

"Kiraz, is a bear."

"No, I'm not! I'm a fox too."

I think she might've gotten a bear instead, I just didn't correct them. Turns out twin girls were the equivalent of red panda cubs. A little wild, a hella curious, and adorable.

Sonya hadn't been the infertile problem in her marriage.

We had gone to the doctor a few months into me staying with her Sonya had gone to see a specialist and the doctor thought we were pranking her.

Because Sonya had been very pregnant.

With twins.

To my surprise we'd both walked out of there a little stunned.

Sonya had motioned to me stunned. *Your fault.*

I had hysterical laughing bubbling up. *My fault?*

Yes, it is your...superhuman parts. You did this to me.

We both burst into laughter realizing we were having twin girls. I honestly think both us had no fucking clue what was coming.

Now? We had two—very active four-year olds.

"Kiraz," Sonya began with a stern look in her eyes. *"Babanın üstüne boya sürmemek konusunda ne demiştik?"*

"Sorry, Mama." Both of them climbed off me and I grinned as Selin rubbed my face. I cuddled them both closer with laughter.

I was learning Turkish was a hard as fuck language. But the girls spoke it after their Mom. I only talked to them in Gaelic at night to tell them stories. Multi-lingual kids were something else.

Sometimes the girls spoke English but they chattered in whatever they wanted to and then they ran around with the other Titan kids who all spoke garbled mixtures of languages.

Alexei leaned in with white on his face. "She is telling them about not putting paint on your face." *Right.*

"What are you supposed to be?"

"Alexei is a polar bear…" Kiraz mumbled as she snuggled her full face of paint and all into my shirt. I grinned at Sonya's dismay at me getting smothered in paint.

This was my family.

"Nisha and Killian have their girls finishing up," Sonya said with a laugh. "Do you want to eat now?"

"I'm hungry, Mama." Selin said. "Kiraz is hungry too."

"Is she?" Sonya's eyes twinkled. "Good thing I packed a picnic basket for all of you."

Turns out, family picnics could be nice. With flowers. And my daughters. And my wife. And my son.

I laid back as the girls giggled and crawled over me before finding Alexei much more fun to bother. He entertained his sisters easier.

Sonya and I did find out he was seventeen or eighteen when Sonya had her doubts about his age. That meant I met him as a child.

At eleven. Which explained why he'd been desperate, hungry, obedient, and had done everything possible to learn from me.

Why his reading level was low. Why he acted how he did.

Sonya realized he probably needed a form of trauma therapy or another but Alexei was pleasantly happy with his life.

He lived in the townhouse with us and had turned twenty-two. For real this time.

Sonya realizing I had been raising a teenager this entire time as a fighter shouldn't have surprised me.

Now?

He was letting the girls crawl all over his back while he did push ups and let them hang off him giggling and tumbling and hopping back on him.

Alexei and Sonya went to go grab the baskets of food while the girls crawled into my arms.

"Daddy, boo." Selin pursed her lips at me.

"Daddy, boo." I turned to Kiraz who did the same.

Killian and Nisha had this thing they did when their daughters were younger, they pursed their lips when they wanted kisses from each other without saying a word.

Somehow, Kiara and Marissa and now their youngest Nadia had picked it up and called kisses 'boos' and so the entire family did it.

My girls spending too much time with Kiara, and picked it up and began doing it to Sonya and me when they realized—it did in fact work.

It did.

They were giggling as I kissed them all over.

Being a stay at a home dad to my girls was interesting.

It was strange going from running a whole empire to this.

But Reed had asked if I wanted to go to Titan Midtown and train up some of their recruits instead as an instructor and sometimes I did.

I took the twins with me and they ran around driving them crazy. Today they were giggling in my arms filling my chest up.

Now I knew why Killian dropped the world for Nisha. This was my legacy. My peace.

My girls and Sonya and Alexei were my safe haven.

And it set me free. Sonya had sent me back to school to get my bachelors simply for the sake of learning when I told her I ditched my full ride to run my father's empire.

She paid for it. She wanted me to do it.

I was finishing up a masters degree in cybersecurity and a minor in history because I got bored. I realized I liked being a student.

Nobody would ever guess it, but I did.

Sonya had encouraged me to go after the things I have loved. I had missed.

The other day I went to a gaming convention with the Devereaux's.

Lucas who walked around with his daughter Belle on his shoulders and Evie who fluttered excitedly with me nerding out.

I had found my place in this city that I had formerly despised.

I got away from New York to run from my past, only to realize I couldn't run anymore. Now I ran to things.

I took care of my girls. I cuddled them as they chattered in garbled mixtures of Turkish, English and whatever else they were learning at the manor running around with the Whittaker's and Mattison family.

Everyone in Titan had settled in their own ways.

"I always thought I would be a mother in another lifetime," Sonya murmured. "But no, I am a mother in this lifetime."

Her green eyes welled with unshed emotions.

"You are never the problem," I held her tighter. "There is nothing wrong with you, there was never was."

Sonya nodded. Over the years we'd worked together as a team. Unlikely. But strong.

Fate had led me to her, and I couldn't walk away.

UNDERWORLD KINGS | BOOK III
COMING SOON

Saint

Liam Sullivan & Larissa Ford

AUTHOR'S NOTE

Lilah Lance writes romance for all the girls who dream of being seen, being *accepted*, and being loved for *who they are.*

Get exclusive content and giveaways by signing up for Lilah's newsletter on http://lilahlance.com where you can get sneak peeks and news before anyone else.

ABOUT THE AUTHOR

Lilah Lance writes romance for all the girls who dream of being seen, being *accepted*, and being loved for *who they are.*

For more info check out http://lilahlance.com to contact Lilah.

www.ingramcontent.com/pod-product-compliance
Lightning Source LLC
Chambersburg PA
CBHW061943170626
46813CB00006B/2518